SINISTER ROOTS

ISLAND OF FOG LEGACIES #2

SINISTER ROOTS

by Keith Robinson

Printed in the United States of America
First Edition: August 2016
ISBN-13 978-1537040950

Cover design by Keith Robinson

Visit www.UnearthlyTales.com

SINISTER ROOTS

ISLAND OF FOG LEGACIES #2

KEITH ROBINSON

Chapter 1
First Official Mission

Miss Simone spun around as Travis Franklin and his mom arrived at the small lab. Her usually lovely face was screwed up with irritation, her blue eyes blazing as she stamped toward him. "Why are you late?" she demanded.

Her long, blond hair swirled about her shoulders as though a breeze had swept in through the door.

"Uh," Travis mumbled.

"I'm a very busy person, Travis," she said stiffly. "You're thirty minutes late. I don't have time to stand around waiting for you to show up. If this is going to work—if you want to skip the formalities that other children your age have to go through to be a shapeshifter—if you want me to come here and personally oversee your procedures and hand you missions—then you'd better show me the courtesy of turning up on time. Is that understood?"

"Um . . . yeah." Travis wished his mom would speak up and offer an excuse, but she said nothing where she stood in the doorway. "Um, sorry?" he added.

"Then let's get started," Miss Simone said, abruptly turning away and pointing to a glass of dark-colored liquid. "Get undressed, drink, lie down."

Travis hustled behind the screen, shooting his mom a hurt expression as he went. She stood there quite calmly, a tiny smirk on her face as though she'd enjoyed his telling off.

Some mom you are, he thought as he took off his thick silky shirt and threw it on a chair.

As he was about to pull his pants down, it occurred to him he might not need to undress all the way. He poked his head out. "Uh, Miss Simone? Do I need to take *everything* off? These are smart clothes."

She looked up from her clipboard and stared at him. "I suppose not. Just your shirt will be fine. Come lie down."

So he wrapped his arms around himself and stepped out, a chill finding its way down his spine. He hurried to the bed— more of a stiff board with a suggestion of padding—and climbed up onto it. When Miss Simone gestured toward the glass tumbler, he picked it up and downed the 'sleep tea' in one gulp.

Adjusting his wafer-thin pillow, he lay back and waited for the drink to take effect.

Two doctors entered, and Miss Simone turned to talk to them. Still by the door, his mom had folded her arms and seemed at ease . . . though she gently tapped her fingers, suggesting she was actually a little nervous about the whole thing. No surprise there. She was his mom, after all.

"Where's Dad?" he asked, and blinked in surprise when his words came out slurred. Even his blinking seemed weird, his eyelids heavy. It took all his effort to swallow and repeat his question.

His mom sauntered over. "He'll be along in a while."

In slow motion, he glanced over at Miss Simone, who was now lofting a syringe full of dark blood. "She was kind of angry, wasn't she?" he whispered to his mom.

"Well, we were late. I told you we had to be here by eight, and you goofed off half the morning."

"I was checking my bag!"

"Which you should have done last night." She patted his arm. "Look, you're twelve, I get it. But if you're going to take your shapeshifting job seriously, then you need to learn that some of the people you meet in life—the leader of the naga, the centaur khan, Miss Simone—are going to expect the basic courtesy that comes with being an ambassador."

Ambassador, he thought dreamily.

The title sounded so regal. Emissary, envoy, delegate, deputy, even messenger—he loved them all and couldn't decide which was best.

"I'll be esstra early ness time," he slurred.

"All right. Now relax. Sleep. I'll be here when you wake."

"Sure," he whispered as the room spun slowly.

"Oh, and Travis?" His mom pursed her lips and frowned. "If you wake up feeling an urge to shoot fireballs . . ." She leaned down and kissed him on the forehead. "Just don't, okay?"

The reminder of what he was about to become almost caused him to sit up straight with excitement. *Fireballs! I'm gonna be a three-headed chimera, one of the weirdest and deadliest beasts in the land!*

Drowsiness overcame him, though, and he drifted off worrying if he'd packed everything he'd need for his two-day mission . . .

* * *

He'd done a final check of his knapsack just before leaving for the laboratory that morning. "Firestarter, tinder, small pot for boiling water, fork, compass—*definitely* need that one." He rummaged deeper, nodding with approval at the long length of thin rope but wondering if a change of underwear was really necessary. He was only going for one night, after all. The large plastic sheet, though, was essential—

"Travis!" a voice called from the hallway. "Are you coming?"

He frowned. "Just making sure I've got everything, Mom."

His mom, the famous faerie shapeshifter Abigail Franklin, popped her head around the door frame and smiled. "Got a spare shirt?"

Travis grinned and nodded. "A *smart* shirt. No point taking something that'll rip into pieces when I transform."

His mom slid into the room and folded her arms as she leaned against the wall, her dark-brown hair hanging loosely around her shoulders. "And you're sure you're up for another adventure?"

He nodded. "Totally. It's been a week already since I was a wyvern, and I'm ready for something new." He glanced out the window at the morning sunlight. "What time is it?"

"Just past eight. Simone'll be at the lab by now. Best not keep her waiting."

He slung the knapsack over one shoulder. "I have everything I need. Well, everything except the *package*."

His mom raised an eyebrow. "Yes, the *package*. Your dad's gone to fetch it. He'll meet us at the lab, so you and Rez will be ready to head out straight after the procedure."

Bringing his best friend along on the two-day mission would be a lot of fun, but only if he took it seriously. Patience wasn't one of Rez's strong points.

Travis and his mom left the house together. The large log home stood on the brow of a hill, sheltered on the fringe of the forest, a fair walk to the town of Carter. They walked side by side down the path to the gate, then out into the open fields. Though the air felt chilly this morning, it looked like it was going to be a clear day, at least until the evening when it might rain. *Waterproof sheet*, Travis thought. The rolled-up orange vinyl was probably the heaviest thing in his knapsack.

He'd camped outside before, but never away from home. A day's walk there and another day's walk back. Not too far, but still quite a trek if he ran into trouble.

As if reading his mind, his mom said, "Part of me says I'm crazy to let you go off like this. But another part remembers how it was when I was your age, when your dad and me went off on really dangerous missions at Simone's bequest. Of course, we were a whole gang of shapeshifters and could all turn into something either fearsome or useful. We made a good team. But you're on your own."

"Don't forget Rez," Travis said, picking up the pace a little.

"He's not a shapeshifter. He'll be relying on you to keep him safe from predators."

"I know, Mom. But I'm ready for this."

She smiled at him and grasped his shoulder as they walked together. "If I had any doubts about that, I wouldn't let you go." After a pause, she said, "You brought the cookies, bread, cheese, and—"

"It's all in my bag, Mom. I've checked a million times."

The knapsack felt a little heavier than he'd expected. It was one thing testing it in his room, but quite another marching across a field. He and Rez had a long walk ahead once they got started on their mission.

Though Travis had forged a trail across this field during his walk to and from school every day, his parents tended to fly. His mom usually sprouted faerie wings from her back and buzzed along at quite a clip just a few feet above the long grass. His dad, on the other hand, didn't know how to be subtle; he transformed into a massive dragon and tore through the sky with a heavy beating of wings and occasional happy roars, casting a shadow liable to scare a person to death—that is, if they didn't know it was Hal Franklin, the most famous of shapeshifters.

Travis had always been proud of his parents. Many of his friends were simply embarrassed by theirs, always cringing at things they'd said or done. Hal and Abigail Franklin, however, had a pretty cool reputation around town.

"I still wish I could be a dragon," he said, breaking the silence. "You'd have nothing to worry about if I could transform into a giant fire-breathing monster."

His mom pulled a face. "One's enough, thank you. Besides, a chimera is fearsome enough."

"I guess," he said with a sigh. "For a couple of days, anyway."

Last weekend, he'd gone to the lab and become a wyvern shapeshifter. But the ability to transform into a small orange-and-blue dragon hadn't lasted long. Contrary to popular belief, inheriting super-strong immune systems from both parents actually worked against him, because his boosted healing power had kicked in and turned him *normal* again. Miss Simone expected this would happen with every procedure.

"So what's the package?" he asked his mom for the umpteenth time.

She laughed. "I knew you'd ask me that again before long. Just wait and see, okay?"

"But is it heavy? Big? I don't have a lot of room left in my knapsack."

"It'll be fine," she assured him. "You'll barely notice it."

They reached the bottom of the hill and started up the slope toward Carter.

"So it's small, then?" Travis pressed.

"Or invisible," his mom said in a mysterious voice. "Or it floats on its own. Or maybe it's a living thing and will walk with you."

"Like Nitwit?" he asked, puzzled. "Mom, are you saying the package is Nitwit?"

"Don't be silly. She's still recovering from her injuries. She'll need to rest another week or two before she tags along after you again."

Travis's long-time friend, a very shy imp, definitely needed to recuperate after helping him and his parents out of a deadly situation the previous weekend. "So what, then?"

"You'll see."

He slowed and turned to her. "But I'm delivering something important, right? Not just some random parcel or whatever?"

She frowned. "Travis, we wouldn't patronize you that way, especially not after you rescued all those caged creatures last week. No, I promise you, this is a very important errand." She gave him a gentle shove. "Now, let's hurry. Simone is going to be ticked if you're late for the procedure."

The procedure.

It sounded so ominous calling it that, but really it wasn't much more than drinking a cup of 'sleep tea' and zonking out for two hours while the doctors did their thing with a syringe of blood, some extracted DNA, and a healthy dose of magic . . .

And when he woke, he'd be a chimera shapeshifter.

Chapter 2
The Package

His mom's warning about shooting fireballs echoed in his head, conjuring weird images like curtains of fire all around, and red-hot globs of ceiling dripping dangerously close. Travis spun and gasped, looking for a way out of the choking fumes . . .

"Wake up," a man's voice said in his ear, sharp and loud. "Travis, wake up."

He jolted upright, still breathing hard.

His parents were there, one on either side of the table, grasping his arms to hold him still. "W-what—?" he stammered.

"Relax," his mom said. "You're safe. You just had a bad dream or something. Everything's okay. The procedure went well, and you started to turn just now."

He fought to control his breathing. Realizing he was drenched in sweat, it was probably a good thing he didn't have his shirt on. "I *turned?*"

"Grew pale-brown fur on your shoulders," his dad said with a grin. "Your mouth was full of fangs. You had some pretty sharp claws for a moment there." He held up one arm and showed Travis the back of his wrist, which had four wide-spaced slashes across it.

"Oh!" Travis exclaimed. "Did I do that?"

"It's okay. I've had much worse. It'll heal next time I change."

Travis took stock. The room was undamaged, the ceiling intact. His transformation really had been only partial, and no fireballs had been launched. "You shouldn't have said anything, Mom," he said, checking his hands to make sure they were fully human.

"What are you talking about?" she said with surprise.

He looked at her. "Just before I fell asleep, you warned me not to shoot fireballs, and that made me have a dream about shooting fireballs and melting the room."

Her puzzled expression cleared, and she covered her mouth with one hand. "Oops. Sorry. I was just trying to warn you—well, never mind."

His dad stood. "Come on, let's get out of here. Rezner is waiting outside."

"I need lunch first," Travis exclaimed, his stomach rumbling.

"Relax, there's a sandwich right here in this basket courtesy of the grumpy goblins in the kitchen. One for Rez, too. Put your shirt on and let's go."

Travis ate half of his sandwich before he'd finished putting his silky shirt on. He finished the rest as he hurried along the corridor and outside.

Rezner Malick—or just Rez to his friends—looked bored out of his mind. He sat on one of the tree stumps just outside the front of the laboratory building. Brown-skinned with neatly cropped black hair, he was exactly the same height as Travis, though that changed month by month as one or the other grew half an inch. A knapsack lay at his feet.

Rez jumped up and grinned. "You survived!"

Accompanied by his parents, Travis marched over and handed his friend the extra sandwich. "You weren't worried, were you?"

"I was worried for about three minutes," Rez said, carefully opening the sandwich to peer inside, "but mostly I've been bored. I've been sitting out here for *ages*."

Travis's dad snorted. "You got here half an hour ago."

"That's what I said. *Ages*." Rez gingerly took a bite, looking like he was afraid the cheese was moldy. After a moment, he chewed more vigorously. "Who made this? It's good."

"Gnotnose the goblin," Travis's mom said with a smile.

Rez paused mid-chew. "A goblin made this? Really? Huh."

"What, you didn't know goblins could prepare sandwiches?" She shook her head. "I know. Mind-boggling, isn't it? They can build homes, engineer clever machines, construct fine swords and beautiful armor, harness the power of geo-rocks, plot highly detailed and accurate maps like the one you're holding, and—amazingly—make sandwiches as well."

Narrowing his eyes, Rez peered at her and said, "Ri-ight." He took another bite and turned to Travis. "So did the surgery work?" he asked with his mouth full. "Are you a griffin now?"

"Chimera," Travis corrected him.

"That's what I said. So you can breathe fire and stuff?"

"Shoot fireballs."

"Same thing." Rez swallowed noisily. "Did it work or not?"

Travis nodded. "I guess. Dad said I almost transformed right there on the table."

His dad dutifully showed off the claw marks on his wrist, which elicited a suitably impressed exclamation from Rez. "Wow! That's cool, Mr. Franklin."

"Thanks—I think."

Travis's mom sighed. "What is it with boys and scars? Look, here's Simone. She'll explain your mission."

As the blue-eyed scientist strode along the path toward them, Travis suddenly felt nervous. "I bet it's something easy," he muttered, not sure if he wanted that to be true or not.

"It should be," his mom said. "But make no mistake, it's still a very important task, the first of many that Simone has lined up. Rather than enlisting dozens of different students to complete her To-Do list, this two-day expiration on your shapeshifting ability means you can switch to one form, get the job done, and move straight on to another. Basically, you can do the jobs of many, many shapeshifters at a rate of one a week with no extra training. You're invaluable, Travis."

He grinned, a feeling of pride swelling in his chest. "Yeah, I guess I'm pretty lucky. Unlike you, stuck in one form. If you got fed up being a faerie and wanted to do something else for a change, you'd have to have all your blood drained first."

"A full transfusion, yes," his mom said with a shudder. "A complete flush-through to rid my body of magic. Aside from your dad, I'm not sure a shapeshifter has ever done that—oh, except for some of those shapeshifter scrags we captured twenty years ago, the ones who were too dangerous to release."

Travis stood there staring into space, a bright future opening up. Of course, he'd already figured out that his overly active immune system might have a silver lining, but now Lady Simone herself was planning a long list of missions? The weeks and months ahead looked exciting!

Miss Simone's familiar green cloak flapped around her ankles as she approached. She rarely shifted to her mermaid form, but she still favored her silky green smart clothes as most shapeshifters did. One never knew when circumstances might require a transformation.

"Have you explained?" she asked without preamble, looking at both Travis's parents.

"Not fully," his mom said.

Miss Simone nodded. "Hal, do you have it?"

"Right here." Travis's dad slipped a hand into his pocket and pulled out a slim wooden box not much bigger than his hand. He handed it to Miss Simone.

She in turn handed it to Travis. "Don't try and open it. Just guard it well. Now, here's a map."

Travis took the box with a trembling hand and eagerly eyed the folded map Miss Simone produced. She held it out to him, but Rez was too quick and plucked it from her fingers.

"I'll look after this," he said, quickly unfolding it. "I'm better with directions, anyway. Travis sometimes doesn't know his left from his right."

Miss Simone stared at him with her piercing blue eyes, then gave a quick shake of her head and turned her attention back to Travis. "Now, listen carefully. That map will get you where you need to be. Do not deviate from the map. Somewhere around here—" She jabbed a finger at an empty spot on Rez's unfolded sheet. "—you'll find the home of the Grim Reaper.

Deliver the box. It should be a straightforward mission for a chimera, and I expect you'll be there this time tomorrow around noon. Don't dilly-dally. Remember, your shapeshifting ability may only last two days. One day there, one day back. If you're lucky, your power will wear off around the time you return home."

Travis listened with his mouth hanging open, still clutching the wooden box. The excitement he felt was almost overwhelming. He never wanted this moment to end. His first real, official mission, handed to him by none other than Miss Simone herself, who stood there almost glowing with her mermaid enchantment even though she was in her fifties and well over the hill.

"Uh, did you say the Grim Reaper?" Rez piped up.

A jolt of fear brought Travis out of his daydream. He swallowed and licked his lips, then chuckled. "I'm pretty sure she didn't mean the *real* Grim Reaper."

Miss Simone's brusqueness softened. "I did, actually. And there's nothing to worry about. The Reaper is not as grim as everyone makes out, and he'll be very pleased to receive this box."

Travis blinked at her in amazement, then turned to find his friend looking equally dumbfounded. "I don't get it," he said at last. "The Grim Reaper? The skeleton in a black robe, carrying a scythe? The one who goes around killing people? *That* Grim Reaper?"

Miss Simone raised an eyebrow. "He doesn't kill people. He simply ensures that their soul passes on. You'll be quite safe around him. We wouldn't send you to him otherwise." She brushed her hands together, ending the short briefing. "Now, I'm needed elsewhere. Good luck, boys." She nodded to the parents. "Hal, Abigail—always good to see you."

"You too, Simone," Travis's dad said as she marched away. He watched her go, his gaze lingering. "Does she ever age, Abi?"

"Sure she does. It just doesn't show because of the enchantment."

Travis turned to Rez and held up the box. "This is going to be awesome."

His friend looked equally awed. "Like a treasure hunt, only we're not *finding* treasure, we're *delivering* it." He studied the map. "Looks like we head north across the Parched Plains, through a forest, over a valley, and toward this blank spot."

Travis's dad nodded. "I've been that way. It'll be an interesting walk for you both. You should reach the valley on the other side of the forest before nightfall, and there you can sleep in the open by the river. Build a fire and cook a fish, sleep under the stars, all that good stuff." He grinned. "In the morning, you can head to the Grim Reaper's place."

"Why's it not shown on the map?" Travis asked.

"Because nobody's ever seen it."

Travis glanced at Rez, a shiver going down his spine.

"So how do you know it's there?" He stared at the blank spot some more. "I mean, there must be *something* there."

"Nothing worth noting," his dad said. "But the Reaper lives there, nonetheless. You'll see his home when you get close. Nobody else will. Just you."

Both boys frowned at him, waiting for an explanation. None came.

Scowling, Travis tried another question. "Is it dangerous?"

"All you have to worry about are trolls," his mom said.

"Trolls!"

"Yes. They'll try to charge you a fee for crossing the river in the valley. Don't let them. Show them who's boss. The bridge was built by goblins for travelers."

Rez pointed toward Travis and asked the most important question of the day. "What's in the box, Mr. Franklin?"

Travis's dad smiled. "Nothing you need to concern yourself with. It's locked, anyway. Don't try to break it open. It belongs to the Reaper." He grasped both boys' shoulders. "It's nearly midday already. I suggest you boys get cracking, or you'll end up stuck in the forest at night."

Chapter 3
The Mission Commences

With the slim wooden box stashed in Travis's knapsack and the map in Rez's, the boys set off for the north gate at a brisk pace, the air cool but the sun warm on their backs.

"You don't have to follow us," Travis called back over his shoulder.

His parents were tagging along behind. "Just want to see you off," his dad said. "Also, I want to make sure you can transform okay. Can you show us before you head out?"

"Yeah, Travis," his friend said. "Turn into a chameleon."

Travis frowned. "Chimera." He stopped and carefully placed his knapsack on the ground. "I guess I can try."

They stood on a narrow road of hard-packed dirt to the north of the village, the perimeter fence just ahead and trees beyond. Behind them stood dozens of cottages in a vague semblance of order. A few villagers ambled about. A goblin shuffled past, giving them a friendly scowl that creased his piglike features even more.

Suddenly feeling very self-conscious, Travis concentrated on transforming. *Don't think about it too much*, he thought. *Just do it.*

For a moment, he feared nothing would happen and that he'd spend the entire two days just trying to figure out how to shift. But then the change started, slow at first and gradually speeding up. His legs thickened, his knee and ankle joints shifting and throwing him off balance so that he tumbled forward to catch himself—and as he fell, his hands and arms fluidly altered into the front legs of a lion. He landed on wide, furry paws with impressive claws.

Even as he was gawking at his catlike feet, the rest of his body rippled and morphed, a strange and unnerving feeling when stretched over ten or twenty seconds like this. He heard his friend gasp, and Travis glanced at him with a grin.

Except his new mouth didn't seem to allow a grin. He had a lion's face now, and he suspected his grin was more like a snarl full of fangs.

Despite the oddly slow transformation, everything seemed okay at first. Then he felt movement on his back as though a small person was straddling him and squirming around. He became aware of a voice in his head, saying something that he couldn't quite make out. He tried to twist his neck to see who was back there, but he ended up turning his whole body. Still, he thought he glimpsed a dull-grey shape.

The goat's head, he realized with a shudder.

Though he'd met a chimera the weekend before and seen it in action, not to mention researched the creature in his pre-shapeshifter studies, somehow he'd not really thought too much about one body possessing three heads. He felt that his own presence—his mind, perhaps even his soul—occupied the lion's head at the front end of the body. But what about the goat's head? And the head on the end of his snake tail?

He turned to look again, sticking his tail out to one side. Rather than a lion's usual furry tail, it was clearly reptilian and scaly, a rich golden color, thick at the base where it joined his body and ending with a fairly large snake's head with wide, unblinking eyes. A forked tongue flicked in and out as the snake glared at him. He sensed its voice over that of the goat's head, just a faint whisper that came and went.

"Weird," he said aloud, and his voice emerged as a throaty growl.

Oh, he thought. *The language problem again.*

He'd suffered the same issue while being a wyvern last weekend. It was impossible to form human words with inhuman lips and animal vocal chords. It just didn't work.

"Very good," his dad said.

His mom was a little more glowing. "Beautiful! So gorgeous. Look at that fur, so shiny and clean. And that tail!"

"Not so much the goat's head, though," his dad added. "It looks kind of weird, stuck on your back like that."

A sense of indignation welled up, and Travis opened his mouth to retort—but then he realized the indignation wasn't his. The goat had its own personality, separate to his, though how that could be was a mystery.

He looked at Rez. His friend stood there open-mouthed, rooted to the spot.

"Looks like you're good to go," his dad said, coming over to pat Travis on the shoulder. He ruffled his mane of hair, too. "Stay out of trouble, kids. Just follow the map. See you in a couple of days."

Travis watched his parents turn and leave. They looked pretty relaxed—but then, he was a *chimera*, one of the deadliest creatures in New Earth. Who would mess with him? Even without the fireball-shooting goat's head and the venom-packed snake's head, he was a *lion*, a powerful animal by any standards.

How do I shoot a fireball? he wondered.

That was the goat's job, and Travis doubted he had any control over that part of his body. He could feel the second head twisting about, but it wasn't his own doing. Likewise, the scaly tail seemed to writhe of its own accord, the snake's head peering around with interest.

"Let's walk," Travis said to Rez. "I want to get used to this body and figure things out."

Rez obviously didn't understood a word, but he followed anyway, picking up Travis's knapsack and trailing behind.

It wasn't until they were well outside the village and entering the woods that Rez caught up and started talking. "So, uh . . . you're a chimera."

Finally, he'd gotten the word right. Travis nodded and looked sideways at him as they walked together. Rez had the extra knapsack draped over his shoulder. It would probably be all right to hang it around the goat's head somehow, but there was no way to communicate this.

"And . . . which head should I be talking to exactly?" Rez asked. "Does it matter?"

It was weird the way he looked directly at Travis, then at the goat, then at the snake. "The lion's head," Travis growled.

His friend glanced at him, direct eye contact for a moment. But then the goat bleated and the snake hissed, confusing things.

"*All* of you?" Rez whispered, sounding disturbed.

Travis shook his head, but so did the goat and snake. He couldn't see the goat, but he could feel its vigorous sideways motion.

Rez sighed. "Oh, come on, man. Quit messing with me."

"I'm not!"

They walked on in silence. Travis wanted to talk but couldn't vocalize. Rez clearly didn't know which of the chimera heads to address. Wasn't it obvious, though? Surely the lion's head—at the front of the lion's body—was the most likely?

Travis felt he needed to figure out how to communicate with his goat and snake companions. His *roommates*, since they shared the same body. Travis had control of the legs, so that put him in charge, right? The others needed to fall in line. *Can you hear me?* he thought, wondering if a bit of mental conversation would work.

The goat bleated, and the snake hissed.

Interesting. So we can all hear each other . . . kind of. Or maybe they can hear me better than I can hear them. Maybe they can understand me. I guess this telepathy thing will take time to master. It's so weird for someone who's used to being human to suddenly have three heads with three different—

"Hey, how about changing back?" Rez interrupted. "I don't want to walk all day without talking. And it's not like chatting aimlessly to a dog. I know you're in there somewhere. It's . . . creepy."

Travis couldn't argue with his friend's point of view. And he'd have plenty of time to try again later, maybe get to know his roommates and talk with them.

He paused and concentrated. When he'd been in wyvern form, his first ever alternate body, it had taken him ages to figure out how to revert back. Once he'd gotten used to it, though, it had become second nature.

To his surprise and delight, he shifted to human form without any effort, the transformation fast and fluid. As he did so, his enchanted smart clothes rearranged themselves around him, and his plasticlike shoes wrapped up around his feet. He hadn't noticed where the silky garments had disappeared to, but they'd been there somewhere, safely wrapped around his chimera body awaiting his return to human form.

"There," he said, patting himself down just to make sure everything felt normal. He turned his back on Rez. "No spare heads anywhere?"

"N-no, you're good," Rez said, his eyes wide.

"Did you see where my smart clothes were hidden away?"

Rez frowned. "You call them *smart* clothes?"

Travis rolled his eyes. "I've told you a million times shapeshifters wear smart clothes. They're smart enough to know when a shapeshifter transforms, and they change shape so they don't get ripped apart. What happened to mine?"

"They kinda stayed put, like one of those little sweaters old ladies make for small dogs. Only the material faded out so it was almost invisible—same color as your fur." He reached around and pointed to Travis's upper back. "The silk turned grey up there, though, where your other head was."

Both boys were silent for a moment. Travis sighed. "Like a chameleon changing color."

Rez brightened considerably. "I was right, then, when I called you a chameleon."

"No, you weren't. Come on, let's walk."

Their journey resumed. This patch of woods happened to be very narrow, and less than ten minutes later they emerged on the other side and looked out across endless meadows. Well, not endless—in the distance ahead, the grass petered out, and the soil gave way to dust and rock. But that was a good hour's walk away yet.

They talked about everything and nothing as always, devoured their snacks even though it wasn't long after lunch, swigged from their water bottles, and ended up flinging droplets at each other until it became a full-on assault with streams of water shooting from their squeezable weapons. Laughing, they agreed to save the last ounce or so in case of emergencies.

The lush meadows were easy going, and when the ground hardened underfoot, they speeded up even more, their feet scuffing on flat rock. Nothing beat the grassy hills for beauty, but the Parched Plains were more interesting, full of cracks that might be anywhere between an inch and a mile deep—or so Travis liked to believe.

This dryland stretched a long way north, all the way to the Labyrinth of Fire and beyond, but the map nudged them west toward a forest. They could see the line of trees on the horizon already, another hour or two away.

"My dad came this way when he was twelve," Travis said. "Him and all the other shapeshifters. It was their first real mission. Aunt Lauren had to deal with harpies, and my dad was supposed to visit the labyrinth and persuade dragons to stop eating people."

Lauren and her husband Robbie weren't really his uncle and aunt; they were just very good friends of the family, even more so than the rest of the group.

"They walked all the way to the Labyrinth of Fire?— whoops!" Rez said, stumbling on one of many small rocks strewn about the place.

"No, they rode in a massive six-wheeled machine built by goblins." Travis screwed up his eyes and looked ahead. "I think they headed straight for the forest and cut through instead of going around to the east. We're going to cut through in the same place, but then take a fork to the west. And when we come out the other side, we'll be in the valley."

"And after that," Rez mumbled, "we'll be delivering a package to the Grim Reaper who lives somewhere in the middle of a blank spot on the map."

The moment he uttered those words, the sun drifted behind a cloud and a gloom fell across them. Travis gave a shiver. Their stroll throughout the bright, sunny morning and early afternoon had been trouble-free so far, almost blissful. They'd talked and joked, spilled most of their water, and scoffed their snacks. It had been fun.

But dusk would be upon them in just a few hours. The sun would sink out of sight, darkness would fall, and by then they'd better be hurrying out of the forest and into the Valley of Rocks before it got too dark to see.

"We need to hustle," Travis said, his carefree joy slipping away.

Now it was time to get serious.

Chapter 4
Three Heads Are Better Than One

"Let's rest," Rez said, pointing to a clump of smooth rocks.

Travis had no argument. The plains were far more expansive than they looked, and that was saying something. They'd walked miles and miles, yet the distant forest seemed only marginally closer. It had to be late afternoon by now. The past four hours or so had slipped away.

They laid out their knapsacks on the hard, baked dirt and sat with their backs against the cool, shadowed face of an enormous boulder. Travis twisted around and shielded his eyes against the sun. It was definitely beginning its descent.

"Let's take a look at the box," Rez said.

Travis rummaged and gingerly handed it over. "Don't open it," he warned.

The first thing Rez tried to do was open it. "Can't find a way in," he complained after a while. "I can see where the lid fits—see the line?—but I don't see any hinges or a catch or anything. It won't slide off, either." He strained with it every which way he could think of, his brow furrowed and his hands shaking with the effort.

"Don't break it," Travis said, somewhat relieved it wasn't yielding. He knew how to obey instructions and contain his curiosity, but his friend didn't.

Rez finally gave up and tossed it back to Travis. "Piece of junk," he muttered.

This was the first time Travis had gotten a good look at the slim box. It was unremarkable, made out of a dark cherry or something similar; he didn't know one type of wood from another. He lofted it in the palm of his hand. "Any guesses what's inside?"

"Gold," Rez said. "No, wait. Why would the Grim Reaper want gold? Maybe it's something macabre like an eyeball."

"And what would the Grim Reaper want with an eyeball?"

"I don't know. I just wouldn't be surprised."

Travis dismissed his friend's guess. An eyeball indeed! Maybe it *was* gold, though it weighed almost nothing. It could be anything. Heck, it might be absolutely nothing. His parents might be playing a trick on him after all, simply giving him a purpose for his mission, something tangible to focus on.

If so, it was working.

With disgust, he threw the box back into his knapsack and dug deeper. "What food do you have?" he asked.

Rez had his eyes closed, leaning back against the rock. A bright-orange lizard perched nearby, basking in the sun, perfectly still except for its pulsing throat. "You can't be hungry again."

"No," Travis said, idly wondering if Rez would leap in fright if he spotted the lizard. "But we will be later, and we might not be able to catch a fish."

The whole idea of camping out and feasting on perfectly cooked fish under the stars seemed more fanciful now that the afternoon showed signs of winding down. In his imagination, nighttime temperature was inconsequential, as were bugs and creepy-crawlies. But he knew it wouldn't be as much fun as he hoped. He probably wouldn't find a comfortable place to lay out his waterproof sheet, and they wouldn't be able to keep the fire going all night, and giant spiders would probably scuttle all over the place, and a snake or three would wind its way into his bed . . .

"I have two apples," Rez said, his hands deep in his knapsack, "plus an egg sandwich, a bag of roasted chestnuts, and . . ." He grinned and brought out his carefully wrapped prize. "Small loaf of bread fresh from the market." He sniffed at it and closed his eyes. Then he carefully placed the loaf back in his bag. "We ate the cookies already. I should probably finish the egg sandwich, too, before it goes bad. It was supposed to be my lunch, but we ate at the lab . . ."

Travis sorted through his own contribution. "I have a can of soup from Old Earth, so that'll be great with the bread. And I have two peaches and a hunk of cake with cranberries and raisins in. I guess we'll survive even if we don't catch any fish."

Rez didn't look convinced. "I was counting on catching *something*. I figured you'd be able to pounce on it and then use a fireball to cook it."

"Well, we have to get to the valley first." Travis twisted around again, shielding his eyes against the glare of the sun. "We should get moving. It'll be midnight before we know it."

They slung their knapsacks across their backs and set off, a strong breeze pushing at them. Half a dozen giant rocs flew by, and Travis swore they eyed him as a possible food source. They usually didn't bother with humans—too feisty and not meaty enough to be worth the trouble—but they'd attack if hungry enough.

The hairline fractures across the baked earth were more substantial here, though nowhere near as dramatic as farther north. Travis's dad had regaled him with tales of the shapeshifters' first trip to the Labyrinth of Fire in a monstrous, six-wheeled, steam-powered machine, and he'd told of cracks far too big to leap over, more like chasms. Earthquakes had ripped the region apart long ago, making much of it impassable without long, inconvenient detours. Luckily, the driver, Blacknail the goblin, had already mapped the area, and he steered the steam-powered iron vehicle on a zigzagging but economical path.

Travis wondered if the same goblin had drawn the map Rez had in his knapsack. Someone must have gone to a lot of trouble as it was quite detailed. *Most likely someone who can fly*, he reasoned. Goblins could do it in their usual methodical way, but it would be much easier for, say, a mothman or a harpy. Both had wings *and* human hands with which to draw while flapping about.

Of course, only one harpy would even bother drawing maps, and that was Aunt Lauren. He smiled at the thought of Robbie and Lauren's two children, Melinda and Mason. One of these days, he'd have to go see them and show off his shapeshifting ability . . .

"You're quiet," Rez said.

"So are you."

"I'm only quiet because you are."

The distant forest still seemed a long way off. Travis sighed. "You know, if I transformed, I could probably run pretty fast without tiring."

"You'd tire eventually."

"Yeah, but not as soon as I would in human form." Travis slowed. "What if I shift, and then you sit on my back?"

Rez gave him a look of disdain. "Sit on your back? Are you kidding?" He shook his head and added, "No, that'd be weird."

"What's weird about it?" Travis thought for a second, and shrugged. "Well, maybe it'd be a little bit weird. But what if I were a centaur? Would *that* be weird?"

"You're not a centaur, though. You're a fluffy lion with three heads. Anyway, I'm not sure there'd be room on your back with that great big goat's head sticking out."

"Sure there would."

Rez shook his head. "Forget it. We'll walk. Unless we jog for a bit?"

Travis shrugged. "Okay. Anything's better than this endless slog."

So they broke into a jog. It definitely took away the boredom for a while, and it became a competition to see who could keep running the longest. Gasping, Travis conceded defeat and returned to a steady walk, his throat dry.

At least the forest appeared a little closer now. "I think that helped," Travis said once he'd gotten his breath back.

"We'll run again when you stop being a pansy," Rez said, annoyingly unaffected by the exertion. He hadn't even broken a sweat.

A simple idea popped into Travis's head. "I'll transform, and you run alongside."

Rez looked intrigued by the suggestion. "Human versus chimera in a sprint across the Parched Plains? Sounds good to me. You can carry your own bag, though. I'll hang it off your goat's ear or something."

Travis transformed, excited at the prospect of trying out his ability again.

Only this time, something was off.

He blinked rapidly, staring at the back of the lion's head and its mane of yellow-brown hair. "Huh?" he exclaimed, confused. Meanwhile, Rez reached toward him and slung one of the knapsack shoulder straps over his head. He felt the heavy bag snag around his neck.

He didn't care about the knapsack, though. He cared only for the fact that his consciousness was now inside the head of the goat rather than the lion.

Rez took off running.

"Wait!" Travis shouted, bleating instead. "I can't feel my legs!"

Even as that realization popped into his head, his lion body took off running after Rez, catching up just moments later. His friend looked sideways at him—at the lion's head—and grinned. "I'm not the fastest runner in school, but I betcha I can outlast anyone."

Travis had no argument there. His friend had always been able to escape the clutches of his pursuers during games of tag.

He concentrated on his predicament. This wasn't what he'd expected. So he was the goat's head now? He didn't like that at all. First of all, it seemed demeaning. A goat wasn't half as cool as a lion. But worse than that, he had no control over his legs. He might as well be a passenger sitting astride the lion's back—just like he'd asked of Rez moments before.

Maybe that very suggestion had caused this error. Maybe he'd had the notion in the front of his mind as he was shifting, and his magic ability had somehow interpreted that as an instruction. It sounded crazy, but then again, so was having three heads.

So being the goat meant just hanging back and enjoying the ride? Did he have no say in where the lion went? What if he wanted to stop and look at something?

He gave it a try, willing his legs to freeze up.

It didn't work.

Who, exactly, was up front? Who was driving this hybrid chimera creature? The idea of having some unknown consciousness in charge didn't sit well with him.

On the other hand . . .

He felt a surge of excitement well up from somewhere. Apparently, his brain was wired to the lion's body enough to experience feelings that came from the pit of his stomach or wherever feelings came from. In any case, *he was the goat's head*, and that meant he had control over fireballs.

Rez, running alongside, was pointing ahead and saying something, but Travis only half heard him: something about getting the map out to figure out exactly where to head for. Right now, Travis was more interested in coughing up a fireball. How was it done, exactly? He could feel a stirring in his throat, the slow build of heat as a compact fiery projectile formed. It grew slowly, and though he could release it at any time, obviously a larger ball would be way more interesting than a tiny speck.

Fascinated, he could almost picture the superheated orb turning in some protected compartment of his throat. He imagined it growing too big and getting caught on the roof of his mouth as he tried to spit it out, the flames searing his flesh and tongue . . .

Suddenly fearful, he coughed it up as though it were a gob of phlegm and spat it as far as he could directly ahead.

He barely felt the heat. The projectile shot out of his throat as a compact ball and instantly expanded into something he'd seen many times—a spinning, roaring, glowing deadly mass that arced overhead and smacked down on the dry ground.

It exploded, sending dirt in all directions. Rez yelled and reacted wildly, skidding and veering off to the left.

Whoever was driving Travis's lion body took everything calmly in stride and slowed to a halt before the three-foot-wide crater. As if sensing that Travis might want to check it out, the lion halted and turned sideways so he could look down on it.

"Whoa," Travis said, awed at the smoldering damage. *He'd* done that. Not the lion, and not the snake on his back end, but *him*—the goat.

"What the heck?" Rez yelled.

Chapter 5
Entering the Forest

Rez looked almost comical, standing some distance away with his hands on his hips, scowling at the smoldering crater in the ground. "How about a warning before you start shooting lasers out of your eyeballs?"

Being a mere goat's head protruding from a lion's back, Travis had no way to apologize to his friend or argue the difference between lasers and fireballs. "Sorry," he said anyway, then frowned at the noisy bleating sound he made.

"That boiling furball packed a punch!" Rez said.

Again, Travis wanted to set him right. Boiling related to liquids, not balls of flame. To be fair, though, he had no idea what had erupted from his mouth. If he recalled, his dad's fire gland actually used a chemical reaction to produce fire, and it started off in his throat as liquid. Maybe a chimera's fireball was a glob of chemically unstable goo that ignited when exposed to air.

They continued their journey, and finally Travis felt they were making good progress. He and Rez trotted alongside one another, taking short breaks here and there. The forest grew ever closer. According to the map, the entranceway should be easy to spot.

It was. Numerous travelers over the years had meandered northwest across the plains and converged on this one place to cut through the forest. The ground here was worn smooth, forming the vague outline of a road that became more sharply defined as it entered the forest. Trees had been cut back, helping to funnel travelers into the opening.

"So I guess we have the right place, then," Rez said, grinning as he held up the map. "It can't be any clearer. This is where we enter."

Travis nodded. According to his dad, there had been no such road when he'd made his first trip twenty years ago. The big machine he'd ridden had flattened all the little trees and bushes and started a new route, and everyone had been using it since.

We need to take a left at the fork, he thought, wishing he could speak aloud without sounding ridiculous.

The forest road was nice and wide, at least fifteen feet of dry, flat surface sprinkled with pine needles, cones, leaves, and small twigs. Huge six-wheeled steam-powered machines may not pass this way very often, but horses and carts certainly did judging by the shallow wheel ruts. But as wide as the road was, the trees pressed in tight at the sides and above, forming an almost perfect tunnel of thick foliage so that entering the woods was rather like walking into the great hallway of a vine-smothered temple. Very little sunlight penetrated here; all was surprisingly dark.

The wideness of the road gave Travis a sense of safety, even if that feeling was misguided. After all, a predator could easily jump out of the bushes on either side. He remained in chimera form just in case, ready to let loose with a fireball or two.

Rez, however, quickly grew bored with the lack of conversation. "Come on, man, change back so we can talk. You can shift again if something jumps out at us."

Travis reluctantly reverted to human form, which made him feel exposed and vulnerable. Had the forest darkened? Probably—they were deeper now, the arch of light at the entrance now far behind them. As they rounded a bend, that light source vanished completely. The gloom and unearthly quiet bothered him. All he could hear was a gentle rustling in the branches above as a breeze worked its way through.

"I wonder who maintains this road," Rez said, breaking the silence.

Travis was eager to talk about anything at all. "Goblins and dryads."

Rez started glancing all around. "Dryads?"

"Yeah. Darcy O'Tanner, one of my parents' friends, is a shapeshifter dryad. Ages ago, she told the dryads of the forest it would be better to keep this road nice and clear for people to use, otherwise everyone would just cut through the woods in random places. She convinced them it was in their best interests to keep this road maintained so travelers stayed on the road and out of the woods." Travis grinned. "The goblins come through once in a while to clear fallen branches and stuff."

After a while, Rez said, "So how does it work? The dryads talk to the trees and bushes and tell them where not to grow?"

"Something like that."

"That's nuts," Rez muttered. His eyes widened, and he grinned. "Chestnuts, to be precise. Or walnuts. I'm not sure which, but definitely nuts."

Travis pretended not to pick up on the pun and simply offered a nod.

Rez tried again. "Do dryads bark orders at them?" He paused, then: "Get it? Bark?"

This time, Travis didn't even bother to react. It was best not to get his friend started.

"But why would the trees and bushes listen to instructions like that? I guess the softwoods might, like pine and cedar and spruce, but I can't imagine hardwoods like oak and hickory taking orders from a bunch of shy dryads."

Travis shrugged. "Plant life isn't exactly smart. It just does as it's told." He couldn't be certain, but it seemed like the rustling in the trees fell silent just then. He shook it off. "Dryads have a way of *connecting* and getting their message across, and the plants just kind of obey."

Rez pointed upward. "That branch there is hanging a bit lower than the rest. Is that tree deliberately disobeying? Or is it just a knot head?"

"Don't be rude," Travis said, feeling an inexplicable urge to defend the trees. Or if not defend them, at least refrain from insulting them. "Maybe it's just too old and sturdy to get out of the way."

They passed under it, and Rez changed the subject. "So what's it like having three heads?"

This again. "It's weird. The first time I changed, I was the lion and could hear the goat and snake whispering, but I couldn't figure out what they were saying. I was in control of my legs and everything, so I could walk where I wanted. But the second time I changed, I was the goat and was just kind of along for the ride. I got to shoot a fireball, though."

The shocked look on Rez's face was comical. "That's freaky. But shooting a fireball must be pretty cool, I guess." He thought for a moment. "Remember that field trip to Old Earth last year? That movie we went to see?"

Travis would never forget it. Crossing over into Old Earth was always interesting, the people there so different, so reliant on technology. A visit to a run-of-the-mill movie theater had been almost overwhelming—sitting in a massive dark room with hundreds of seats, a moving picture playing across an equally massive screen, deafening sound and music blasting out of the walls. The Old Earthers had looked so relaxed, sitting there munching that awful popcorn stuff, but his classmates had squirmed with unease. He and Rez had gripped the armrests and shrunk down into their collapsible seats as giant space machines ripped through the blackness of space toward them, shooting laser bolts as they twisted and tumbled . . .

He shuddered. "Never again."

"Well, anyway, if the chimera is a spaceship, maybe the lion's head is the pilot, and the goat's head is the gunner."

Travis thought long and hard about that. "I guess so. And the snake on the end is . . . what? Another gunner?"

"Sure. A tail gunner. It brings up the rear."

"I don't want to be just a gunner," Travis said with a scowl, stamping on a slim dead branch lying in the middle of the road. It cracked underfoot. "I want to be in charge of my own body.

But then again, I want to be able to shoot fireballs when I want to. I feel like I'm sharing with two other people I don't even know."

"Well, they're *you*, surely?" Rez said, looking surprised. "Who else would they be?"

"But if they're me, how come I'm not in control of everything at once?"

Rez shrugged. "You're headstrong, but not *that* headstrong. You're human and not supposed to have three heads. Something like that could seriously mess you up. I mean, imagine if you—"

He broke off suddenly, coming to a halt as he grabbed Travis's arm.

Travis followed his wide-eyed gaze.

Peering out of the darkness of the trees to one side was a large, hairy face with fangs sticking up from the corners of its mouth. The creature had to be eight feet tall, and it didn't look friendly. It slipped out from behind the tree trunk and waded through a bush, revealing oversized hands on the ends of thin arms covered with shaggy greyish-brown hair.

Travis swallowed. "It's a troll," he muttered.

Rez remained absolutely still. "That's bad, right?"

It could be worse, he thought absently. He knew some troll clans were bigger, more like twelve feet tall. These were forest-dwellers, a little smaller. But still huge.

The troll took slow but deliberate strides toward them, hunching over a little and glancing from side to side as it came. Travis spotted movement in the bushes behind it, and to his dismay, three more trolls emerged. The four converged in the middle of the road, and the leader tilted its head as it glared at Travis and Rez.

"Pay," it said in a deep, guttural voice, holding out one of its large hands.

Travis sighed. This, it seemed, was what trolls were known for—blocking passage and making travelers pay a fee of some kind. They typically didn't speak the language of humans, but if they had to learn just one word, it would be "Pay."

"We don't have any money," he said loudly.

The troll's expression hardened. "Pay."

Travis considered everything he had in his knapsack. A tiny bit of food, a plastic sheet, a few bits and bobs—and a valuable box belonging to the Grim Reaper, which the trolls absolutely must not get their hands on.

He spoke quietly to his friend. "I guess this is where shapeshifting comes in handy. I don't know how this is going to turn out, so go find a place to hide, okay?"

"I'm not leaving you," Rez murmured.

The trolls shuffled closer, and the leader's eyes roamed over the bags Travis and Rez carried, its intentions clear.

"Hide," Travis whispered urgently—and then transformed, wondering how easy it would be to dodge these trolls if they ran at him. He found himself in the head of the lion, and he let out a roar as he planted his clawed paws into the dirt and made a stand. Behind him, he sensed the goat head was already busy working on a fireball.

All four trolls stopped dead, their eyes widening in unison.

The leader gave a curious bark and gestured wildly. The other three let out howls and launched themselves toward Travis, baring their fangs and reaching with their massive hands.

"Stay back!" Travis growled, though he knew they couldn't understand him. "Fireball!" he urged the goat's head.

But the trolls were too fast. They fell on him before the goat was ready, and suddenly Travis found himself pinned to the ground, laying on his side with the weight of three eight-foot trolls spread over him.

The goat finally let loose with a fireball, but it missed its targets and shot straight upward. It arced sharply and headed back down, smacking into the road just five feet away. The explosion threw dust and spatters of hot liquid over them all, and the trolls cried out as the sizzling droplets burned their flesh. Travis felt a drop or two himself, but he was too busy wriggling to care.

The trolls wrenched at his knapsack, which he realized he hadn't taken off when he'd transformed; it was still slung across his back and somehow caught around the goat-head's chin as they yanked at it. The trolls viciously punched the goat in the face, and it bleated continuously.

Travis thrashed and twisted, furious that he was so helpless. He glimpsed the fourth troll, the leader of the pack, loping closer to join in the battle . . . but it went for Rez instead, who yelled and ran for the trees.

One of Travis's attackers let out a yelp, sounding oddly like a dog in pain. Travis heard a savage hiss, then another yelp. Two trolls tumbled off his back. They scrambled away, leaving the third alone. With the much lighter weight on his back, Travis wrenched himself loose and leapt to his feet, slashing with his claws as he did so, catching the last troll across the face.

Travis became aware of his tail swinging wildly back and forth of its own accord, the snake head hissing with anger. He shook himself and snarled, turning from one troll to another, daring them to attack again.

Two nursed snake bites, one on a shoulder, the other on its rear end. Neither of the creatures looked willing to jump back into battle. They backed away, leaving the third alone. When it realized this, it gave a cry of rage and turned to face them, urging them to help.

The goat's head chose that moment to release another fireball. It shot through the air toward the trolls, smacking into the ground at their feet. As before, the small but powerful explosion sent up a shower of dirt and splashes of lava, and the three of them yelped and batted at their smoldering hair. All three raced off the road and into the trees, and after a frenzy of rustling bushes, they were gone.

"Rez?" Travis growled, spinning around.

There was no sign of him. Sniffing at the ground, Travis picked up his friend's scent and scurried into the trees.

Finding him should be easy enough—if the leader troll didn't find him first.

Chapter 6
Scent of the Troll

"Rez!" Travis yelled, succeeding only in roaring noisily. He tore after his missing friend, knowing he would probably come across the troll leader first. The creature's nasty scent was much stronger than Rez's.

As he zigzagged between the trees, he could feel his goat companion working up a new fireball. But he had to wonder about the dangers of letting one loose in the middle of a forest. It hadn't rained much in the past week, and everything was dry. Those fireballs exploded and flung what seemed like lava around the place. Any one of those drops might set dry brush alight.

"Rez!" he roared again.

He gave up and focused on following the scent instead, slipping easily through the thick vegetation, spotting occasional prints in the soil and broken fronds where something large and clumsy had blundered past. As far as he knew, trolls preferred mountainous regions; their oversized hands and long fingers were adept at scaling rock faces. But he supposed they were equally agile among the trees, too.

He marveled at how quickly he moved. His lion body was far better than a clumsy wyvern when it came to trekking through woods.

When a strong troll smell assaulted his nostrils, he froze for a second, then eased forward in stealth mode. He saw and heard nothing through the bushes ahead, but he was close. The troll had a musky scent.

Pushing carefully through some ferns, he froze again. There it was, directly ahead. The gangly creature was busy studying the ground, probably looking for tracks, searching for signs of

Rez. Travis grinned to himself. His friend had given the troll the slip.

He waited. There was no sense fighting the troll unless he had to. Maybe it would give up and head back to its lair.

With a soft cry of excitement, the troll pounced on something. It stared at what Travis guessed was a footprint or a cracked twig on the ground, and then it looked up, searching ahead. It moved on, slowly, parting the ferns with the greatest of care as though they were delicate, treasured things.

Travis padded after the troll, amazed at how perfectly he placed his paws to avoid snapping twigs and rustling dry leaves. He'd never been so furtive before, utterly silent, less than twenty feet behind his quarry. Even his goat head was silent.

The troll stopped again, staring at something just ahead. Travis could see a large patch of white against the dark greens and browns, like an ivory column of some sort. But what would a manmade structure be doing out here in the dense woods? He frowned, creeping forward for a better look.

When he was just ten feet away from the troll, he became aware that the goat was working up a fireball again. It sounded like someone swallowing and regurgitating over and over. *Not yet*, he thought with a touch of annoyance. *Who's in charge here, anyway?*

The goat continued working one up, and Travis returned his attention to the troll.

It let out a guttural exclamation and took two steps forward—but then it paused, looking up and around as if noticing something for the first time. Travis looked, too, and saw thin white tendrils threaded through the undergrowth and dangling from the branches above. They looked so out of place in the woods that he felt a chill. So did the troll, apparently, because it backed up, crouching low to avoid getting close.

Abruptly, it turned to leave—and faced Travis.

It swung its arms wide and roared with anger.

If you're going to use that fireball, Travis told his goat self, *then now would be—*

A fireball shot over his head and smacked into the troll's chest with enough force to knock it five feet backward. Spots of orange bounced off in all directions, each droplet sizzling angrily on contact with the surrounding foliage. Several leaves developed round, smoking holes, and a few burst into flame and flickered for a second before dying out.

The troll lay spread-eagled on its back, completely still except for the gentle rise and fall of its smoking chest. Its entire upper torso was blackened, and smoke curled upward along with a nasty smell of burning hair.

Shocked, it took Travis a while to edge closer for a better look. The wound was terrible, the hair scorched off to reveal bare skin underneath, which itself was reddened and blistered. *Wow*, he thought. *I mean, it's a fireball, what did I expect? But still . . .*

"About time you showed up!"

Rez's voice jolted him from his slack-jawed study. He sidestepped the motionless troll and headed into the clearing. Straight ahead, the white column he'd spotted earlier turned out to be the trunk of a bizarre plant as thick as a tree at its base and spreading into at least a dozen thin, smooth branches that arced overhead. They in turn split into fine tendrils that wound through nearby boughs and hung down into the undergrowth, so tightly curled in places that it would take days of hard work to disentangle it all if anyone wanted this creepy plant removed.

But Travis doubted anyone knew it was here. This was one of his dad's infamous white-tentacled monsters, quite possibly one he was not aware of. He would have mentioned it otherwise. Heck, he probably would have marked it on the map.

Rez was busy extricating himself from a hidey-hole at the base of the white trunk. Travis sucked in a breath at the realization his friend had been *leaning against it*.

"What took you so long?" Rez said, his words vaguely slurred. He slowly climbed to his feet, took his time checking for his knapsack, and shuffled forward. "That troll was too fast for me, so I hid, and just when I thought I was going to be there forever, it showed up and stood there for about an hour!"

Travis needed to explain something to his friend. He reverted to human form and checked that his smart clothes were back in place. His own knapsack, while hanging around the goat's neck, had been yanked about by trolls. Now it was beaten and torn. He adjusted it and waved his friend closer. "Come away from that thing."

He led Rez away from the clearing and past the prone troll. In single file, they hurried back through the woods toward the road.

"Man, we're never going to get out of this forest before dark now," Rez moaned. He looked up. The canopy of trees was too thick to see through, but daylight showed in places. "I reckon we lost a good two hours or more. Where _were_ you, Travis?"

Travis sighed. "I was right behind you the whole time. You happened to find one of those tentacle-monsters my dad studies. He knows of eighteen in this region, so this one makes nineteen. I can't wait to tell him."

Rez stopped dead. "Wait, what? Are you telling me _that_ was one of those weird white plants he goes on about?"

"It's not a plant," Travis said. "Scientists have done studies and agree with my dad that these things are more animal than plant, but they won't accept what he says—that they're actually the tips of something much larger below the ground. Something sentient, my dad says. He thinks it's one giant organism, like a gigantic brain, wrapped halfway around the planet just below the crust."

Rez was speechless. He shook his head, and they both resumed their return journey to the road. "Okay, so you've told me about this before, and the stuff about the brain is still completely nuts. But that's the first time I've seen one in real life. I hid in a hole right next to it. I actually _leaned_ against it!"

38

"Which is why time slowed for you. The monster made your brain go into hyperdrive while it absorbed your thoughts, and that interfered with your senses."

"Yeah, I get it," Rez said with a sigh. "I know all about it, I've just never seen one in person. There's another plant just like it in the Prison of Despair near Carter, right? Prisoners serve a week behind bars and come out feeling like they've been there for months, and that's about how I felt just now—like hours had passed."

Travis nodded. "You were only there a few minutes. Imagine if you were a prisoner, unable to walk away from it. You'd have tons of time to think things through, maybe even start feeling sorry for whatever crime you committed. It's prisoner rehabilitation sped up."

"It's torture," Rez muttered. "You'd think about your family and friends moving on with their lives while you're stuck behind bars, and you'd eventually do your time and feel remorse and everything . . . when actually just a week or two has passed in the real world. Freaky stuff!"

Travis smiled. "Dad came up with a name once, but he doesn't use it because it's a little goofy. He calls them Treentacles."

Rez laughed. "Ha! Like 'tree' and 'tentacle'? That's my kind of name. All right, they're Treentacles from now on."

"You know," Travis said, scratching his chin, "I sometimes wonder if one of those Treentacles is wrapped around the walls of our classroom. It would explain why Math drags so much."

"Yeah. I bet the class is really only about two minutes long."

They emerged onto the road exactly where they'd veered off earlier. Travis looked for trolls, but they seemed to have made themselves scarce—for now. "We'd better hurry in case they come back."

After a few minutes of hurried walking, Travis felt marginally better. Around the next bend, they came across a fallen tree and eyed it suspiciously, wondering if it was a trap.

It had to be a fairly recent collapse. Such a big tree would take some serious work to clear before any travelers with carts used the road. But it didn't slow Travis and Rez; they simply clambered over it and moved on.

"Let's look at the map," Travis said.

With a bit of fumbling, Rez dug it out of his knapsack and unfolded it. They walked slower, peering at the map with interest.

"Doesn't tell us much," Rez complained. "It's hard to say how far we've come into the forest and how far we have to go. It should tell us how long it takes overall."

"Yeah, but some people walk and others ride horses and carts," Travis argued. "So it can't just say 'An hour's walk' or whatever. I don't think it's to scale, either. We've come around a few sharp bends already, but they're not really shown in detail. I guess we just keep walking until we get to the gnarly tree."

The words *Left at Gnarly Old Tree* were printed on the map. It indicated a narrow path through the woods that would lead them to the western fringe of the forest. That, at least, gave them an estimate of how long it would take: *Fifteen Minutes' Walk to Valley*. This also suggested the path was too narrow for carts.

"So we're not out of the woods yet," Rez said with a smirk. He glanced sideways at Travis. "See what I did there? Not out of the woods yet? With the trolls still around—"

"Yeah, I get it, thanks," Travis said, putting on his most bored expression. Rez's puns were awful at the best of times. "Keep your eyes open for a gnarly old tree."

Rez shook his head. "How stupid is that? Our only marker is a tree in the middle of a forest."

"It must be a *particularly* old and gnarly one, then."

They kept walking, lapsing into silence for a while, now studying every single tree on the left-hand side of the road. Quite a few might be considered old and gnarly, but none really stood out, and Travis felt that the one they wanted had to be something really special, something unmissable.

"I can't see the tree for the forest," Rez quipped. To make it worse, he started emphasizing his keywords to make his puns extra clear. "Sorry, you must think I'm *barking* crazy. Did you *twig* my joke just then? What a *sap* I am! I'd better quit before you walk off and *leaf* me alone out here . . ."

Travis tuned him out. When Rez started in on the puns, it was best to just offer a polite smile and look away. Getting annoyed just made Rez laugh and work harder.

He had more important things on his mind. What if they'd missed the gnarly old tree? They hadn't been paying attention earlier because it seemed too soon to come across it, but what if the map was completely out of scale and the left fork was just a hundred yards into the forest? They might have passed it already. But he didn't want to turn around and go back, either.

Just keep looking, he decided.

"I was thinking about *branching* out and being a comedian," Rez continued. "Sorry, that's *knot* funny."

Travis clicked his tongue. "Are you still going on? I hope you're looking out for this gnarly old—"

He broke off, and his mouth fell open.

There it was—possibly the oldest, gnarliest tree he'd ever seen.

Chapter 7
The Narrow Path

The ancient monstrosity loomed ahead, jutting into the road in defiance of the dryads and goblins, its branches hanging low. Even its coloring was off, a far more reddish brown than any other tree in the forest. The bark looked like scabs on top of scabs. A massive burl stuck out to one side. Carpenters might one day make some fine furniture out of such a desirable deformity, but right now it looked like a cancerous growth.

This was most definitely, unquestionably the gnarly old tree mentioned on the map.

And right alongside the thick, twisted, knotty trunk, a narrow path cut deep into the woods, so narrow that a traveler would probably have to twist sideways in places to avoid being snagged on the prickly bushes lining its sides. It barely qualified as a path at all.

Travis and Rez came to a halt at the junction. "Gnarly old tree," Rez said. "And a path."

"Another fifteen minutes' walk, and we'll be out of this forest," Travis said, pleased. "Good thing, too, because it's starting to get dark."

Without another word, Rez folded the map and handed it to Travis. "You keep it. I got to thinking earlier that I might have lost it when that troll came after me. If I'd lost it, you would have failed your mission. I don't want that. So you keep it. That way, it's your own fault if you lose it."

"Thanks," Travis said doubtfully. "Well, let's go."

He tucked the map into his pocket and stepped off the wide road, edging past the gnarly sentry and onto the narrow path. Prickly bushes immediately snagged at his smart clothes, but rather than rip, the fabric peeled apart to release the thorns before melding together again.

Behind him, Rez wasn't so fortunate. "Ow! Oh, hey, that's not fair. What the heck?"

Travis twisted around to see his friend yanking loose with a tearing sound. "Crowded, isn't it?" he said. "Mind these roots on the ground. I nearly tripped."

Indeed, the path bore little resemblance to a well-worn route. It was full of ups and downs and protruding roots, and so overgrown with weeds it was obvious nobody had passed this way in quite a while. Anyway, if it were a frequently used path, the goblins would have chopped the bushes back on either side.

Still, the dryads must have been at work, because they'd gotten the dense vegetation to part down the middle and lean out of the way, otherwise there would be no path at all.

"This is going to be a long fifteen minutes," Travis muttered, raising his arms high so he could squeeze through the gaps a little easier.

Thankfully, the path widened a little deeper in. At least he and Rez were able to walk comfortably now. They followed the gentle curve around to the left.

"Quiet, isn't it?" Rez whispered from behind him.

Travis understood exactly what his friend meant. If the main road through the forest was like an ivy-smothered temple corridor complete with a reverent hush, then this path was a secret passage behind its walls, steeped in deathly silence. Whatever soft breezes had rustled the trees earlier had faded. Now the boys heard nothing but their own footfalls.

To break the oppressive quiet, Travis said, "So why don't you want to be a shapeshifter?"

Rez clicked his tongue and tugged his shirt free again. "Huh? Oh, well, it's just not natural. Nobody is meant to be able to change shape like that."

"But we *can*," Travis said, puzzled. This wasn't the first time they'd discussed this, and it wouldn't be the last, but he'd hoped his friend's attitude had changed in the past week or two. "So you still won't even consider it? After seeing me become a chimera?"

"Look, shooting laser beams from your eyeballs is impressive, but it's not for me. Nor is a life with Portal Patrol, guarding portals against unruly types from Old Earth. And as for being an emissary or delegate of whatever—forget it. All that diplomatic stuff? Sorting out problems between humans and nonhumans? That's just not me."

Travis laughed. "No, you're not the most diplomatic person I've ever met. If you were a centaur shapeshifter dealing with some complaint or another, you'd end up starting a war the moment you opened your mouth. You'd probably address the khan as 'chief' or 'big boss man,' and you'd make some comment about stinky rear ends."

"Centaurs *do* stink," Rez said. "Have you seen all the flies that follow them about? And as for a centaur shapeshifter . . . Why would any self-respecting human want the rear end of a horse?"

"But what about a wyvern? I wish you'd seen me last week, Rez, flying about in the sky. It's the best feeling in the world, and it's *so easy*."

Rez grunted. "Not for me. I'd crash and leave a wyvern-shaped indentation."

After a pause, Travis said, "So you just want to be a carpenter when you leave school?"

"Yep. It's a solid, respectable trade. My dad is always busy, and he has a good reputation in Carter. I'm gonna be a full apprentice with him a few years from now. That massive burl on the gnarly tree back there? He'd love to salvage that. If you cut the tree down and sliced that burl the right way, it would make an awesome table or a one-piece armchair—"

They both stopped walking as a sudden rustling swept through the forest. Travis expected a gust of wind to hit him any moment, but none came even though he could see branches moving and the tops of trees swaying. Not *all* the trees, though. Just some of them.

He stared in surprise, noting how one nearby seemed to *twist*, its boughs turning, while neighboring trees stood absolutely still. Another caught his attention, and he swore it moved a few yards closer. He blinked and rubbed his eyes, and when he refocused, all was still again.

"Did you see that?" he whispered, turning to his friend.

Behind him, Rez was frowning. "Uh . . . maybe. Was that wind? I saw the trees moving."

"I saw *some* trees moving," Travis said. "Just a few. Most didn't move at all."

"Wind can do that. Probably a squall."

"A what?"

Rez looked thoughtful. "Like a mini-storm ahead of a bigger storm. But . . ." He looked up, squinting to see through the thick canopy of branches and leaves above. "I don't know. Everything is so calm. They said it might rain, but I don't think that's going to happen."

"No. It looks pretty clear."

They waited a while longer, but everything seemed quiet now. Travis tried to find the trees he thought he'd seen moving, but he wasn't sure anymore. Thick bushes obscured much of his view, and what little he could see was almost lost in the ever-darkening gloom.

"We should hurry," he said at last. "Shouldn't be much farther now."

They continued their trek. A minute or two later, they came upon one of those odd reddish-brown trees standing right in front of them. The path veered sharply to the left, and Travis figured he had to be heading southwest now, which surprised him because the map had indicated more of a northwesterly direction. Or maybe he'd just lost his sense of direction in the oppressive woods.

To his relief, the path widened a little farther. The prickly bushes to the sides seemed to lean backward even more than before, leaving a good three feet of space, almost enough for both boys to walk side by side. The branches above thinned, too, and a pale-purple sky peeked through.

"We're getting there," Travis said, picking up speed. "I think the woods are ending."

"What kind of trees are these?" Rez asked as they passed another reddish-brown trunk. It seemed as gnarled and twisted as the first one they'd come across back on the main road. "I don't recognize them."

Travis couldn't help scoffing. "And you know all about trees, do you?"

"My dad does. He knows them all." Rez stooped to pick up a fallen leaf, and he walked with it held between finger and thumb. "Hmm. Is this cross-venulate or pinnately lobed?"

"Huh?"

Rez grinned. "Did you know leaves have different skeletal structures and vein patterns? Usually reticulate or parallel . . ."

Travis peered at the leaf. It looked no more interesting than any other leaf, just green and leaf-shaped. "How can you tell the difference?"

"I can't. I have no idea what I'm talking about." Rez tossed it and brushed his hands off. "My dad keeps showing me leaves and spouting all this weird tree jargon, but I never have learned what's what. He keeps telling me I can't be a carpenter without knowing my trees. I need to learn this stuff one day."

An idea popped into Travis's head. "Maybe you should be a dryad shapeshifter. Then you'd know everything you ever needed to know about plants and trees, and that would help you in your job as a carpenter."

Rez pursed his lips, then shook his head. "But then I wouldn't want to chop up wood and build stuff. I couldn't hammer nails into planks. I'd probably feel the pain. Using a plane to shave lumber would be like peeling back the flesh on a good friend's leg."

"What?"

"Being a dryad carpenter would suck. For every house I built, I would hear the screams of the forest. Their agony would haunt me in my sleep."

"You're such an idiot. Lumber is just dead wood."

"Is it, though?" Rez demanded, grinning broadly. "Is it really dead? When you hammer a nail in, did you know that blood seeps out?"

Travis shook his head. "Do you mean sap? We have a beam on our ceiling at home that leaks sap. It kind of oozes out and forms a little orange glob."

"Yes, Travis, I mean sap. *The blood of trees.* And as a dryad, I'd weep every time I swung the hammer, and I'd probably wail with despair with every push and pull of the handsaw."

"You don't know what you're talking about, Rez," Travis said, getting annoyed now. "It's probably a good thing you don't ever want to be a shapeshifter. You wouldn't know what to do with your power. It'd be wasted on you."

Rez laughed. "Probably. Hey, shouldn't we be out of this mess by now? Feels like we've been walking for ages."

The narrow forest path wound on ahead, trees and prickly bushes crowding in from both sides, so thick that Travis felt like they might start closing in at any moment. He slowed, puzzled. His friend was right. They should have emerged from the forest by now.

"Did we take a wrong turn?" he wondered aloud.

Rez looked back the way they'd come. "We took a left at that gnarly old tree just like it says on your map. There's nowhere else we could have gone wrong."

Travis fished in his pocket for the folded piece of paper and smoothed it out. "Maybe the map's wrong."

But it looked pretty clear. The forest path meandered for miles, then forked. It was clearly marked *Left at Gnarly Old Tree*, and they'd gone left. They should have made it to the valley shortly after. It actually said *Fifteen Minutes' Walk to Valley* from the fork, but they'd been walking much longer.

"Are we lost?" Rez said with a scowl.

At that moment, a deep, booming moan sounded from the trees.

Chapter 8
The Trees Are Alive!

Travis and Rez froze as the low, eerie moaning continued for ten seconds or more. It trailed off eventually, but new sounds took its place—bushes rustling, branches creaking, twigs cracking, birds taking flight with a frantic flutter of wings. But despite the noise, hardly anything moved, certainly no more than a few trees here and there . . .

A few trees, Travis thought, his heart thumping in his chest. *A few trees are moving.*

He could clearly see one in the evening gloom beyond the hedgerow. The short, stout tree moved slowly through the woods, lurching to one side as it slid around a stationary neighbor, its branches twisting out of the way to avoid getting caught up, the entire trunk bending as though made of rubber. He saw another tree moving to the left, and another—three of them advancing on Travis and Rez.

The hairs on the back of Travis's neck stood on end, and he swung around, realizing two more trees were closing in from behind.

"Run!" he squawked.

He and Rez ran onward, having no choice but to follow the narrow path, hemmed in as they were by bushes. Travis hoped they'd burst from the forest into open land any second now. It couldn't be far. *Fifteen Minutes' Walk to Valley*, the map had said. They'd walked fifteen or twenty already, maybe more. They had to be right on the outer fringe by now.

As another booming moan echoed through the woods, the prickly bushes on both sides shivered as if caught in a cross-breeze, though Travis felt no such gust. The meandering path narrowed until there was only just room to walk single file. The walls of vegetation seemed taller now, making it impossible to see what lay around the next bend, and all he could do was keep running and hope it ended.

The path *did* end, but not in the way he'd hoped. Ahead loomed a familiar splash of white—the weird Treentacle they'd come across earlier that afternoon, with its wide-spread tendrils.

"No, no, NO," Travis moaned, coming to a halt with thorns snagging at him from all sides. "Why are we back *here?*"

To his horror, one of the creepy white tendrils dangled just above his head. He jerked away from it, lashing out with a fist. When he hit it, the thing actually recoiled like a snake, twisting away in slow motion. As if that wasn't enough, he swore the nearest bushes flinched. He swung around, eyeing them suspiciously.

"Did you see that?" he whispered.

Intrigued, he boldly reached for the tendril and gripped it tightly in one hand, squeezing as hard as he could, trying to squash it flat. He remembered his dad had tried to inflict all kinds of damage on one of these tendrils a long time ago, and it had seemed impervious to harm. A strange, numb feeling swept over him as he dug his fingernails in, ignoring how it squirmed like a worm. He held it as long as he could, squeezing until his knuckles turned white and his fist trembled, wondering if prolonged pressure would strangle it in some way.

All around him, bushes recoiled. Was that horror he sensed? Fear? Of what, though? As he looked closer, he saw something within the dense and prickly foliage, something that shouldn't be there, something that moved among the thin branches . . .

"Let that thing go," Rez demanded. "We gotta go back."

Travis sucked in a breath and let go of the tendril. He felt like he'd just woken from a light nap, and he blinked in confusion.

Rez was right. Going back was the only option if they wanted to avoid being sucked into a deep, month-long slumber in the presence of that awful milky-white Treentacle. There was nowhere else to turn thanks to the impenetrable walls at their sides.

"Back," he agreed, and the two of them spun around and ran back the way they'd come, this time with Rez in the lead.

The booming moan had stopped, but the rustling in the trees continued. Travis glimpsed movement again, one tree or another moving ponderously through the woods, getting closer all the time. He imagined it sliding along, obliterating brush and leaving a massive trench in the dirt . . .

But how could that be? Trees didn't move. They *couldn't*.

"The path's closing in again!" Rez shouted from ahead.

It didn't seem possible, but it was true. The path narrowed to a point, finally ending.

"We just came this way!" Travis exclaimed. "How can—?"

He stared suspiciously at the prickly bushes. They quivered in a nonexistent breeze, and as he watched, one *moved*.

Startled, he ducked down to look underneath. At first glance it looked like any other bush, with a thick stem sprouting from the ground. Behind that stem, he could see a short trail in the soil where the bush had obviously come from.

Then he spotted reddish-brown tentacles.

He yelled and scrambled back in horror. "It's alive!"

Rez knelt to see for himself. The tentacles were somehow part of the bush, descending like snakes from higher up, wound tightly around the thick stem, so heavily camouflaged they only showed when they wriggled. There were four of them, spreading outward across the soil, digging in deep like roots . . . only they *moved*, walking the bush inch by inch, closing in.

Shocked, Travis leapt to his feet again. "This isn't even a path," he said through gritted teeth. "Something's gone wrong. We have to get out of here."

Rez jerked around, sweat on his forehead. "How?"

It was clear their path was designed to marshal them toward the Treentacle, though for what possible reason Travis had no idea. He had no intention of succumbing to the time-skewing effects of the eerie monster. But they couldn't stand around, either. The trees were still moving out there in the darkness. He could see one less than ten or fifteen feet away, its limbs swinging around in slow motion as the trunk swayed and lurched, still advancing. High up, just below where the branches sprouted, Travis thought he saw a knothole opening wider like the jaws of a monster . . .

"Stay close," he told his friend. "I'm getting us out of here."

He transformed, thinking of fireballs in the hope he would become the goat's head. To his relief, that was exactly what happened. He started working on a fireball straight away, wishing it were a quicker process.

Rez leaned close, breathing hard. "Hurry," he muttered.

The trees loomed closer, ready to—what? Chomp them? Flatten them? How exactly did walking trees kill people?

Travis belched up his fireball. It shot straight into the bushes, tearing a hole through and then exploding as it hit the ground just beyond. But the hole wasn't much good, just a blackened tunnel through the upper half of the nearest bush, too high and too small to struggle through. The bush shook and shivered, and Travis thought he heard a high-pitched scream, but he might have imagined it. In the clearer area beyond, flames licked high as a fire took hold of the dead leaves coating the ground.

"It didn't work!" Rez shouted. "Do it again! Aim lower!"

Again that awful, booming moan, this time much louder. The nearest moving tree was almost upon them, as gnarly and ancient as the others, its reddish-brown bark somehow surviving the dramatic twisting of the trunk. It had to be far more supple than it looked, an immensely tough but stretchable living skin like that of a scaly dragon.

Travis frantically worked on another fireball, but he knew it was too late. And could he really blast a hole through the wall of bushes anyway? The projectile was powerful but small, most of its destructive force ripping loose as it smacked into the ground or some other solid surface. The last one had torn right through the bushes with ease—*too* easily, because it had only left a small hole.

The tree, Travis thought. *Hit the tree.*

The massive trunk lurched suddenly, its branches spreading out overhead. Bushes quivered in its presence, like evil minions rallying around their master. If the situation weren't so terrifying, Travis might have laughed at the idea.

Almost there, he thought as the volatile liquid-fire puffed up in his throat.

"Travis!" Rez urged. "Do it!"

He spat it out, aiming for the trunk of the slow-moving tree. The fireball roared into life and shot over the tops of the bushes, skimming the top of one and causing it to sizzle. With a resounding *smack!*, the flaming orb exploded dead center of the trunk.

Chunks of bark and wood flew outward amid a flash of bright yellow flames and orange lava droplets. The damage was staggering, a giant hole fringed with black where it had been charred. Scorched tentacles were visible through the hole, leaking yellow blood. Around the damage, the trunk was split and broken.

For a long, terrible few seconds, a deathly silence fell over the woods. Then a knothole higher up opened wide, and the tree let out a mournful howl. Travis gaped in amazement and horror as he made out a face surrounding that mouth—two slits for eyes, a shapeless nose, even a chin of sorts. The face was vague at best, easily missed if the thing was stationary as a tree should be . . . but animated like this, screaming in agony, it stood out plainly.

If the position of the face high on the trunk was anything to go by, then Travis's fireball had hit it in the chest. The tree swayed and continued howling, and as it bent from side to side, the whole thing began to crack and splinter around the wound. All the surrounding bushes quivered and fell into disarray, shuffling apart and leaving gaps everywhere, moving away from Travis and his deadly fireballs.

Suddenly finding himself with a good six feet of space all around and a number of escape routes, he turned and let out a growl, then took off with Rez following closely behind. *Please let us be somewhere near the edge of the forest*, he thought as he hurried along. *We're done with this place now.*

It concerned him that the path he'd been on earlier, so tightly hemmed in on both sides, no longer existed at all. The map clearly showed a path, so there had to be one somewhere . . . but this wasn't it. He and Rez had never found it in the first place. The trees and bushes had tricked him.

He shoved his way through whatever gaps in the undergrowth he could find, noting that most of the bushes were the same variety—all thorns and reddish-brown leaves, standing five or six feet high. And they all seemed to be quivering and jostling, moving about on their tentacled roots.

As Travis ran, the forest opened up, the undergrowth thinning and the suspicious thorny bushes well behind him. He watched the trees closely, looking for movement, but he saw nothing out of the ordinary even in the ever-darkening gloom. It would be night time very soon, and then visibility would be nil. He and Rez *had* to escape this place.

Another booming moan sounded in the distance behind them, followed by a terrible cracking and splintering, the familiar sound of a tree falling. Travis didn't want to think about it. Destroying a tree was one thing, but a mobile treelike creature with a *face*?

It was going to eat us, he told himself as he scampered into a far more open part of the forest. *It wanted to lead us to the Treentacle and make us lose our senses so it could nibble on us while we slept.*

The trees here were spaced ten feet apart, and there were almost no bushes. Pine needles coated the soft soil. This was more like it! Travis picked up speed, aware that Rez was still puffing and panting along behind him.

If it were daytime, he would probably be able to see the valley through the trees and head toward it. But it was dark now, and he saw a blanket of darkness all around. Still, he trotted on. The forest had to end somewhere.

He remembered a riddle his dad had asked him once: "How far can you walk into a forest?" Travis had immediately asked how big the forest was, and his dad had replied, "It doesn't matter. Now, what's your answer?" Travis had pondered the riddle for ages, unable to fathom how he was supposed to know the answer when he had no idea how big the forest was. A mile? Two? Ten? His dad had finally provided the answer: "Halfway. After that, you start walking out."

But it was just wordplay. That simple truth meant nothing to someone lost in the woods. Even if he had passed the halfway point, the forest could be four miles across, in which case he might still have two miles to go. Two miles was an awful long way to stumble through the dark woods at night when being pursued by nightmarish tree monsters and their bushy minions.

And what if he and Rez were just going around in circles?

Chapter 9
Lost in the Woods

"I need to rest," Rez gasped.

They paused to take stock. Travis looked all around, studying the silent trees to see if any had that monstrous, ancient, gnarled quality about them. They seemed normal enough, mostly pine trees, tall and straight with greyish bark.

He reverted to human form and checked for his knapsack. It was still there, though he had to adjust it again. "What was *that?*" he demanded, jerking a thumb over his shoulder.

"You tell me," Rez said breathlessly. "You're the expert."

It was true that Travis had done a lot of studying over the years to prepare for his shapeshifting career. He knew quite a bit about eighty percent of the magical creatures dwelling in New Earth. There were others he recognized from pictures and descriptions but hadn't gotten around to researching. But animated trees?

He squinted in the darkness, looking for any sign of movement. "Well, obviously I've read about talking trees. Everyone has."

"Not me," Rez muttered.

"There are old stories about them, but they're not real."

Rez scoffed and threw up his hands. "They looked pretty real to me!"

"But they *can't* be." Travis shook his head. There was no point denying what they'd seen tonight. "How can they be living here in the woods without anyone knowing? People use that road all the time. Why has nobody run into these moving trees before?"

"Maybe the ones who saw the trees got themselves eaten."

That was a sobering thought. What if many passed by without any deadly encounters, but those unfortunate enough to be trapped by prickly bushes and flesh-eating trees met with a sticky end? What about the trolls, though? Surely they would have—

Travis clicked his tongue with annoyance. "I bet the trolls know about the trees. They probably charge a toll for safe passage through the forest, and those who avoid the fee wind up getting lost like we did, never heard from again."

"How could they get lost?" Rez argued. "Most people would probably just continue on the main road. We only got lost because we turned left at the gnarly old tree like it said on the map."

The gnarly old tree . . .

Travis would have fished the map out again, only it was now too dark to see. "It was one of *them*," he said bitterly. "Same color, same ugliness. That's why it stuck out into the road more than other trees. That wasn't the left turn we were supposed to make. The tree could have wandered out and stood anywhere it wanted, and the bushes lined up behind it. We were tricked."

Rez sighed. "So the path we wanted was a bit farther on? We turned left too early?"

And now we're lost, Travis thought. He looked around again. Any lingering feeble light had faded, and the woods were black. They could try to stumble on, but it would be a treacherous journey. *But so is staying here waiting for monster-trees to sneak up out of the darkness.*

"Should we carry on?" he asked his friend.

Rez shrugged. "I'm game. Better than sitting here."

So they set off again, feeling their way. The trees were almost solid black now, and the earliest signs of moonlight showed through the branches above. Travis knew it would be easier to pick his way in the darkness if he transformed, but he remained human for now so they could talk in low voices.

"I'm pretty sure I would have read about walking trees if they existed today," he whispered. "But there's just a few ancient myths. Miss Simone's never mentioned them, either. Or my mom and dad."

"What's your point?"

"Just that this is something new."

Rez was silent for a moment as he trudged alongside. "Why did that bush have tentacles hanging down? You saw it, right? Like there was an octopus in the bush, and it was dangling its tentacles down the trunk and lifting the whole bush off the ground."

"I saw that," Travis agreed. "And we were being led toward that white Treentacle back there, which also has tentacles. Coincidence? Is there a connection?"

They discussed it for the next few minutes while they plodded through the woods, then fell silent, aware that every step they took caused a terrible scuffling noise that might be heard for miles. Then again, the walking trees made even more noise.

They don't walk, Travis reminded himself. *They slither and slide.*

"Gnarlers," Rez said.

"Huh?"

"Those gnarly old trees that move? I hereby name them Gnarlers."

"Uh, okay," Travis said.

"And the bushes that shuffle everywhere? Shufflers."

"*Shufflers*? Seriously?"

"Got a better name?"

Travis didn't. And since he also didn't care either way, he shrugged and agreed.

"This is hopeless," Rez said at last. "We could be going in circles. I can't see a thing now."

The feeble moonlight barely helped at all. Travis slowed and looked around, a sense of despair settling over him. He saw nothing but vague silhouettes now. Rez was right. They *could* be going in circles.

"I'm going to transform," he said. "Maybe I can sniff our way out. Stay close."

He shifted to his chimera form and set off, making sure his friend followed. He quickly realized he had no useful scent to pick up on, at least not one that would lead him out of the woods. It was certainly easier to traverse the rough ground, and he didn't mind as much when protruding branches and brambles tried to snag him, but he was still directionless.

Keep going, he told himself. *Maybe we'll get lucky. The edge of the forest could be just a few paces ahead for all I know. We might blunder out of the trees any minute now.*

"Watch what you're doing with that tail," Rez muttered from behind.

Travis instantly became aware of his snake's head swinging about, but he couldn't control it. The entire tail—a serpentine body—writhed and twisted into tight loops, then somehow slipped loose of its own knots and started over.

"Some trip this is turning out to be," Rez said with a sigh. "Maybe you should have been an ogre, Travis. Don't they have a great sense of direction?"

They walked and walked until, with an unspoken agreement, they both halted and stood in silence listening to the forest, mostly the sounds of cicadas chirping and bullfrogs croaking. There was a breeze, but just a faint one, whispering through the trees from time to time. Occasionally, a twig cracked somewhere. It could be a squonk shuffling around, or it might be dryads. Or trolls. Or even a walking tree.

Travis reverted to his human form. "This is pointless. We're gonna have to wait until it's light again. Even if we had a torch to carry around, or a lantern, it wouldn't show us anything in the distance. We still wouldn't find our way out." He took off his knapsack and threw it down. "Let's start a campfire."

"Start a fire?" Rez looked doubtful. "They'll see us."

"Who? The walking trees and bushes? Yeah, they might—if they have eyes. If they *don't* have eyes, then they must sense us some other way, like smell or movement . . . which means our fire won't make a difference."

"They might smell the smoke."

"Yeah, well, what else can we do? It's too cold not to have a fire. Anyway, it might keep bugs and snakes off us."

"Let's make a fire," Rez agreed.

They sat on pine needles and delved through their knapsacks, wishing for even a tiny bit of light to see by. Feeling around, Travis eventually found his firestarter and small pouch of tinder. With the utmost care, he pulled out a cotton puff and placed it on the ground next to him, then arranged the delicate splinters on top.

"Need some twigs," he said quietly, as if speaking louder would cause a draft and blow it all away.

"Already on it," Rez said, his voice equally low.

Fumbling in the darkness, he handed the twigs to Travis, who added them to his pile. "And get ready with some bigger stuff."

While Rez scrambled around nearby, Travis began striking the firestarter's striking blade against the magnesium block. Sparks flew immediately, like miniature flashes of lightning, and he scraped rapidly to get a good sense of where his tinder was located. Then he was able to bend lower and aim at it.

After the twentieth try or thereabouts, the cotton caught alight. He watched breathlessly at it glowed orange. Was he supposed to blow on it? Maybe if it started dying down . . .

But it didn't. The tiny, newborn flame crept over the blackening puff of cotton and sniffed curiously at the splinters above. When they started catching, more flames sprang up, then more as they found the larger twigs.

"It's working," Travis said, fighting to contain his delight.

Rez moved closer. "Here are some logs."

They weren't so much logs as thin, brittle, long-dead branches snapped into pieces. But they were bigger than the twigs, and perfectly dry, so Travis gently added them to the fire.

With flames growing hotter and brighter, his friend came into view at last while their surroundings darkened further. A campfire made all the difference—warm, friendly, and a source of safety against creepy-crawlies. Plus, they could cook over it.

"Let's heat up our soup," Travis suggested. "When the fire's nice and hot, we'll pour it into my tin pot."

Rez nodded and rubbed his hands. "Yeah—soup and some nice fresh bread. Sounds good."

They spent the next fifteen minutes setting up their camp. The large plastic sheet meant something clean and relatively bug-free to sit on; being orange, it would be easy to spot any critters crawling toward them. Both knapsacks were emptied and sorted through in the light of the fire. Their first priority was food, and they divvied their rations while waiting for the soup to heat.

"This would be fun if it weren't for the Gnarlers," Rez said.

"Yeah, killer trees kind of spoil the atmosphere a bit. Maybe they'll stay away. Maybe we gave them the slip."

"How are we supposed to sleep tonight with those things out there?"

Travis thought of the long, long night ahead. It was still only early evening. They had at least eight or nine hours to get through before the sun rose. "We'll probably have to take shifts," he said. "It's a pain, but if we're not careful, those Shufflers will creep up on us."

The soup and bread were impossibly delicious, and all their worries faded for a good ten minutes or so. Even afterward, as they burped and lay back with their eyes closed, it seemed their night out in the woods might not turn out so bad after all. With a fire, food, supplies, and the knowledge that civilization wasn't a million miles away, they just needed some daylight to find their way out. Until then, taking shifts and keeping the fire going was essential.

Oh, and stay on the lookout for trolls, Travis reminded himself.

He opened his eyes and sat up. Falling asleep would be disastrous. Rez already looked like he was snoozing. If so, it would be best to let him.

Resigned to a first shift, Travis carefully fed the fire with a few more short lengths of brittle deadwood, then got up and moved away from the orange sheeting. He could better hear the sounds of the forest without being so near to the crackling fire.

I'll climb a tree, he thought. *Or sit next to one, anyway. I'll listen out for trolls and killer trees, and I'll transform the moment I hear anything. Let Rez sleep.*

And so he leaned back against the trunk of a tree—an ordinary one, not one of those Gnarlers—and psyched himself up for a long, patient wait.

Ten minutes later, he was too cold to sit there any longer. He returned to the plastic sheet and huddled over the fire, warming his hands while feeding the flames with a handful of fresh twigs. Whether or not he needed to watch out for lurking trolls or lurching trees, it was going to be a full-time job just keeping the campfire going.

It occurred to him then that he could try switching to chimera form. Maybe three heads were better than one. He could sleep while one of the other heads stayed awake and kept watch.

He experimented, ending up in the snake's head. This suited him fine. Let the others stay awake awhile, and then he could switch places a little later on. He settled down, resting his snake body on the plastic sheet fairly close to the fire, enjoying the warmth. He began to feel drowsy.

Then he scowled, seeing that the goat's eyes were closed. It looked like the lion was asleep, too, though it was hard to tell from this angle. "Hey, guys," he hissed. "That's not fair!"

Or was it? Why should *he* get to sleep first and not the others?

As it happened, both the lion and goat jerked awake just then, and over the next fifteen minutes of trying to drop off again, he came to the conclusion that all three heads shared the same sleep cycle. It seemed when the body shut down for the night, it affected them all. This made sense. After all, his heart rate and breathing slowed, his body temperature fell, and his natural senses dulled, and none of these things could happen while one or more heads remained fully alert.

It's up to you and me, Rez, he thought. He reverted to human form and resolved to stay awake for an hour or two.

Only he didn't.

Chapter *10*
Creepy-Crawlies

Travis woke suddenly. He stared up at the trees above, seeing an orange sky through the leaves. A ray of sunshine had worked its way through and warmed his cheek.

He sucked in a breath. He'd fallen asleep!

Horrified, he struggled to sit upright but found that his legs were pinned. He pushed up on his elbows, fearful of what had fallen across him—and let out a gasp of terror.

Reddish-brown Shuffler bushes stood all around, completely encircling him and his friend as well as the plastic sheet and the white ashes of the smoldering campfire. Travis shivered. The brambles and shrubs looked innocuous enough except for their coloring and the fact that they hadn't been there the night before. They'd crept up on the campsite and might have been standing there for hours.

Outside the circle stood at least five of the stout Gnarlers. He must have been in a truly deep sleep to ignore the noise those giants had made on their approach.

But it was what pinned his legs so tightly that made him shudder with revulsion and fear. A hideous dog-sized creature had crawled onto his shins, a giant scorpion only with four substantial tentacles arcing up and over from the back instead of a segmented tail and stinger. Being an arachnid, it had eight legs, and it was these that bound his own together like shackles. The thing the same reddish brown as the Gnarlers and Shufflers. Its head had stubby feelers and multiple eyes. The pincers were smooth and shiny, the body long and flat.

Travis let out a dry, rasping scream.

"What—?" Rez exclaimed, jolting awake.

"Get it off me!" Travis yelled.

Instead of rushing to help, Rez scrambled backward, his face a mask of horror. But then he crawled closer, his jaw tight, looking like he'd rather be someplace else. "I—I don't think I should touch it. I mean, what if it bites?"

Travis was busy trying to kick it loose. He thrashed, but it simply tightened its grip and stared balefully at him with expressionless eyes. The raised tentacles quivered, each tasting the air like tongues. Though he could move about on the orange plastic sheet, the thing moved with him. It was heavy, three times the weight of his knapsack.

All around, bushes trembled with anticipation. Gnarly trees leaned closer.

I can transform, Travis realized with a surge of relief.

He did so, and he suffered a dizzying change of perspective that befuddled him. His lion body lay on its side. His front paws flailed in the air, and his back paws remained clamped together by the arachnid legs. His goat's head bleated in anger at being squashed into an awkward position. And his snake's head—

Travis swung from side to side, feeling like he was floating. *He* was the snake's head this time, and it was the weirdest feeling, like he was separated from his body and hovering above the ground. He glimpsed Rez still crawling toward him, his eyes wider than ever.

The hideous scorpion-creature tightened its grip.

Without giving it a thought, he bit the thing on its back. His fangs glanced off the tough carapace, so he tried again, this time farther along its back where the soft, fleshy tentacles projected. His fangs sank deep.

The scorpion jerked and thrashed, immediately letting go and leaping clear. It swung around, and its tentacles swung with it, each coiling tight and then unfolding again as the creature assessed the threat.

"Want some more?" Travis hissed, darting toward it. He couldn't reach though, tethered as he was to the back end of the chimera.

Rez had frozen in place as the scorpion stood and quivered. Its short feelers moved fluidly, tentacles crawling.

Travis climbed to his feet and, to his annoyance, found himself facing away from the action as the chimera advanced on the threat. He twisted around. The scorpion seemed to have disregarded him already, instead staring up at the lion's head on the front end. Travis hissed savagely, suddenly feeling left out.

A fireball erupted from the goat's head and smacked into the scorpion-creature. The fiery explosion blew the bug to smithereens, legs and bits of its carapace flying out in all directions along with a nasty dark-red mess. The four tentacles flew away, landing in the surrounding bushes and hanging off the delicate branches, still wriggling. The orange plastic had a smoldering hole along one edge now.

For a second, nobody and nothing moved. Even the reddish-brown vegetation had frozen.

Then Rez jumped to his feet. "Run!"

Only he had nowhere to run. The prickly bushes burst into a frenzied quiver all around, but they held their positions, walling the boys in.

Meanwhile, the goat's head worked on another fireball.

A low, mournful boom sounded from the nearby trees. It was loud enough to echo through the forest, and it caused Travis to flinch and hunker down with fright—or his lion's body, anyway; Travis himself, deep in the mind of the snake's head, remained stiff and upright like a cobra poised to strike.

The moan ceased, then changed to something more familiar—a human voice, deep and rumbling. "Stop!"

Travis and Rez froze again, shared a glance, then looked around at the trees. Each of the gnarly monstrosities swayed and twisted with obvious dismay. *They're scared of me,* Travis thought with fierce satisfaction.

One of the Gnarlers, the fattest of them all, lurched forward with a dozen massive tentacles sliding about at its base. The entire trunk lifted and moved, and then the tentacles repositioned and lifted again, hoisting the colossal weight of the tree in one unified effort.

Stunned, Travis couldn't help being impressed. And repulsed. It was the most bizarre thing he'd ever seen.

"Ta-a-a-a-lk," the tree moaned.

The trunk's surface *shifted*, the rough bark morphing into the vague shape of a human face. Eyes appeared, then a nose, and a mouth, and the whole visage deepened and clarified until it looked like a formidable old man wearing the deepest of scowls.

"What do you want?" Rez shouted, his voice wavering despite his balled fists and wide-footed stance. "Why are you following us around?"

The Gnarler with the face lurched again, and some of the quivering Shufflers moved aside so it could enter the circle. Travis studied every inch of it, his gaze roaming up the trunk to the widespread branches and somewhat lackluster leaves. He sucked in a breath as he made out the shapes of half a dozen giant scorpions high among the boughs—a whole nest of them, their greatly expanded tentacles threaded into the top of the trunk itself as though the wood had been eaten out by termites.

Travis's gaze dropped to its base where the same tentacles emerged. The tree *was* hollowed out. It had no natural roots nor even real substance. It looked like a tree from the outside but was flesh and blood on the inside. The giant bugs wore the bark-covered skin like a coat. Maybe some of those tentacles threaded through the larger branches, too . . .

"Need . . . help," the stoic face of bark said in a long, drawn-out boom. "Please . . . do not . . . hurt us."

It took a moment for the words to register. Travis wondered for a second if he'd misheard. The words were so deep and rumbling that it was possible he'd simply got it wrong.

"I think it said it needs help," Rez whispered out of the corner of his mouth. "Is that what I heard? It asked for us not to hurt it?"

Travis let out a hiss of agreement, and Rez glanced at him—actually looked directly at him as though recognizing that Travis was inside the snake's head.

With the likelihood of death fading, Travis suddenly felt overcome with curiosity. He had questions to ask, and for that to happen, he would need to be human again.

"Uh, is that a good idea?" Rez whispered as Travis reverted to his human form. "I like you better as a chimera right now. I think you should keep a fireball ready to go at all times."

"Yeah, but I need to know what's going on," Travis said, absently checking his smart clothes were intact. He also glanced around for his knapsack. It lay right where he'd thrown it down the night before, though completely empty, its contents pulled out onto the sheet. The valuable wooden box peeked from beneath a spare shirt. "Sorry I fell asleep," he added. "I, uh . . . I guess I failed as a watchdog."

"We slept good," Rez agreed. "It's just a shame we woke to *this.*"

The Gnarler had sidled to within ten feet by now. Meanwhile, the army of Shufflers had eased back a little. Travis couldn't help noticing the wriggling tentacles in the shadows beneath their foliage. Exactly four appendages for each scorpion-like bug, one bug per bush. Except in the trees, where teams of them were needed.

"Hard . . . to communicate . . . this way," the tree grumbled.

Travis felt the vocal vibrations under his feet, even through the plastic sheet. "What do you want?"

"Allow us . . . to bind."

As the Gnarler spoke, its thick wooden lips moved up and down to emulate speaking, but its lip-syncing was poor and the effect lost. The voice came from the tree, but it wasn't like conversing with a true humanoid.

"What do you mean?" Rez demanded. He pointed to the scattered remains of the dead scorpion. "If you're talking about letting one of those things crawl all over us, you can forget it."

"We meant . . . only to . . . converse . . . through our minds."

Travis shared a glance with his friend. "Telepathy?" he guessed. Raising his voice, he said, "So that thing pinning me down was going to . . . what? Stick a tentacle in my ear and connect with my brain?"

After a moment, a strange rumbling swept across the woods, and all the bushes shook. It sounded like the trees were angry at his flippant remark.

But then the rumbling changed and became more familiar, a sort of chuffing bark. Travis frowned, listening hard. Then he put his hands on his hips. "Are you *laughing*?"

The noise died down, and the tree spoke again. "Allow us . . . to bind."

Rez looked at Travis. "He's a pretty slow talker. It'll take ages if he has a long story to tell. We'll be here for days."

Travis gaped at him. "You *want* a tentacle stuck in your ear?"

"I want to get on with our mission. How about I volunteer? That way, you can stand guard and blast them all to bits if things look weird."

"If things *look weird*? You mean weirder than a giant scorpion with tentacles?"

Rez ignored him and raised his voice. "I volunteer to, uh, to bind—but only if you promise it won't hurt. Because I warn you, if anything happens to me, my friend here will shoot fireballs at you."

Another long, low rumble sounded. This time, some of the nearby Shufflers moved. One approached the orange sheet and stopped at its edge as though it were an unspoken boundary.

Travis watched in amazement as the tentacles slowly unwound from its thick stem. The creature they were attached to descended from the bush, backing its way down until all eight legs were firmly on the ground. Then it turned to face them. It was the same size as the one Travis had destroyed.

A replacement.

The bush sagged and fell sideways. Now that its guest had detached itself, the foliage slowly darkened in color, turning from a vibrant reddish-brown to near black. Its leaves wilted and curled, and the bark began peeling. The entire bush died before his eyes, drying up until it looked like it had been uprooted weeks ago.

"Ugh," Rez exclaimed, standing perfectly still as the giant scorpion scuttled toward him. He breathed hard and fast as the creature reached around his legs and clambered up. "This is just—Oh my gawd!"

Travis steeled himself, prepared to transform and start lobbing fireballs. Then again, it occurred to him he couldn't just fire one at Rez's feet, at least not without severely injuring him. All he could do was shoot at the rest of the forest. "Rez," he said shakily, "maybe we should rethink this."

"Let's get it over with," his friend said through gritted teeth, sweat standing out on his forehead. "They could have hurt us in the night, but they didn't."

He had a point.

The scorpion moved higher, clinging to Rez's thighs. Its tentacles slithered about his feet, then wound around his ankles until he was truly bound from the thighs down. Rez raised his hands out to the sides, obviously uneasy about losing his balance.

"Okay," he said in a shaky voice. "So far so good, no harm done. How do we talk?"

The booming voice of the gnarled tree made Travis jump. "Do not . . . fear us. Open . . . your mind."

Rez shrugged. "My mind is always open. My mom always said I was the most open-minded person—"

He gasped and jerked, then started to topple backward as his eyes rolled up.

Travis leapt toward him, then paused as his friend halted at a weird angle. One of the tentacles had slapped down onto the ground behind him to arrest his fall. It had to be incredibly strong to hold such a weight upright with so little leverage. But then, those same tentacles held entire trees upright.

Rez slowly eased back to a standing position, though he was clearly out of it. His eyes were now wide and staring, his mouth hanging open.

"I'm warning you," Travis growled, torn with indecision. Transform or not? Were they hurting his friend, or was this merely part of the binding process? Maybe both. Maybe binding with humans hadn't been done before. It might be dangerous.

Then his friend spoke. "Thank you. Now I may speak openly."

Chapter 11
The Seer

Rez spoke in an even tone, his gaze fixed on an unseen point in the distance. "We apologize for scaring you. It's difficult for our kind to communicate our harmless intentions. We tried to delay you deep in the forest to explain before you ran away. But you ran nonetheless. So we approached while you slept and waited for you to wake. We would prefer to bind only with your permission."

"You pinned me down!" Travis exclaimed.

"And waited for you to wake," Rez repeated. "We were hoping to persuade you to open your mind to us. Alas, your transformative powers are impressive."

Travis stared at his friend. He seemed unharmed, standing perfectly still with a glassy stare, a huge tentacled scorpion wrapped around his lower legs. It looked like a few greyish-white filaments bound his feet together, too, as though a spider had started spinning a web. "What—" he started, then swallowed and tried again. "Who are you?"

"We are the Seer," Rez intoned. "We emerged from our nest several days ago. It appears you have injured another of your kind."

Travis frowned. "What?"

"You were attacked by four bipeds. One was badly hurt."

Light dawned. "Are you talking about the *trolls*? They're not our kind. And they deserved everything they got."

Rez—the Seer—remained silent for a moment. Then: "I see. Forgive our impertinence. From our point of view, these 'trolls' are very similar to you."

Travis had to think about that. "I guess. Same way that you look like giant scorpions. But you're not scorpions at all, are you?"

He realized he'd been addressing Rez the whole time, which wasn't quite correct. He looked at the creature wrapped around his friend's feet and wondered if he should be directing his questions at it instead. But then again, the Seer spoke as a collective group, like an army of ants or a swarm of worker bees.

He looked at the Gnarler. "Who should I be looking at? You? Or my friend?"

Rez spoke. "It does not matter. We are one. You dispatched several of our kind yesterday, but that's no different than a tree losing a small limb. However, *your* kind—including the trolls—are entirely individual souls, each as important as the next. We would not like your troll to die."

Travis could hardly believe what he was hearing. He hadn't quite known what to expect from a talking tree—or more accurately, talking scorpions!—but he definitely hadn't reckoned on *this*. "You're . . . you're worried about the troll I threw a fireball at? He was breathing the last time I saw him. I'm sure he's fine, just a bit sore."

"No, he is dying."

The words from Rez's mouth sounded so matter-of-fact and certain that suddenly Travis felt bad about what he'd done. Still, he was confused. "Why do you care?" he asked. "How do you even know about souls and all that stuff? You're just giant bugs!"

He regretted his choice of words as soon as they left his lips. However, the Seer barely skipped a beat. "Our physical form is not pretty in the eyes of your kind. But the 'giant bugs' you speak of are simply tools. Our hands and feet, if you will; a means to bind with what's important, which is nature itself. Vast knowledge lies within the trees, which have stood for many decades. There is a chasm between the animal and plant kingdoms that only a few species can bridge. The dryads are one such species. We, the Seer, are another."

Travis stared at Rez, suddenly noticing a change in his friend's complexion. His normally dark-brown skin had turned a more reddish color to match the creature clamped around his ankles. Eyeing the dead bush the scorpion had abandoned, he felt a sudden need to break the connection.

"Let my friend go," he said, edging forward. "I don't like what's happening here. If he's hurt in any way, I'll—" He broke off, then swallowed. "Let my friend go, please."

Rez, as sightless as ever, said, "Certainly. But please do help the troll. Take him to his people and save his life."

"Well . . ." Travis said doubtfully.

"We will guide you back to the road. There you will find the troll, whom we moved while you slept. Fetch help. Return him to his people. The trolls live outside the forest to the north. We have safely cocooned him to protect his burns. Leave him wrapped up until you arrive."

Frustrated and more than a little befuddled, Travis said, "But if you can carry the injured troll back to the road and cocoon him, why can't you take him to the trolls yourselves?"

"There is a river running through the valley. We cannot cross the river. And our pace is slow. Help the troll. Thank you."

And with that, the giant tentacled scorpion released its grip on Rez's ankles and scuttled away. It seemed to sniff at the dead bush it had vacated earlier, but then it turned and made a dash for the deep woods.

Travis shuddered. He hurried to help his friend, who now stood alone, swaying and blinking rapidly.

"Wh-what—" he stammered.

Travis caught him before he fell. "You okay?"

Rez's natural dark-brown skin color returned, the weird redness fading. "I feel like a lemon with all the juice squeezed out. What's this around my feet? It's sticky—like a spider web. Ugh!"

"But you're okay? You're *you*?"

As Rez plucked the last of the greyish-white strands from his feet, all the ancient Gnarlers began to move. The scowling man's face seemed to melt away, the usual rough bark texture taking its place. With branches bending, giant tentacles flopping about, and leaves rustling, the Seer turned away and began its slow, steady departure.

Many of the bushes shuffled away, too. But a few remained. They quivered like nervous tour guides waiting to point the way.

"We'd better pack up," Travis said. "Did you catch any of what you said?"

Rez rubbed his nose. "Uh . . . something about a dying troll?"

"Right. We need to take him to a troll village or whatever."

"Of course we do."

* * *

With everything packed up in their knapsacks, Travis and Rez headed out, following the excruciatingly slow-moving Shufflers. It wasn't a direction Travis would have guessed they needed to take, but that only proved how turned around he was.

"The troll will be dead long before we get there," Rez grumbled loudly, watching the tentacles slip and slide at the base of the prickly shrub ahead. "How about coming down out of that poor bush and scurrying along like a proper giant insect?"

"Scorpions are arachnids, not insects," Travis muttered.

"Yeah, well, scorpions don't have tentacles."

Travis thought it was probably a good thing the bugs stayed put. If they emerged, the bushes would wither and die. Somehow, that didn't seem right.

Sighing, he thought about the Gnarler he'd shot a fireball at the previous evening. He'd obliterated that tree. It had fallen and died, and its occupants—probably half a dozen of the Seer—had scuttled loose and gone off to find some other host, probably relegated to simple bushes, like a king and his staff ousted from their castle.

He regretted that now. But he also hated to think of all the poor bushes taken over by these creatures. Their relationship was—what was the word?—yes, *symbiotic*. He couldn't think of any parasitic creatures in New Earth except for basic wildlife, mostly bugs, but the Seer certainly fit the bill. They attached themselves to plants and ate through them, replacing vital roots with their own tentacles, which presumably continued to channel necessary nutrients out of the soil and into the remaining trunk and limbs. But they moved around, too, so there had to be some risk there. What if they sat too long on barren ground like rock? Would the plant then starve? He guessed it would.

"What are you thinking about?" Rez whispered as they trudged.

Travis shrugged. "I'm just amazed that I care more about the trees than I do about a troll I shot a fireball at."

"Well, it attacked us."

"Yeah . . . although I shot it after it had decided to leave you alone."

"It turned toward you and would have attacked if you hadn't stopped it," Rez argued.

"That's true. But I still never really cared about it afterward. It was alive, and that was all. I didn't stop to check it over."

Rez was silent for a moment. "You were in chimera form. Do you think a real chimera would have cared after shooting a fireball at something? The question is why *I* didn't care."

"Because your head was all foggy from sitting next to the white-tentacled monster."

They left at it that, accepting each other's reasoning for now. They continued their trudging without another word for the next few minutes, the trek so painfully slow that Travis considered ditching the guides and finding his own way.

"We're wasting so much time," he groaned after a while. "It's bad enough that we got waylaid last night and didn't make it out of the forest. Now we're supposed to help an injured troll? How? Pick him up and *carry* him?"

"Maybe we should leave him and go fetch help," Rez said. "Other trolls can carry him. It's their problem, not ours."

"Yeah!" Travis exclaimed, cheering up. "Yeah, that's what we'll do. *They* can carry him."

Even so, the prospect of seeking out trolls and approaching them, trying to *talk* to them without being attacked . . . He wished he'd never bumped into that gang in the first place. What a nuisance! He couldn't help thinking he and Rez were better off just forgetting about the stupid trolls and carrying on with their mission.

The slow-moving shrubs continued through dense undergrowth, the terrain dipping and rising. It was such a tedious pace that Travis and Rez found it better to sit down for a minute, catch up, sit down again, and so on—otherwise it was a case of waiting a few seconds between each step, which was somehow more tiring.

Then Travis spotted the road ahead. He let out a whoop and tore past the Shufflers to the flat road surface. It felt wonderful to be free again. He took long strides and walked around in a large circle until Rez caught up.

"Finally!" Travis said. "Now let's get moving and—"

He paused. Just a short way along the road behind him to the south, he spotted a strange and disturbing mound. He wanted to ignore it and move on, just continue north and resume their mission . . . but his curiosity got the better of him.

"Is that the troll?" Rez whispered as they ambled back along the road.

"I think so. They said they cocooned it."

The mound was in fact an eight-foot-long cylindrical object. As they approached, Travis saw three or four giant scorpion-creatures scuttling away with tentacles trailing. They vanished into the woods, their task apparently completed.

The troll lay there, his head exposed but his entire body wrapped from the neck down in a greyish-white stringy substance with a sticky sheen, tightly bound to form an elongated oval shape. Travis imagined the troll's arms pressed tightly to his sides somewhere deep within the cocoon, his legs pinned together, unable to move an inch.

He and Rez stared in silence, their shared horror almost tangible.

The troll was unconscious, and thankfully so. To wake up now would be unimaginably terrifying. Even though these brutes had ganged up on Travis and Rez and tried to rob them, *nobody* deserved this.

"Is he breathing?" Travis whispered.

They both bent to check, feeling a little awed at being so close to a troll. He had a strong odor of pine or some other earthly scent. His mouth hung open, nostrils flaring every few seconds. The whites of his eyeballs showed through not-quite-shut lids.

"Should we cut him loose?" Rez asked.

"I want to," Travis answered, "but what if he dies on us? The trees said the cocoon is protecting his wounds." The white shell started just below the troll's ears, wrapped tightly around his throat. As Travis watched closely, he could see a faint pulse beneath the coarse hair. He reached out with one hand to touch the cocoon's surface. It was surprisingly thick and tough, and it made a dull thud when he rapped his knuckles on it. The stickiness had dried already, the sheen faded. "I don't like this at all, but maybe he's better off staying inside this thing until we get him back to his people."

"We can't carry him, though." Rez paused. "Maybe roll him?"

"Don't be an idiot. I'm wondering if . . ."

"Wondering what?"

"Do you think a chimera could *drag* him?"

Chapter 12
Cocooned

Travis padded at a slow, steady pace, dragging the cocoon behind. Rez walked alongside.

They'd spread out the orange plastic sheet and rolled the unconscious troll onto it, then bunched the ends together and tied them off. The scrunched bottom end prevented the troll from sliding out, and the plastic sheet protected the cocoon against the harsh road surface.

With a long rope looped around his chest, Travis felt like a horse plowing across a field. Rez had tried pulling the load on his own and only managed a yard or two. Travis found it much easier in chimera form, but even he was feeling the strain now. They'd only been walking ten minutes.

"Look at that," Rez said suddenly, pointing ahead.

The road split. Unlike the narrow path they'd mistakenly attempted the day before, this was a proper fork in the road. To the right, the road continued into the distance, as wide as ever. To the left lay a modest four-foot path that had obviously been there a long time, well-trodden and flat, with no sign of those tightly clustered Shufflers.

And there was a gnarly old tree standing between the two routes. Not a reddish-brown Seer-occupied monstrosity, just an ordinary aged hickory. It didn't even stand out as particularly gnarly. It might have gone unnoticed had it not been positioned smack in the middle of the fork.

"This is the *real* trail," Rez said. "Now we're in business!"

And, according to the map, it's just a fifteen-minute walk from here to the valley, Travis thought, wishing he could speak out loud in a human tongue.

Fifteen minutes, though. He wasn't sure he could drag the cocoon that far. His chest ached from the strain of the rope, and his leg muscles were already worn out. But if he stopped, he'd never get started again, so he gritted his teeth and pressed on.

Rez talked nonstop. ". . . fifteen minutes to the valley, and then maybe we can just leave the troll by the river and go find some of his friends to help . . ."

Now that he'd switched to chimera form, Travis had reservations about helping the injured troll at all. He was once more inside the lion's head, and perhaps now he felt the way a lion might, with far less compassion. Dragging an injured creature of *any* kind seemed a colossal waste of effort unless he planned to eat it later.

And maybe I will, he thought lazily.

"Get a grip," he growled to himself.

He wondered if his goat aspect shared the lion's indifferent sentiment. And what about the snake? He delved deeper, trying to peek into their minds. It was hopeless, though. They might as well be completely separate creatures grafted onto his lion's body.

". . . can't think why these Seer people care so much about a troll anyway," Rez went on. "I mean, they're giant bugs with tentacles! Okay, I get that they're not *just* bugs, they're some kind of unified intelligence, but still, why should they care about a troll?"

Travis wanted to answer that he'd been wondering the same thing, but he grunted instead, pouring all his effort into forcing one step after another.

The trail meandered for a while, then straightened. The forest began to thin, and Travis renewed his efforts when he saw bright light through the trees in the distance, signifying the outer fringes of the wooded area. Beyond that, he expected to find endless grassy hills and a river, perhaps a bunch of trolls frolicking about, one of them wearing a doctor's smock, a stethoscope around its neck as it came running over . . .

He smiled. *Unlikely—but a nice thought.*

"We're nearly there," Rez announced. "Can't you speed up a bit?"

Travis growled, straining at the load and trying to ignore his screaming muscles. Oh, he was going to be sore after this!

". . . so I guess we're not *too* far behind schedule because we got such an early start this morning and probably would have slept in if we'd woken in the valley as planned. We might even get ahead . . ."

Rez trailed off and slowed. Travis had been staring at his own plodding forefeet, but now he looked up.

Ahead, figures materialized from the trees on either side of the four-foot path. They were humanoid and slender, wearing rather large headpieces that stuck up like jagged rocks. *Or splintered wood*, Travis thought. *Yeah, it looks like they're wearing hats made out of tree bark.*

There were seven in all, each standing with arms at their side, waiting. The coloring of their bodies, including what little clothing they wore, blended in perfectly with the background.

Dryads, Travis realized. Utterly harmless and extremely shy creatures, part of the forest itself, as comfortable talking to plants as he was to other humans.

So why were they out in force, blocking the way?

As he and Rez continued walking, ivy crept out from the undergrowth ahead, snaking across the road. At the same time, more sprouts erupted from the middle of the dirt trail, quickly shooting upward as though time was fast-forwarding.

"Uh . . ." Rez murmured, slowing.

Travis veered sideways and gave him a shove from behind. "Keep moving," he growled for good measure.

They closed the gap to forty feet, thirty-five, thirty . . . and as they continued on, the vegetation across the trail ahead thickened—ivy, vines, weeds, even grass, all of it sprouting in record time. The dryads remained, but it was almost impossible to see them now, they were so well camouflaged. Travis glimpsed one as it moved, a mere blur out of the corner of his eye, yet when he tried to look closely, he saw no sign of the creature.

They're see-through, he thought with awe. He knew a dryad shapeshifter named Darcy, but he'd never seen real dryads in the forest before, at least not up close like this. And never so many!

At just fifteen feet away, a sudden blur of movement made him and Rez halt. Without tension, the rope fell from around Travis's chest—a huge relief, though right now he was almost too distracted to notice. The dryads scattered in all directions, rushing back into the trees at both sides of the trail. It seemed their nerve had broken.

But their work was already done. Three thick vines blocked the way like a fence, descending from the trees on one side and threaded through the bushes on the other. Ivy had snaked its way around the vines and become a tangled mess. Weeds stood tall and straight like posts, completing the illusion of a fence. And knee-length grass transformed the dirt ground into a lush carpet.

"Well, that's just plain rude," Rez said at last. "How are we supposed to fight our way through this jungle?"

Actually, Rez could probably manage quite easily. Travis and his load . . . not so much.

Travis reverted to human form, straightening up as he did so. His legs and arms felt wobbly, and his chest ached. He stretched and groaned, then shook the kinks loose. "Why would they do this? I'm getting a bit fed up with this forest. First the trolls, then the Seer, now the dryads . . . Everyone just needs to *leave us alone!*" He shouted these last words, glaring into the woods all around.

The dryads were either long gone or they'd hidden themselves in plain sight. It didn't matter. Nobody had ever been hurt by a dryad, at least not directly. They could make plants do weird things and cause an inconvenience, and that was about all. In this case, they'd simply created a temporary barrier, nothing more.

Rez approached and ducked between the middle and lowest vines. The ivy came alive, winding tighter like a writhing mass of alarmed serpents. Some of it reached for Rez and encircled his wrist, and he yelled and jumped back. The moment he was clear, the ivy settled down and became still. At his feet, the grass swayed as though a breeze had swept through.

"Well, that was interesting," Rez said, glancing back at Travis with a sheepish grin. "Nearly strangled by ivy. Not how I expected to leave this Earth."

"Let me try," Travis said.

He stepped forward, already realizing that even if he managed to cross this living fence, he'd have to come back for the troll. But first things first. He boldly stood on the carpet of swaying grass and waited to see what it would do. It merely swished back and forth, so he made a scoffing sound and put his foot on the lowest vine.

The moment he did so, the ivy came alive again. Not only that, the nearest weeds bent toward him. Their stems were as thick as two fingers, and they stood five feet high with prickly, ugly leaves and deep-red berries. He let out a cry as the sharp leaves scratched his face, and he moved aside only to find another weed attacking him just as viciously.

Determined not to be outdone by a bunch of plants, he battled against the weeds and climbed the vines as though hurdling a fence. Everything bounced and wobbled, and it took all his concentration to avoid being thrown off. As he straddled the top vine, ivy wrapped around his legs and wrists, and he found himself completely unable to go any farther.

"Argh!" he yelled in frustration, wrenching loose and tumbling backward.

"You okay there?" Rez called, sounding only mildly concerned.

"Fine." The grass swayed around his feet as he sidled over to join his friend. "Well, that's annoying."

"Burn it," Rez whispered.

Travis didn't like to, though. It was one thing burning deadwood, but seemingly intelligent ivy? And he doubted his fireballs would be effective against such a stringy mess. A solid wall, yes, but not a collection of vines. "Let's see if we can go around," he suggested.

They left the cocoon where it was and headed into the woods. To their dismay, the dryad blockade continued through the trees, an even bigger tangle of vegetation, impossible to navigate. A quick check revealed it was the same in the woods on the other side of the road.

"This is such a pain!" Travis exclaimed as they returned to the cocoon. "Why did they do this?"

"Maybe the trolls are a bad influence," Rez said. "Now dryads are demanding tolls as well. What are we supposed to pay them?"

Travis clicked his tongue. "Well, I hate to do this, but I'm gonna try a fireball."

He transformed and, in the head of the goat, spent a minute developing a sizeable missile. While he worked on it, he studied the dryad's plant-fence and decided it would be pointless targeting any particular vine. Even if he severed one, the others would remain intact, and the ivy would still be there. Heck, the severed vine might be replaced by two new ones. No, his best bet was to hit the ground directly in front and cause an explosion, perhaps blast everything asunder.

Aiming carefully, he lobbed his fireball at a stretch of grass and weeds directly below the horizontally hanging vines. As expected, the ground erupted in a shower of dirt and clumps of roots, and the entire barrier shuddered and wobbled. Ivy writhed, and the closest weeds twisted and swayed, then stood up straight again.

As the dust cloud drifted away, the boys stared at the crater and the largely unaffected fence.

In a sudden rage, Travis pounced into the crater and dug deeper, his claws cutting through the hard-packed earth and sending it flying out between his rear legs. He felt like a dog going after a buried bone, and he knew he looked ridiculous, but right now he didn't care.

To his amazement, plant roots wormed their way out of the crater's sides and got in his way. He ripped at them, but they kept on coming, and finally he had to quit because the entire base of the hole was thick with vegetation.

He reverted to human form and stamped around in a circle, his fists balled. "I can't even dig under!" he yelled.

"I see that," Rez said.

On impulse, Travis raced to the foot of the troll cocoon. "Help me with this."

Together, one at each end, they lifted the impossibly heavy eight-foot troll off the plastic sheet and struggled with him to the vine-fence. Travis led the way by walking backwards, and he dropped his end when weeds nudged against his ankles and he could go no farther.

Rez maintained his grip as Travis rushed past him. "What are you—?"

"Wait there," Travis said. He scooped up the orange sheet and ropes, bundled it all very roughly, and lobbed the whole package over the fence. He turned to help Rez. "Okay, lift. Up and over."

"Ah. I think I get what you're doing."

With the two of them now at the head of the troll, they hoisted the deadweight higher and higher until it stood upright, then gave a hard shove so the troll toppled face down onto the fence. The highest vine on its own did little to support the sudden weight, but the middle one helped some, and the third held firm. The cocoon bounced and jiggled there, held off the ground at one end by the three taut vines as the ivy and weeds went crazy.

"Now!" Travis urged.

One at a time, they ran up and over the cocoon as though it were a bridge, wrenching free of the grasping ivy as it tried to snake around their limbs.

Once on the other side of the fence, the boys turned and grasped the cocoon, digging their fingers into whatever crevice they could find. With a concerted heave accompanied by determined yells, they yanked the cocoon free of the tangled mess and onto smooth dirt. They didn't stop pulling until they were well clear of the dryad's blockade, at which point they collapsed, gasping but triumphant.

Finally, when he'd gotten his breath back, Travis stood and looked back to see the vines withering and cracking, the ivy turning brown, the grass drying up, and the weeds slowly bending in half. He felt pity for the dryads' soldiers. They'd done what little they could to block the way, and now they'd failed and paid the price. He doubted they'd been deliberately punished, though. It was more likely that the hidden dryads had simply given up and relinquished control, and now the plants—traumatized by the unearthly incident—had died.

"Let's keep moving," Travis said quietly.

Rez helped him lay out the cocoon on the orange sheet and secure the ropes at the ends. Then, after shifting to chimera form once more, Travis took up the slack and marched onward.

Chapter 13
The Troll Valley

They left the forest at last.

Travis wanted to revert to human form and talk about the dryad incident. Why had the timid creatures done such a strange thing? He couldn't recall a single incident of a gang of dryads attacking innocent passersby—except perhaps when Darcy O'Tanner, the first dryad shapeshifter, had poisoned a platoon of dangerous soldiers twenty-odd years ago. Using her eerie powers, she'd weakened the potency of a deadly hemlock plant and put it in a pot of soup over their campfire just to make them feel nauseous. She'd also caused grass and weeds to grow in and around their weapons, rendering them useless. Her mission had succeeded in delaying them.

But a concerted dryad attack on two innocent boys? Something was off.

Then again, it hadn't exactly been an attack. Maybe this, too, was a delaying tactic. Maybe they'd hoped to block the way until . . . what? It was a mystery.

Travis held his lion tongue in check until they'd left the forest behind and were heading downhill into a grassy valley. A powerful river flowed out of the mountains in the west, heading east toward the vast expanse that made up the Parched Plains. In fact, the river flowed into a lake not too far away, and Travis knew from the map that it was the last significant body of water for a long, long way.

The trolls had to be near the lake, and he wasn't looking forward to meeting them.

He rested again, dropping the rope and wandering around in circles to stretch his four aching legs. This was torture! He envied the goat and snake heads right now. They probably didn't feel a thing.

This notion hit him like a thunderbolt. Suddenly, he felt cheated. He reverted to human form and stood there for a moment, scowling, while Rez looked him up and down.

"What's eating you, Trav?"

"It just occurred to me that the other two heads probably don't feel the same aches and pains that the lion does. So I really should just be the goat for a while."

Rez laughed. "Bet you feel a bit of a chump now. Hey, what do you suppose that dryad wall was about? Trying to stop us heading into danger, do you think?"

Travis frowned. "Danger?"

"The trolls. Maybe the dryads saw us as a couple of helpless kids and wanted to warn us not to go any farther."

"I hadn't thought of that." Travis scratched his head. "But we *weren't* a couple of helpless kids. There was just one helpless kid. The other was super-powerful, dangerous, and awesome."

"Well, that's true," Rez agreed. "But I wouldn't say I was *super*-powerful . . ."

"What? No, *I'm* super-powerful, dangerous, and—" Seeing Rez's triumphant grin, he broke off and muttered, "Yeah, all right, you got me. Whatever."

They surveyed their surroundings. In the distance ahead, low hills loomed out of a mist that seemed out of place under the clear sky. Somewhere among those hills was their destination. Before that, they had to cross the river. The grass petered out near its edge, giving way to rocks. The water flowed at a fast pace, though it couldn't be more than waist deep. But it had to be twenty feet wide, with no stepping stones. Crossing would be a very wet affair.

Except that a narrow footbridge spanned the river nearby, just as his mom had said. It made sense. Why have a well-used trail but no bridge? Travelers on horseback could probably wade across, but those on foot would naturally gravitate toward the quaint, humped wooden bridge.

Unfortunately, two trolls waited there, leaning idly on the railings at the bridge's highest point over the river.

Travis groaned. "It costs a fortune to travel in these parts."

"What are we supposed to pay with? We don't have money."

"They don't want money. Trolls always want food. Like live chickens. Something they can kill and eat."

"We don't have any chickens that I know of," Rez said. He looked at Travis's knapsack. "Unless you brought some along? Maybe half a dozen of them tucked away in there?"

"Sorry, no."

"Didn't think so. I'd have heard them clucking." Rez huffed with annoyance. "I guess you'll have to go all chimera on them like your mom told you. I'm surprised your parents are okay with this. You know, encouraging violence and all that."

Travis scrunched up his nose. "I think they probably wanted to give us a challenge."

Rez looked aghast. "With trolls? That's harsh, man."

"Mom and Dad saw much worse when they were my age," Travis said softly. "Dragons, harpies, a demon in a temple . . . Look, I'm a chimera. If I can't deal with a few trolls, then what hope do I have?"

"Fine, have at it. Go fireball them or something."

"How about we talk to them first?" Travis gestured at their cocooned patient. "Look what fireballing did last time. How about we hand him over? We'll pretend we found him like that. They'll be grateful and let us through."

Rez raised an eyebrow. "Unless the other three trolls in the woods came right back here and warned everyone to be on the lookout for us, and to kill us on sight."

They stood there a while longer, debating their course of action.

Travis sighed. "We have to do something. Maybe we forget the bridge and just swim across. Or do they charge for that too? Come on, let's check it out."

Together, they dragged the plastic sheet and unconscious troll the rest of the way down the grassy bank to where it grew rocky. As they did so, the two sentries on the bridge stood up straight and split, one heading across to the north side of the river, the other to the south and along the shore toward them.

"He's coming," Rez whispered. "And he doesn't look happy."

"Do trolls ever look happy?"

They stared into the water. Up close like this, it looked much faster as it gurgled and gushed over the treacherous rocks below. Wading would be difficult. Swimming might be impossible without getting swept downstream into the heart of the troll settlement.

"A bridge sure would be handy," Travis admitted.

It seemed they would have to face a troll after all: either the one stomping toward them, or his colleague on the other side of the river. Without another word, Travis and Rez turned and waited for the approaching troll.

He was a big one, much broader than usual. Coarse grey hair ruffled in the breeze. Over his shoulder, hanging on a strap, he carried a long-handled ax with a massive blade. "Pay," he barked without preamble as he stomped closer.

Travis pointed to the cocoon. "We have one of your friends. He needs help. We just wanted to get him to your village. Isn't that payment enough?"

He held his breath, wondering if his gamble would pay off.

The troll peered down at the unconscious patient. He stared for a long time, his eyes roaming from head to toe—not that he could see the toes inside the elongated greyish-white casing. He moved closer and nudged the cocoon with one enormous foot. Then he bent and studied it even more carefully.

Finally, he straightened up, turned his back on the unconscious troll, and shrugged. "Pay."

Travis gaped at him. "That's it? You still want us to pay you? What about *him*?"

The troll reached up and grasped the handle of his long ax. "Pay," he growled.

"What if we don't want to cross your stupid river now?" Rez demanded. "We'll go back the way we came. I'm fed up with—"

The troll whipped the ax off his shoulder and held it high. "PAY!"

Travis was about to transform when something unexpected happened: the cocoon started moving as the injured troll woke and stared around with wide eyes. Then he began howling and thrashing, trying in vain to sit up or roll over.

The ax-wielding sentry backed off a little. He pointed and said something in a foreign language. Some trolls were known to be familiar with more than the word "pay," but not this one. He spoke fast and angrily, a stream of gibberish, as he looked from Travis to Rez and back at the wriggling cocoon.

"He needs help," Travis explained. He pointed east. "Take him to your village and get him out of that thing. He's hurt, but maybe your doctors can fix him."

Doctors. Yeah, like trolls have doctors. Maybe some kind of witch-doctor with a collection of crazy spells and remedies, but that's about all.

The sentry dug around in the thick hair around his waist, and suddenly a belt came into view. He withdrew a dagger and approached the howling troll, bending down with the clear intent of cutting the cocoon open.

"No, not yet," Travis urged, daring to touch the sentry on the arm. He pointed east again, more forcefully this time. "Take him to your village. He needs help. If you cut him loose now, he might die. Do you see?"

As he spoke, he realized that probably wasn't likely now. The patient seemed pretty lively.

Still, the ax-wielding troll paused, then nodded and stashed the ax over his shoulder again. He reached down, got a decent grip on the cocoon, and heaved the entire thing off the plastic sheet and up onto his shoulder. He staggered under the weight, his feet planted wide, then swung around with the bizarre cocoon balanced horizontally across his shoulder. He marched off along the rocky bank, heading east.

"Well," Rez said finally, "that's that, then. One mission accomplished. Now we can get on with the main one."

"Not so fast," Travis said.

Something bothered him. He couldn't quite place it, but this whole business with the Seer trying to help the injured troll, insisting that Travis and Rez take him to the troll settlement, and advising not to open the cocoon until they arrived . . . It just seemed *off*. And why had the dryads laid that barrier? Maybe to warn of trolls ahead . . . or maybe some other reason.

The other troll sentry, who had watched everything from the other side of the river, watched the boys warily. He pointed at them and mouthed the word "Pay," then gestured toward the bridge.

We're still no better off, Travis thought. *But at least we only have ourselves to worry about now.*

The trouble was, he worried about the injured troll as well. Perhaps *all* the trolls. He had the awful feeling he'd just played into the Seer's imaginary hands. And the dryads had tried to prevent his mistake.

The notion hit him like a thunderbolt, and a chill ran down his spine.

"We need to follow him," Travis said at last, pointing east.

Rez almost choked on his words. "*Follow* him? What? Follow *him*? Why do we care if—Let's just get across this river!"

"We'd still have to pay the troll something, and we don't have anything to give. And he's not gonna let us swim across, either."

"So fireball him!"

Travis shook his head. "Part of being a shapeshifter is acting responsibly. I can't go attacking everyone just because I can. This is troll territory, so we need to play by their rules." Before Rez could work up another sputtering fit, he added, "Anyway, I want to see what happens when they cut the cocoon open."

Feeling Rez's flabbergasted glare on his back, he bent to fold up the plastic sheet and unravel the ropes. It took a few minutes to get it all stashed neatly in his knapsack, and by then, Rez had calmed down and even offered a hand at the last moment.

"Yeah, this is why I wouldn't make a good shapeshifter," he muttered. "All this *acting responsibly* stuff. One fireball, Travis. One fireball, and that troll would run a mile. We could walk on and be done with the trolls. Instead, you want to walk right into their camp."

Travis grinned. "Sorry to be a stick-in-the-mud. I blame my parents, always trying to do the right thing . . ."

They headed east along the riverbank. The troll sentry stalked them on the north side until he realized nobody planned to swim across anytime soon. Then, frowning, he headed back to resume his watch on the bridge.

In the distance ahead, Travis could see the bigger troll stomping along with the heavy cocoon balanced on his shoulder. And not too far in front of him, movement on the hills indicated the location of the troll settlement.

The place was swarming with them.

Chapter 14
Opening the Cocoon

As it turned out, two more bridges spanned the ever-widening river at the heart of the troll settlement. Well-trodden dusty paths crisscrossed and meandered all over. The vast majority lived on the north side, many in wooden shacks with roofs of woven willow, others in numerous caves that pockmarked the nearby rocky hills. Campfires littered the place, some of them smoking. A hundred or so trolls milled about—hulking brutes, slender females, a surprising number of youngsters, all shaggy and loping with long arms and oversized feet.

On the south side, where Travis and Rez walked, a few more unkempt shacks and dens were clustered together on the open grassy fields, looking like they'd sprouted directly from the earth. The trolls there were mostly male, maybe hunters or relief sentries.

Travis and Rez took all this in as they shuffled along the river bank, easily fifty paces behind the troll with the cocoon over his shoulder.

"I'm not sure we should be getting this close," Rez whispered.

Travis had to agree, especially as one of the sentries had spotted him. The troll nudged another, and pretty soon, the entire south-side regiment was looking their way. Travis slowed. "Okay, well, I guess we'd better turn back. I wanted to see them open the cocoon, but I feel like I'm walking into the lion's den."

"*You're* the lion," Rez said. "And maybe you should think about that if some of these ugly brutes come after us. Can't we just head back and maybe cross the river somewhere halfway where nobody's looking?"

"Sounds like a plan," Travis said.

Yet still he paused. On the other side of the river, the sentries seemed very interested in the cocoon. The troll carrying it on his shoulder marched straight past his colleagues and to the nearest bridge, a narrow structure that bounced as he stomped across to the north side. A few trolls followed, but three stayed behind, glancing back at Travis and Rez with narrowed eyes.

Not for long, though. Their attention kept being drawn to the strange cocoon as it was lofted to the other side of the river and dumped at the feet of several females there. Odd barking shouts went up, and a very pale-grey troll came hobbling toward them, scowling at the disturbance. His expression changed to one of surprise when he saw what had been delivered.

The females pointed down at the cocooned troll, who began rocking from side to side again, yelling for all he was worth. His noise brought the rest of the settlement to a standstill, though nobody came closer. Everyone watched from afar.

The ax-wielding sentry pulled out his knife and bent. With a sawing motion, and starting at the neck, he gradually sliced the cocoon open along its entire length.

Travis and Rez watched in silence from their own side of the river.

Several trolls bent to wrench the shell apart, and a few brittle snaps and cracks sounded. The injured troll thrashed, bolted upright, and rolled violently from the casing, yelling and brushing himself down the whole time.

"What the—?" Rez muttered. "Do you see that?"

Travis did, though now he wished he'd never insisted on coming this far east.

A teeming mass of palm-sized scorpions spilled from the cocoon and spread outward across the rock, scuttling between the feet of the startled trolls, some running over their shaggy toes. The sheer number of the bugs was frightening; they must have been packed in tight with that poor injured troll, wriggling around the whole time. And he'd known. Or at least he'd suspected. He must have felt the squirming, writhing mass crawling over his body and pushing against him from underneath . . .

Barking trolls danced about, trying to stomp as many as they could. But they didn't do very well. The bugs were *fast*, zipping this way and that, many seeming to vanish into thin air as they found holes in the ground or rocks to hide under. A stream of them poured like liquid into a grassy patch, and from there headed toward the trees.

Travis gasped. The trees! He stared in mounting horror at the fringes of the forest on the north side of the river. "Did you see the tentacles on those bug?" he said in a strangled voice.

"Yeah," Rez agreed. "They're tiny versions of the ones we left behind. You don't think they'll take over the forest, do you?"

"The Seer said they couldn't cross the river," Travis moaned. "That's why they bundled up their young in a convenient package and asked us to deliver it."

Rez shook his head. "We've been suckered. Conned by a bunch of trees!"

"No, conned by the nasty scorpions that *took over* the trees," Travis corrected him. "And now there's a whole load more."

"They're small, though. Too small to take over trees, surely? They need to grow."

"And they will. Look at them all, running to hide. I bet the trolls squished a handful at most. The rest made it to safety."

They watched with despair. With a heavy heart, Travis knew this was all his fault. The Seer had used him and Rez, sweet-talked them into 'saving' an injured troll. And that troll didn't even look very ill despite his severely burned chest. He danced about with the rest of them, still batting at his legs as though he had creepy-crawlies nesting deep in his shaggy hair.

Before long, several trolls pointed across the river toward Travis and Rez. A few angry shouts filled the air, and then a gang of ten or so ran toward the nearest bridge. On the south side, three sentries had a head start and were already stampeding along the shore.

"Run!" Rez shouted.

Travis gripped his arm and said in a no-nonsense voice, "Climb on my back."

He transformed, and his knapsack tugged at one side while slipping off the other. He quickly shook it off and waited for Rez to pick it up and fling himself aboard. "This is ridiculous," his friend muttered.

Once again, Travis found himself inside the lion's head, probably because he'd been thinking about running away rather than shoot fireballs. He felt Rez's weight on his hindquarters and had to assume he'd somehow gotten a good grip around the goat's neck.

Okay, so not as cool as riding a dragon, he thought as he sprinted away, heading west along the riverbank. *But I can still run faster than a human.*

It was hard going, though. The added weight on his back made a huge difference, not to mention two knapsacks, one of them banging against his side. He quickly began puffing and panting and knew he wouldn't be able to run forever like this. Still, he covered a lot of ground very quickly, and when he paused to glance back, he saw the gang of trolls far behind.

The humped bridge came into view ahead, with its sentry standing guard in the center high over the fast-flowing water. Travis ran onto the wooden platform, feeling it vibrate under his paws. The troll stomped toward him, making the whole structure shake. His eyes blazed under his deeply-furrowed brow. "PAY!" he roared.

You still want me to pay? Travis thought, sensing that his goat's head was busy working on a fireball. *Even though I'm a chimera now, and with everything else that's going on? All you're interested in is a couple of chickens or something to eat?*

Of course, this troll had no idea what had transpired at the settlement. And it seemed fearless against a three-headed lion-monster.

Travis's goat belched up a fireball. It flew over his head and toward the troll, who skidded to a stop and only just had time to leap backward as the fiery projectile slammed into the bridge's decking. It punched a hole straight through and knocked several uprights loose, which in turn caused the railing on one side to sag.

The troll, his eyes wide, backpedaled and spun around, then ran for his life to the other side. He eventually disappeared into a distant thicket on the hill. Travis leapt over the damaged decking and hurried over the bridge with no further trouble. Across at last!

Rez leapt off, choosing to run alongside. Travis slowed to match his pace, and together they continued straight up the grassy slopes to where it leveled out. Open meadows lay directly ahead. To the east, a forest sprawled for miles on the hilltops. He shuddered at the idea of the Seer swarming up tree trunks and into the branches above . . .

They ran and ran, distancing themselves from irate trolls and nasty bugs. The pretty meadow scenery fell behind. Ahead, the terrain grew ever more depressing, almost devoid of life, a grey landscape of loose dirt and gravel, a dead tree here and there, and thickening fog. Panting hard, Travis stumbled onward until his legs gave out, and then he reverted to human form and rolled onto his back, exhausted.

Rez collapsed next to him and dropped both knapsacks. He studied Travis for a long time before speaking. "Well, that was fun. You okay?"

Travis nodded. "Yeah. Just tired."

"I think we gave them the slip. I doubt any trolls will chase us this far." Rez brightened. "I bet we made up some time. We ran for *ages*. I reckon we're back on track."

Sitting up, Travis groaned and shook his arms vigorously. "So you think we should carry on?"

Rez frowned and shrugged. "Why not? We came this far. I don't see any point heading back home now. Might as well finish what we started."

"It's just that . . ." Travis sighed and stared into the mist ahead for a moment. He shook his head and jerked a thumb over his shoulder. "All those bug things. They'll grow and start taking over the trees, and the whole forest this side of the river will be controlled by the Seer. They already took over the forest to the south, and now we've helped them spread to the north."

"Well, I don't like it either, but what can we do? I reckon we carry on, go see the Grim Reaper, give him his little wooden box, and head home. Then you can tell Miss Simone all about the Seer."

"Why *me*?" Travis protested.

"Because you're the son of the famous shapeshifters Hal and Abigail Franklin. Miss Simone will forgive you no matter what. Not me, though. I'm just a nobody. She'd probably accuse me of destroying a forest or something, and send me to the Prison of Despair."

Travis scoffed at his friend's statement. He pointed to the knapsacks. "How about we have our breakfast—or lunch, or whatever it is now.'

"Brunch," Rez agreed, pulling the bags open.

They spent the next fifteen minutes sitting on cold rocks and dividing up whatever meager rations they had left. They finished every last scrap, agreeing that lighter knapsacks would be much easier to carry.

When they were done, they slipped their knapsacks onto their backs and climbed to their feet.

"Oh, man," Travis groaned. "I'm all wobbly."

"At least our bags are lighter now." Rez raised an eyebrow. "Do you need a walking stick, old man?"

They set off, continuing their journey north. All being well, the Grim Reaper's home should be just ahead. If they arrived by noon, that would mean a day's travel so far. Travis nodded with satisfaction. Not too bad, all things considered. They'd been delayed, but they'd gotten an early start and done a lot of running. The forests were now behind them, as were the trolls and the Seer.

In just an hour or two, they'd be face to face with the Grim Reaper.

Chapter 15
Into the Mist

Mist curled around them, a living thing that clung to their clothes as they moved, *sniffing* at them as though curious to see who would be fool enough to wander about this dismal region. Travis and Rez quietly agreed they had never seen mist this thick before. They kept their eyes down most of the time, watching as they took one step after another. They saw nothing but a wall of impenetrable gloom just four or five feet ahead.

"My mom and dad grew up in mist like this," Travis said, lowering his voice for reasons he couldn't explain. "Imagine that. Their entire lives walking around in thick fog, never seeing a blue sky. Stuck on an island with the same friends and their parents, going to the same school building every day, same teacher, same everything. They left the island when they were twelve."

Rez looked doubtful. "The mist wasn't *this* thick, was it? How'd they even find their way to school and home again? I can't see anything ahead. Or behind."

"Well, maybe not quite this thick," Travis admitted. "Tell you what, though: I hope we've stayed straight, otherwise we could end up miles off course. It's like walking blindfolded."

They'd looked at the map just once. From the forest exit and over the bridge, it was a straight shot almost directly north to the blank spot on the map. Travis had relied completely on his compass. Still, finding the Grim Reaper's home seemed like a long shot.

The ground had been dry and fairly loose for much of their journey since leaving the scenic valley and meadows. Now, amid the thick gloom, signs of moisture came to their attention—an abnormally soft patch of dirt here, a slight squelch there. The dry terrain gave way to damp gravel, then occasional puddles, and after that the kind of sticky mud that sucked at their feet with a *schlock!* sound.

When Rez lost one of his shoes for the third time, he hopped around for quite a while trying to pull it loose. When he did, he took a moment to hang both shoes and socks off his knapsack. Barefoot, he rolled up his pant legs to his knees and nodded with approval. "If I'm gonna walk through this mess, I might as well enjoy it."

Travis did the same. His smart shoes had no laces, so he tossed them into his knapsack instead. Everything would get very muddy in there, but so be it.

They continued trudging, now sinking ankle deep in increasingly wet mud. Shortly after, the mist thinned a little, and they suddenly realized they were at the shoreline of a bog. They stopped, looking around.

"Is this right?" Travis murmured. "Seems pretty big. Are we supposed to go around or wade through?"

"I vote we keep going straight," Rez said.

Neither said much after that. Travis couldn't decide if he was wading in thick water or thin mud, but either way it sucked all his energy. Every step meant yanking his foot completely free of the marshy ground, and it made a *shloop!* sound every time. And the mist was still too thick to see anything ahead. The Grim Reaper's home could be ten feet away, and they wouldn't know it.

He guessed Rez had to be thinking the same thing. But what else could they do but keep moving onward?

And so they did, slogging north for another twenty minutes or so. It remained knee-deep most of the way. Travis wondered where the ground ended and the bog began. Or was this marshland? Was there a difference? When exactly did a lake become a bog? How deep was the water farther out?

"Well," Rez said, breaking the silence and making Travis jump, "this must go down as one of the best days out I've ever had. Plodding through a bog. Great."

"Just like being at the seaside," he said. "Only without the golden sand."

"Or the sun," Rez retorted. "Or the sea. So nothing at all like being at the seaside."

Travis smiled. Though panting from the exertion of repeatedly pulling his feet free, he couldn't help enjoying their adventure. "Oh, come on, this is *fun*. Live a little."

Wading like this kept him warm, otherwise he'd be shivering from the cold, clammy fog. His clothes felt damp and clingy. His hands were icy, his feet numb. But a fire burned in his chest, and he wondered if Rez felt the same or if it was just the chimera in him.

"Hey, look," he said. "Fog's thinning out a bit."

He found he could see twenty to thirty feet all around now. Not that there was much to see. He spotted a dead, jagged tree trunk sticking up out of the water, and endless reeds, but otherwise it was a still mirror of murky water except where his clumsy wading created thick, wobbly ripples that never ventured too far.

They kept going.

"Why's it so misty, anyway?" Rez grumbled. "Everywhere else is sunny and clear, but it's dismal where the Grim Reaper lives. Does he attract terrible weather? Or does he live here *because* it's terrible?"

"Maybe the Reaper needs the mist," Travis answered after a moment's thought. "Keeps people away, or at least makes it harder to find him."

Rez let out a frustrated sigh. "I guess I'm not cut out for this adventuring thing. This trip has been useful. It's reminded me how much I hate traveling and being in weird places. I'll stick with carpentry."

"Well, you're good at that stuff. Remember the little unicorn you carved for old Mrs. Treacher?"

Rez laughed. "Treacher the teacher. How could I forget? I miss her. She wasn't nearly so hard on us in Math. And yeah, she liked that unicorn I made. Shame the horn broke off."

Travis thought his friend could probably make a living carving ornaments for the home, but he knew Rez would pooh-pooh the idea, saying that kind of work was best left to wrinkly old men in rocking chairs. He was far more interested in construction—framing houses, building workshops and barns, the big stuff. Meanwhile, Travis could barely hammer in a nail without mashing his thumb.

"*This* is what I like," he said, now thigh-deep in grey water. "Going on missions, seeing the world, making a difference." He glanced at Rez. "Not that carpenters and builders don't make a difference, it's just that . . ." He trailed off, uncertain how to finish his thought.

"Carpenters and builders are too *ordinary* for you," his friend teased. "I get it. You want to be famous like your mom and dad."

Travis shook his head. "That's not it. I mean, maybe a little bit . . . But mostly I just wanted to be a shapeshifter. I spent ages choosing what I wanted to be for the rest of my life, and I picked a wyvern, but it didn't work out. Two days! That was all I got in that form before my stupid immune system kicked in."

"But now you're a chimera. And next week you'll be something else. It's better that way, right? A bit of this, a bit of that. Something with wings one week, breathing fire the next, maybe an underwater creature or a giant another time."

Travis nodded. "I think Miss Simone's going to send me on lots of missions, and she'll turn me into whatever I need to be for that mission. Pretty cool, huh?"

Their conversation petered out for a few minutes as they continued their endless wading while peering through the mist. The Reaper's home had to be somewhere close.

"Have you figured out what's in the box yet?" Rez asked.

"The box?" Travis said with a frown. "Oh, the little wooden box we're delivering to the Grim Reaper? No clue. Something worthwhile, I hope."

"Yeah, something worth walking miles waist-deep in mud for."

"It's not waist-deep," Travis muttered, though it seemed to be getting that way.

Then they stopped dead.

"See that?" Rez whispered.

"Plain as day," Travis agreed.

An island loomed ahead. The grounds of Miss Simone's sprawling laboratory complex *might* fit on the island, but only just. As islands went, it was tiny. And not much farther. The problem was that the thick boggy water now seemed runnier somehow, more like ordinary lake water. They sank to their waists over the next few steps, and they paused again.

The mist seemed pretty thin out over the water, and hazy sunshine shone down on the humped island. In its center stood a crumbling mausoleum, trees spread around its sides. The bog was eerily calm and silent.

"That has to be it," Rez murmured. "The Grim Reaper's home."

"Gotta be. Amazing how we walked right to it. There it is, dead ahead."

Dead ahead. An accidental pun.

"Are we supposed to swim?" Rez asked.

"Can you fly?"

"No."

"Then I guess we'll swim."

Still, they stood there a while longer, taking the place in. So the Grim Reaper actually lived here? It seem apt. A mausoleum housed tombs, after all. Where else would the Reaper live?

The legendary harbinger of death, a hooded figure whose very appearance signified the end of a life, wasn't exactly the sort of person one usually volunteered to pop in and visit. Oddly, despite countless evenings researching numerous magical creatures, Travis realized he knew very little about the ominous being known as Death. His knowledge was spotty at best. Some said the Grim Reaper actually took souls when it suited him, thus ending lives prematurely. Others said he merely appeared when tragic death was imminent, a terrifying portent that only the victim could see.

Travis shuddered. Why on earth had his dad sent him and Rez to this place?

"Well," he said finally, "there's no point standing around. I don't see a boat lying about, and Mr. Reaper doesn't seem to be coming to meet us. We're on our own. I guess we'll have to wade a bit deeper, and swim if we have to."

Without waiting for a reply, he checked his knapsack was secure and started toward the island. The ground sloped away under him, and the water rose to his belly. His pants were already soaked, and now his shirt would be, too. And the stuff in his knapsack.

He paused, then turned back. "Let's leave everything here. We'll just take the wooden box."

And so, after a few drawn-out minutes of retrieving the slim wooden box, they both slogged over to the nearest dead tree and hung their knapsacks on a twisted, broken limb. Rez hung his shoes up, too. Better to be barefoot on the island than lose their shoes altogether and face a painful journey home later.

Feeling a bit lighter, they resumed their watery march toward the island.

The bog rose past their waists and up to their chests. Underfoot, sticky mud sucked at them even more, making every step a real nuisance. But other than their splashing and grunting, the silence was oppressive.

The mausoleum lurked in the hazy mist ahead.

Chapter 16
The Mausoleum

Halfway out to the tiny island, Travis and Rez paused again. The unusually still water was up to their chests now, though not quite as cold as expected. Occasionally, Travis felt something brush past his legs—a fish, or an eel, or perhaps a snake. He tried not to think about it.

"Might as well swim," he said. "It's not too far. Want to try for it?"

Rez shrugged. "I'm game. But are you going to cry like a girl if you get tired and find you can't reach the bottom?"

"I might," Travis agreed, nodding and putting on a serious expression.

They surged forward and started swimming, a gentle breaststroke to avoid churning up the water too much. Both agreed that moving quietly and calmly was better, though neither could explain quite why they felt that way.

The mausoleum stood forlorn in the hazy mist on the island. It looked like a miniature temple with its grand stonework and four columns out front, yet it stood no larger than a small cottage. It had seen better days. It looked old, its walls coated in grime and moss, a few cracks here and there. Ivy smothered one corner, though it looked dead and leafless. In fact, the nearby trees seemed to have expired as well, their limbs black and rotten.

Travis couldn't imagine anyone building such a place to honor the dead. How dreary!

Their swim was surprisingly relaxed, though Travis got a mouthful of murky water and spat it out in disgust, imagining all kinds of nastiness floating around on the surface.

They tried to touch bottom a few times, and finally Travis's feet found solid rock. He hopped in slow motion until he was able to rise out of the water, and then he splashed ashore with a sigh of relief, suddenly feeling very heavy.

Free of the bog at last, they climbed the steep, rocky bank onto remarkably dry flatland. The mausoleum stood in front of them, a little more impressive up close. Stone steps led to an ornate door that looked as grimy as the walls.

"Well, let's see if Mr. Reaper is in," Travis whispered.

"Is that what we're calling him?" Rez asked. "Mr. Reaper sounds weird. I doubt that's actually his name, you know."

"Well, we can't call him Grim. I'll stick with Mr. Reaper until he tells me different."

"How do you know it's a he?"

Travis had no answer, so he said nothing. Dripping wet, he padded up the stone steps to the door, noting that he was leaving wet footprints behind him. As he stood before the door, drops spattered around his feet. It seemed rude to enter someone's home and leave such a mess, but what could he do?

He knocked sharply with his fist.

"Nobody's in," Rez said after about two seconds. "Shame. Oh well, let's go. Just leave the wooden box in front of the door."

Travis ignored him and knocked again. "Mr. Reaper?" he called in a decidedly croaky voice. He cleared his throat and called a bit louder. "Mr. Reaper! Hello? Are you in?"

Rez grabbed his arm and glared at him. "Just to remind you," he hissed, "this is the *Grim Reaper* we're visiting. You know, the Angel of Death?"

"He's just a guy in a hood," Travis muttered. "My parents wouldn't send me here if there was any real danger. They're nuts, but they're not crazy."

Still, nobody answered. Travis felt his nervousness slipping away and irritation settling in. They'd traveled across a corner of the Parched Plains, through a forest filled with moving trees, over a river guarded by trolls, and swam through a disgusting bog. They were tired, cold, and wet. And the Grim Reaper wasn't even home?

"I'm going in," he said, reaching for the wrought-iron door handle.

"Travis," his friend warned.

The handle swung down easily, and the door moved inward. *Unlocked, then*, Travis thought. *No great surprise there. Who would loot the home of Death?*

Pushing the door open, he stepped into a small, dank lobby—if indeed that was the correct term where mausoleums were concerned. Four lanterns hung from the walls, two on each side, and they were alight, the flames flickering gently inside the tiny glass casing. Travis glanced from one to another, a sense of relief sweeping through him.

"At least we're in the right place," he told Rez. "*Someone* lives here."

He moved toward a door directly ahead. He pushed it open, and it creaked. The room beyond was similarly lit with lanterns on the walls, but it looked a bit more homey than Travis had expected. He ran his gaze over a small dining table, noting the gleaming silver candelabra in its center and the four chairs tucked in at the sides. He saw a wall full of old books, a spacious armchair facing a cold fireplace, a writing desk with a massive tome spread out on it, even a simple bunk in the corner, partially obscured by heavy drapes . . .

"What the heck?" Rez mumbled by his side. "Where are the dead people? I thought there'd be coffins. Isn't that what mausoleums are for?"

"Well—" Travis started.

Just then, a scuffle behind them made them jump and swing around in alarm.

Death was ice-cold. Framed in the doorway, the black-clad hooded figure held a scythe exactly as depicted in any number of illustrations. The crop-cutting implement, which could equally be called a fearsome weapon, had a pole long enough to stand on the floor while grasped at chest height. The long, downward-curving blade stuck out like a frozen flag. The sharp edge of that blade gleamed in the light of the lanterns, and Travis had no doubt it could cut a man in half with one slash.

He wanted to say hello, apologize for intruding, and introduce himself and his friend. Instead, he opened and closed his mouth a few times, the words choking in his throat. The problem was that the Grim Reaper had no face, just a pitch-black abyss deep within his hood, and this threw Travis for a loop.

Rez was equally dumbstruck. The two of them gaped, and Death waited in silence.

With a monumental effort, Travis choked out a word. "H-hello."

Silence.

He tried again. "I'm Travis Franklin, and this is Rez Malick. We, uh . . . we came to give you something." He started fumbling in his sodden pocket as his words rushed out. "My parents sent it, I don't know what it is, we asked but they wouldn't tell us, and we couldn't get the box open—not that we tried, it's just that—"

He broke off as the wooden box fell from his shaky fingers and clattered onto the floor. He froze, noting the barely perceptible tilting of Death's hood and the tiniest shifting of the scythe.

"Pick it up," Rez urged.

Travis tentatively bent to retrieve the wooden box, realizing as he did so that he might as well be offering himself up for execution. One swipe of that fearsome weapon, and his head would bounce and roll across the floor . . .

He scooped up the box and leapt to his feet, backpedaling to where Rez waited. "Here," he said, holding out his gift to the Reaper. "It's yours."

The Grim Reaper did nothing at all for a few long, long seconds. Then, still grasping the scythe with one hand, he reached for the box with the other.

His fingers were skeletal—long, white, and fleshless. The second finger was missing, something Travis noticed as the hard bones brushed against his hand. An ice-cold feeling swept up his arm, and he reeled backward with an awful sense of dread.

Having accepted his gift, the Reaper leaned his scythe against the wall behind him, then edged out of the shadows. The slight shift allowed light from the lanterns to fall on his face—or rather his skull. The sockets were empty, the teeth-filled jaws set in a perpetual grimace. "Thank you for bringing me this," he whispered.

Travis could almost hear icicles forming as the Reaper spoke, perhaps on the door frame behind him, or higher on the ceiling. "Y-you're welcome," he muttered, his heart thudding. He heard Rez breathing hard next to him. "What, uh . . . what is it?"

"It doesn't matter," Rez said in a strangled voice. "It's none of our business, right?"

The hooded figure switched the box to his fully-fingered hand and raised the other above, palm down as if trying to sense an aura. The wooden box promptly opened, the lid silently sliding lengthways.

Rez gasped.

Travis strained to see into the box, but it turned out he didn't have to. Something rose from it, a white object, jointed in two places—the Reaper's missing finger, complete with a slender gold ring. It turned in midair, then neatly moved into place between the first and third fingers of the Reaper's outstretched hand. And just like that, it was a part of him again, wiggling freely as he tested it.

"I am complete," the Reaper whispered. He returned the empty box to Travis, who took it dumbly, once more feeling that cold wave sweep up his arm.

Travis finally found his tongue. "H-how did—I mean, it just floated up and—How did you even know it was—It's like you knew your finger was in the box before you—"

He broke off again, annoyed at himself for stumbling over his words.

The Grim Reaper tilted his head. "The fact that you're here indicated you had my missing bones. You could not have found my resting place otherwise. Is there something you seek in return?"

Travis glanced at Rez, who stared back wide-eyed. "Well," Travis said, "no, not really. We were just told to give you the box."

"And who told you?" The Reaper held up his newly restored hand and added, "Wait." He snatched up his scythe—and promptly vanished.

Dumbfounded, Travis and Rez stared into the vacant space by the door. The ambient temperature slowly warmed.

"Okay," Rez said shakily, "I guess we're done here, then."

He moved toward the door, but Travis grabbed his arm. "He said to wait."

Rez looked incredulous. "Wait for what? Come on, we should go."

But Travis held firm. "Hold on. Just give him a second. He's not going to hurt us. We did him a favor by bringing him his, uh, missing finger. I don't know where he's gone, but—"

The Reaper appeared as suddenly as he'd gone, and both boys leapt backward with a yell. Travis bumped into the table, and the candelabra wobbled and nearly fell over.

"Who told you?" the Reaper asked in that dreadful whisper that seemed to freeze the air around him. "Who sent you here?"

"M-my dad," Travis said. "Hal Franklin? He . . . he said to bring you the box."

The hooded skull already looked like it was laughing at him, but Travis swore that grin widened now. "Tell him I am pleased."

"I will." Travis swallowed. "Uh . . . so, how exactly did he—I mean, why did he have your finger? Not that there was anything wrong with him having it! At least, I guess not, right? I suppose he found it somewhere. But why—uh, how come you lost it?"

"Travis," Rez hissed. "Will. You. Shut. *Up.*"

"I was just wondering." Travis studied the silent, heavily shadowed, ice-cold figure. "So you're actually the Grim Reaper?"

The personification of Death moved toward him. Travis and Rez backed up in a hurry, then sidestepped as the scythe-carrying specter continued past them into the middle of the room. He seemed to glide, his black robe dragging lightly across the smooth flagstones. "I am a Reaper," he confirmed. "One of many. We come in various guises, each with a ring that allows us to commune from afar. I have been isolated since its loss. But my work, nevertheless, continues unabated."

His words floated eerily about the mausoleum, slipping in and out of the shadows, sometimes whispering in Travis's ear.

"And you . . . you live here?" Travis pressed, his curiosity getting the better of him. His dad wouldn't have sent him if there was any real danger.

"I exist here."

The Reaper's simple statement filled Travis with sadness, a heavy feeling in his heart. Rez looked equally dismayed, his eyebrows raised in the middle, his eyes wide, mouth hanging open.

Travis was about to ask another question when the Reaper abruptly vanished again, just winking out of existence. "What the heck?" Travis muttered.

The feeling of sadness dissipated. Rez frowned and visibly shook himself. "Okay, Travis, we really need to get going. The Grim Reaper can kill with one touch. We've been lucky so far, but—"

"Wait, what? That can't be right. He accidentally touched my hand earlier when he took the box from me."

Rez shrugged. "Well, maybe he *chooses* to kill with one touch, then. The point is, he *can*."

"So? Why would he kill us? We brought him his missing finger!"

"Yeah, well, earlier he only had nine bony digits to kill us with, and now he has ten. Way to go."

They both froze as an intense cold descended on them. They'd been facing toward the living room area, if it could be called that. Now they turned to find the Reaper standing just behind them, the gleaming blade of the scythe reflecting their white faces.

The expressionless skull looked down at them. "All this talk of death . . ." He raised a hand. "Allow me to demonstrate exactly how I take lives."

Chapter 17
The Grim Reaper

The mausoleum fuzzed out, replaced by bright daylight. The Reaper's skeletal hand remained poised in front of Travis and Rez as they gasped and staggered with the abrupt scene change. Things quickly came into focus around them—a highway in Old Earth jam-packed with cars and trucks, the rumble of engines filling the air, people running about, acrid smoke pluming from a raging fire, sirens in the distance . . .

Several cars were twisted and crumpled, turned in different directions, skid marks on the road, bits of glass strewn everywhere, a fender lying nearby. Another car's rear end stuck up out of the ditch at the edge of the highway. That car belched flames and smoke, and frantic drivers darted back and forth, trying to get close but too frightened of the flames.

The Reaper moved toward the wreck. Travis felt himself tugged along behind as though he and Rez were a couple of balloons on strings. Neither had the capacity to resist. When Travis looked down, he saw that his legs were faded out, not even touching the ground. *We're dead*, he thought in horror.

But he knew that wasn't so. Not yet, anyway. He and Rez were merely spectators.

Ignoring the shouting drivers, even passing through one of them, the Reaper descended the slope of the grassy bank and approached the crumpled car. The car's hood had popped open, and flames roared high from the engine, though Travis felt no heat. He felt nothing. Inside, the flames had worked their way through to the car's interior on the passenger's side, and grey smoke rolled fast and thick from the smashed windshield and side windows.

The driver lay motionless in his seat. Travis didn't want to look any closer. Nor did Rez, who tried to pull back.

"He is dying," the Grim Reaper whispered, his voice somehow cutting through the rest of the noise. "There is no hope for him. His legs are trapped, his injuries are fatal, and the smoke will fill his lungs before the fire reaches him."

"So . . . so you're going to put him out of his misery?" Travis exclaimed bitterly. "Take his soul?"

"Not take his soul," the Reaper replied. "Simply pass it along."

He reached into the car. Something happened just out of sight, something that caused the dying driver to jerk. Then the Reaper stood up straight and turned to face the boys, and from one hand dangled a dark-grey aura, long and wispy. "We are done."

Abruptly, the daylight faded to darkness, and all the shouts and sirens cut out. Silence fell, and the interior of the mausoleum came back into focus, now a welcome relief.

Travis stamped around on the flagstone floor. *I'm real*, he thought. *Not a ghost.* He then reached out and grabbed Rez by the shoulder to make sure his friend wasn't some kind of phantom. Everything seemed okay.

"I don't take lives," the Grim Reaper whispered, standing quite still with his scythe. He held up his other bony hand, and the creepy smudge of an aura hung there, roughly the shape of a person but with the lower half faded and insubstantial. "Fate does that. I simply ensure the soul passes on."

Travis had been eyeing the soul with awe, but now he caught his breath. "To . . . to the World of Darkness. To the Lady of Light."

The Reaper tilted his head to one side. "Call it what you will. Souls are processed, their energy returned to Earth—not Old Earth from whence they came, but to New Earth in the form of magic. Every life that ends is reborn as magic. Wait here while I deliver this soul."

With that, he winked out of existence.

"You see?" Travis said, backhanding his friend across the arm. "Dad told me all this stuff ages ago. He visited the World of Darkness when he was our age, when he was turned to stone by a gorgon and trapped there until a phoenix reversed the spell."

"Yeah, yeah," Rez muttered. "But I seem to remember you didn't believe his story, either."

Travis had to admit that was true. He felt ashamed now. His dad had talked of floating around in darkness along with glowing balls of energy, and an ethereal woman who marshaled souls into a pit of light . . . It had all seemed crazy, especially as nobody could confirm his tale. Plenty of other people had been in his predicament—other gorgon-calcified victims, plus comatose patients who lingered somewhere between life and death—but nobody else remembered the World of Darkness if and when they woke. They weren't *supposed* to remember, his dad had said. Yet he, for some reason, had been deemed special, granted the privilege of recollection just so he might carry out a mission, which in turn had led to mines exploding, thousands of portals opening between the worlds, and the unification of Old and New Earth.

What the Grim Reaper had shown Travis today gave weight to those tales. Now there was no doubt. Everything his dad had ever said was true.

The Reaper returned just then, now without the soul. "It is delivered."

Rez cleared his throat. "Well, we can't hang around here all day." He looked meaningfully at Travis, then nodded toward the door. "I guess we'll be heading out, right?"

The Reaper made no move to stop them. He remained standing behind the spacious armchair, apparently lost in thought. Still, Travis lingered, overcome with curiosity. "Why was your finger missing?" he blurted.

"Travis—" Rez hissed.

"Just a minute, okay?" Before Rez could say another word, Travis moved closer to the Reaper and repeated his question. "What happened? How did you lose it?"

The black-robed figure placed a skeletal hand on the back of the chair. The ring—gold with a white stone—glinted in the light from the wall-mounted lanterns. "It is a simple tale. A woman was attacked one night several months ago, in a town south of here. Three men set upon her in a dark alley to rob her of a few meager items. She was murdered. I arrived to ensure safe passage of her soul. As for the three men . . ."

Travis leaned closer. He remembered hearing of an incident like this in Carter. The woman had been a lifelong resident, while the men had been from Old Earth. "What about them?" he asked.

The Reaper turned his hood toward him, revealing his shadowed skull. "They should have escaped alive. As I said, I do not serve death despite what some will have you believe. However, the dullahans do."

"Doola-what?" Rez broke in. Despite his urge to leave moments ago, now he crept closer, obviously drawn to the Reaper's tale.

"I mentioned that I am one of many Reapers." He lifted his scythe and tapped it gently on the floor. "I am perhaps the most recognized, yes? But I am not the only one who takes and delivers souls. We come in many forms. None of us decide who dies. We simply arrive at the moment of death and—" He cocked his head. "Please wait. I will return in a moment."

As before, he vanished in the blink of an eye.

In the silence that followed, Rez let out a long breath and turned to Travis. "Why are we still here? Let's *go* while we still can."

Travis shook his head. "You heard him. He doesn't take life. That's not his job. We're perfectly safe."

Rez snorted. "Safe! We're in the Grim Reaper's living room, listening to one of his amusing anecdotes about life as the Angel of Death. What could possibly—"

The Reaper appeared again, standing in the same place but his posture a little different, his scythe gripped in both hands.

"No soul?" Travis croaked.

"I have delivered it," the Reaper murmured. He relaxed and turned again to Travis. "As I was saying, there are many of us, and we have a never-ending task. We divide the work by region. We don't catch every death, and in those cases the soul is displaced upon death and tends to linger, confused and unable to move on. They become haunts. Ghosts."

"Ghosts . . ." Travis mumbled, transfixed.

"But then there are the dullahans," the Reaper continued, his whispery voice causing the surrounding air to drop a few more degrees. "They defy the natural order of things. They are empowered to manipulate the physical world, nudge things to ensure a different outcome. One destined to survive an accident might die instead thanks to a visit by a dullahan, who will appear out of nowhere on a black stallion, his severed head under his arm, eyes wide, a grin stretched from ear to ear. He will state the name of his victim, thus bringing instant death. For dramatic flair, he will lash out at the victim with a whip made from a human spine."

Travis gasped, and Rez muttered something under his breath.

"In any case," the Reaper went on, "the chosen victim will drop dead. On this particular night in the town of Carter, a dullahan made his appearance as I was lifting the soul from the murdered woman. He laughed and pointed at one of the three men, and that man suffered a heart attack and died on the spot. I cared not for this evil man's well-being. But his soul, tainted by the dullahan, was rendered useless. Such a waste. I've witnessed dullahans in action countless times, and I usually say nothing, because they are very powerful. But on this occasion, without thinking, I swung my scythe and caught the dullahan across his chest, slicing him wide open."

"You killed him!" Rez exclaimed.

"Alas, no. It is hard to dispatch a dullahan. I simply angered him. He came at me with his whip, and I raised my hand to protect myself—"

"And you lost your finger," Travis finished.

The Reaper bowed his head once. "My other fingers were bent backwards, but *this* one—" He lifted his hand and wiggled the second finger. "It flew off, and it was lost to me."

"You couldn't find it?" Rez said. "It couldn't have gone far."

"It didn't. It landed at my feet. Unfortunately, once disconnected from my body, it became one with *your* world. I could not pick it up. It was as insubstantial to me as I am to the living."

This confused Travis. "But . . . you touched me earlier, when you took the box from me. You're not insubstantial at all."

"That's because you're *here*. You carried my finger back to me. You crossed into my realm."

Travis and Rez stared at him. Then Rez said, "So . . . we're *dead?*"

The Reaper gave a single shake of his skull. "No, you're simply visiting. When you leave my presence, you will return to the land of the living."

So that's that, Travis thought. *The story of how Death lost his finger—lopped off by something called a dullahan.* He imagined Miss Simone must have visited the scene of the crime the next morning and found the severed finger. Seeing that ring, with its distinctive stone, she'd figured out who it belonged to and vowed to return it.

The Reaper must have caught him staring because he held out his skeletal hand and flexed the bony fingers. The stone caught the light and glinted. "This ring allows me more freedom. It gives me the power to choose destinations and relocate in a more substantial manner. Without it, I'm a mere puppet drawn to where souls are in need of saving."

"How did Miss Simone figure out where you lived?" Rez piped up.

He immediately shrank back behind Travis as the Reaper turned and offered him what could only be a withering glare. The ambient air temperature dropped a few degrees. "I left clues within my limits. An infestation of flies, the stench of corpses, frigid temperatures in the summer, isolated mists at night. All these things I could do without my ring. This region—" He gestured vaguely. "—has quietly become known as a place of death. I am pleased my subtle messages were noticed."

"But it's a mausoleum," Rez muttered. "I would have thought it was obvious."

Travis frowned. "Actually, it's just a blank spot on the map." He paused. "I get it. We're not really in our world right now, are we, Mr. Reaper? This is, like, a ghost world."

The Reaper inclined his hooded skull.

"And Miss Simone figured delivering your ring would be a neat first mission for me," Travis concluded. He nodded and smiled, then rubbed his hands briskly. "So, any chance of a ride home now that you have your power back, Mr. Reaper?" Receiving another of those withering glares, he swallowed and shrugged. "I guess not. Okay, well, we'll be on our way, then. Got a long walk ahead of us."

He and Rez turned and headed toward the exit. Just before they passed through the doorway, the Reaper spoke softly. "Wait. I will escort you to dry land."

And with that, the Grim Reaper seemed to flow toward them, his black robes dragging behind. Travis shuddered. Now he regretted asking for a ride home, even in jest. His clothes were still damp, and he was already cold enough without having an icy phantom creature of death by his side!

He longed for the sunshine of the Parched Plains.

Chapter 18
Ferry Across the Bog

Outside the mausoleum, the Grim Reaper led the way to the bog. Watching from behind, Travis was even more convinced the skeletal creature had to be floating across the flat dirt. No swaying from side to side, no bobbing of the hood, just a smooth forward motion. The black robe dragged but not once snagged on protruding roots or small rocks.

At the water's edge, the Reaper stopped on a rocky ledge and lifted his scythe. When he banged it down hard on the rock, it made a *clack* sound that reverberated through the light mist. Silent ripples on the surface of the bog spread out from where he stood even though he couldn't have touched the water.

"What's he doing?" Rez whispered.

Travis shrugged.

To their amazement, something emerged just three yards out—a man's head and shoulders, rising smoothly and quietly. Gaunt and grey-robed, he had a pallid face and long grey hair. He gripped a pole in both hands, held vertically. As he rose higher, it became evident he was standing at the bow of a long, very narrow boat, which broke the surface with a bubbling, gurgling noise. A torch fixed to the slender, upward-curving bow sputtered into life the moment it was clear of the bog. Though the shallow boat was understandably full of murky water, it quickly emptied in a way that made no sense, simply draining through cracks in the bottom. Seconds later, the boat—glistening wet but impossibly seaworthy—turned ninety degrees and eased closer until it bumped its side against the rocky bank.

The Reaper turned to face Travis, his hood so low over his head that only his bottom jaw showed. "Go now. My ferryman, Charon, will see you safely to dry land. Return home and pass on my thanks to your father." He raised a hand and wiggled all his bony fingers.

"I will," Travis said, edging toward the boat. "Uh, can we come visit again?"

The Reaper gave one barely imperceptible shake of his head. "You found this place only because you had a part of me in your possession. Now you do not."

Travis gingerly stepped onto the boat. It yielded slightly under his weight, and he sat down on one of the flat, hard seats. Rez sat on the next one along, facing him.

Without a word, the ferryman dipped his long pole into the water and pushed off. The boat gracefully and silently moved, turning ninety degrees until it was angled correctly.

Travis twisted around so he could see the Reaper. The black-robed figure stood watching from the bank, the mist curling around him. Twenty seconds later, he faded from sight.

"So that's that," Travis said, facing front again. He watched the ferryman over Rez's shoulder. "Not many can say they've visited Death at his home."

"And lived," Rez agreed. "Well, I'm glad to be heading back. Hey, I hope we can find our stuff on the other side."

The journey across the misty bog was surprisingly relaxing. Travis turned to look over his shoulder several times, though he saw less each time, just a dreary whiteout. He felt almost sad that he might never get to come back and see the Grim Reaper . . . creepy though he was.

Ahead, black and lifeless twisted trees began to appear in the gloom. The mist, which had thickened dramatically, began to thin again. Before long, the boat nudged up onto firm ground and halted, and the ferryman turned to give the boys a piercing stare with grey eyes. He grinned, showing rotten teeth.

"I guess we're here," Rez said, standing. He looked at the ferryman and apparently decided not to try and squeeze past him to the bow. Instead, he grimaced and eased himself over the side into thigh-deep water.

Travis followed him in. "Thanks, Mr. Charon."

As he and his friend splashed ashore, the ground quickly hardened underfoot. In fact, nothing seemed as wet and boggy as it had before. They padded out of the mud and onto thick grass that definitely hadn't been there before. Travis looked toward the south, amazed at how ordinary it seemed—plains of grass and rock, dry and pleasant, stands of leafy trees here and there. "There's no mist," he remarked. "And it's dry. On the way here, we walked through mist and mud for ages before we made it to the water."

"Tell me about it," Rez grumbled, shielding his eyes against the sun. "We must have come a different way, maybe farther along the—"

He broke off. He'd been about to gesture to the left along the length of the bog, but they both turned to see a single tree standing not more than twenty feet away, healthy and full, its leaves moving in a faint breeze. Hanging from one of its lower branches were their knapsacks.

Travis gasped and swung around. The bog had gone. So had the ferryman and his boat. The last of the mist lifted to reveal miles of open meadows, dry and grassy, with forests and mountains to the west and north, and sun-baked plains to the east.

There was absolutely no sign of the mausoleum.

"I feel like we just woke from a dream," Rez muttered.

They retrieved their knapsacks and opened them up. They'd both brought an extra shirt, and they took a moment to change. Their wet shirts could hang off the straps at the back. It felt good to put shoes back on. Unfortunately, neither had a change of pants, so they'd just have to dry off in the sunshine.

They closed up their knapsacks, slung them over their shoulders, and started their march south. With the sun directly ahead, their moods lifted dramatically. The oppressive cold of the Grim Reaper and the mausoleum seemed a millions miles away now—or as Rez had suggested, it had simply faded away like a dream in the night.

"It has to be mid-afternoon," Travis said. "I reckon we'll camp out again tonight and be back home in the morning."

"Can't we just be home tonight?" Rez said with a sigh. "We don't have any food left now. And I'm not sure I want to mess about trying to set up a camp and all that stuff."

Travis clicked his tongue. "You're so boring. We'll be over the river and past the troll valley soon, then in the forest, and we'll be back out in the Parched Plains before dark. Maybe we can camp under those huge rocks we stopped at on the way here. We'll get a nice fire going, make it all cozy and warm, and—"

"Make a fire with what? We need wood for fire. Are we planning on toting a load of branches out there?"

He had a point. But Travis was sure they'd figure it out. "Let's just avoid talking trees and giant scorpions this time. And if any trolls try to charge us a fee like last time, they'd better watch out."

He looked forward to a relaxing night in the Parched Plains—a roaring campfire, maybe a couple of fat groundhogs roasting on a spit, him and Rez talking the night away while staring up at the clear starry sky, then sleeping soundly in the shelter of those big rocks . . .

He grinned. "This is gonna be great."

Rez rolled his eyes.

* * *

They approached the troll valley with trepidation.

"Let me carry your bag," Rez said quietly when the narrow humped bridge came into view. "You'll probably need to transform."

It was certainly looking that way. Two trolls waited on the bridge, leaning on one side, deep in conversation. Travis couldn't imagine what kinds of things trolls talked about.

Maybe a few grunts here and there, one suggesting he was bored, the other agreeing and wishing it were dinnertime . . .

Travis and Rez stopped near some trees, not wanting to be spotted just yet. The terrain to the east was forested and hilly. They could easily creep through the trees and along the foot of the hills, then make their way to the river unseen and cross somewhere downstream. But that would involve a long detour and getting drenched.

The bridge looked so simple and tempting. It stood at the bottom of the slope directly ahead, beckoning them to cross. If only the trolls weren't waiting there . . .

"I don't want to get wet again," Travis said, looking down on the fast-flowing water. His pants were thoroughly dried by now, his shirt safely stored in his knapsack.

"Me neither."

"Okay, so I guess I'll transform, then rush at those two trolls and spook 'em. You follow as fast as you can, okay? We'll just make a run for it."

He wasn't quite sure how it would work out. Hopefully they'd see him coming and flee across the bridge to the other side of the river, then dash to safety. If they stood their ground, then it would get tricky.

"Ready?" he whispered, handing his knapsack to Rez. It was much lighter now than it had been when they'd started their mission. It felt empty apart from the plastic orange sheet.

"Ready," Rez agreed, slinging the extra knapsack across his shoulder.

And it was at that moment Travis heard a sudden scuffle behind him. He swung around and just had time to see four trolls descending on him before a heavy fist whacked him around the side of the head. He went down, dazed and confused, his ear ringing. A tremendous weight fell on his back.

Then another blow to the side of his head knocked him senseless.

* * *

He was dimly aware of being picked up and carried, strong fingers pressing into his wrists and ankles. Rez yelled from afar. The sounds of guttural conversation drifted through Travis's hazy consciousness. When he forced his eyes open, he saw trolls all around, glaring at him as he was hauled along. He blinked furiously, saw shacks in the background, trees on the hillside, cave openings and rocks, and a river with two rickety bridges. The troll's lake.

"Lemme go . . ." he mumbled, finding that his words came out thick and slurred. His head throbbed.

Amid the grunts and excited troll barks, he heard the squeak of a heavy door opening, and suddenly the bright sunshine dimmed as he was carried indoors. He forced his eyes open again and looked up at a ceiling of crisscrossing logs lashed together with rope and covered with a thick canopy of branches. A sturdy structure, bigger than a shed and smaller than a barn. He saw a few pinpricks of daylight, but mostly it was tightly woven, a well-built roof.

The trolls threw him to the floor. He gasped and lay still with his eyes shut, convinced his head was about to explode. He heard shuffling, stamping feet and grunted conversation, and then a door slammed. A bolt slid across. Then more stamping, and another door slamming.

Peace and quiet descended.

Chapter 19
Prisoners of the Trolls

Travis groaned and held the left side of his head. His cheek was all puffy and tender, and it hurt like crazy when he touched the bony part surrounding his eye. One of those trolls had clobbered him good! Twice, if he recalled. He lay there a moment, thinking this was going to be the worst headache ever.

Rez!

He bolted upright, then winced. It took all his effort to squint around and figure out where he was. He couldn't be certain if it was supposed to be a jail of some kind, but it sure looked like one—a roughly triangular room with a small barred window and a single, very stout door, also with bars. The floor was flat, hard-packed dirt with one wet patch in the corner where rain evidently leaked in.

No Rez.

Breathing hard, he looked around one more time in case his swollen eye was causing a blind spot to one side. The room was shaped rather like a wedge of cake—two longs walls across from one another, a short inner wall where the door was, and a curved external wall with a window in the center. The cell couldn't be more than twelve feet lengthwise.

Definitely no Rez.

He climbed unsteadily to his feet and stood there swaying a moment. Then he staggered to the door and gripped the bars, which were set three inches apart in a small square opening at head height. He found that odd, since the trolls were all much taller. A single bench seat stood against one wall, and it looked too short for a troll to sit on. Clearly this jailhouse was intended for human travelers, perhaps those who tried to skip paying a toll. Or, more likely, the place had been built by humans and abandoned long ago.

He saw the rest of the building through the bars—basically another two cells shaped like his own, their doors within spitting distance. The rest of the building consisted of a large open room with a couple of windows and a main door. Everything smelled musty thanks to half-dried pools of water. The place had some serious leakage problems. Maybe that was why the trolls used it as a jailhouse.

"Rez?" he called.

No answer.

He tried again, louder this time. "Rez!"

Still no answer. Wherever his friend was, it wasn't here. Unless he'd been clobbered as hard as Travis had been. He might be unconscious in one of the other cells.

Travis fretted over this. He couldn't help thinking of the steel cages he'd been locked up in the previous weekend. Mr. Braxton had kept all manner of magical creatures in his warehouse, and Travis—new to shapeshifting—had been stuck in wyvern form. Now, however, he—

Sucking in a breath, he almost slapped himself across the face for forgetting what he was. He could take care of his throbbing head in no time.

He transformed, and to his relief had no trouble becoming the familiar chimera monster. This time he found himself inside the goat's head, and he instantly thought about blasting a fiery hole in the door to escape.

But first, he needed to repair himself. The pain had already subsided a little thanks to his healing power. A few more transformations would do the trick. He switched back and forth, and each time he arrived inside a different chimera head—first the snake, then the lion, then the goat again. He stopped. The pain in his head was almost nonexistent now.

He backed up to the curved external wall and started working on a fireball. As he did so, he wondered briefly how the lion had known he'd wanted to back up. Perhaps it had simply thought of it simultaneously. It probably happened that way all the time. A chimera's three heads had to be in tune with each other if they were to exist as one. Their unity was instinctive.

Travis, on the other hand, was a stranger to this multifaceted way of life. He put the matter aside and concentrated on the fireball.

There's no room, he thought suddenly as he peered over the lion's mane at the door. If he blasted a hole in it, he'd be showered in bits of wood and gobs of fire. But it was also possible his fireball would be ineffectual. He'd experienced that problem already back in the woods. He needed some distance from his target.

He tried it anyway. The fireball was already forming in his throat, and it seemed a pity to waste it. He backed up as far as he could, squeezing his rear into a corner. It meant his aim would be at a fairly sharp angle to the door, but it gave him more space.

He fired his red-hot projectile. It glanced off the door with a weird spatter, and liquid fire coated the frame and adjacent wall. The door itself didn't budge an inch. Flames sputtered and flickered as the steaming acid burned holes and dribbled to the floor in smoking rivulets. Luckily, nothing stayed alight. It wouldn't be much fun being locked inside a burning room.

What a washout, he thought with disgust.

Just another six feet of space would be enough for his fireballs to harden and intensify as they flew through the air, making them far more explosive. Instead, it was like flinging acid.

He sighed. Well, he could always spit his burning phlegm at the trolls when they came to torture him . . .

Shoot a fireball through the bars! he thought with a sudden jolt of excitement. But his enthusiasm died almost instantly. The bars were set too close together. It would never work.

He paced the room, growling softly. What was the point in being a shapeshifter if he couldn't escape from a simple cell?

He looked up. This corner of the roof was like the rest, a series of sturdy logs with a thick roof of woven branches and probably other kinds of thatch on the outside. He could set it alight if he aimed high . . . but how would that help?

He clawed at the hard-packed dirt. Maybe dig his way out? He padded over to the sodden area and found it a lot softer, and he grew excited at the prospect of tunneling under a wall. But he quickly gave up on the idea when he hit rocks and gravel. The original builders had actually laid a solid foundation.

He leapt at the door and rattled it in its frame. Then he snarled and paced the room some more. There *had* to be a way out.

A commotion caught his attention. Outside his cell, the main door swung inward and a group of trolls burst in. They dragged Rez into an adjacent cell and dumped him, then left and slammed the door shut, bolting it as they went. Two trolls remained.

"Rez!" Travis shouted, but his voice came out as a roar.

This caught the attention of the trolls, and they scowled at him. One of them had a badly burned chest, all the hair scorched off and the bare skin a much darker brown than it should be. Travis stared in dismay.

The burned brute pointed at Travis and uttered something intelligible. He sounded angry.

Next to him, a smaller troll with pale-grey hair spoke in a low but clear voice. "Zoth say you will hurt for this."

Travis had never heard a troll speak more than one word in English. He opened his mouth to retort, then remembered he was still in chimera form. He stepped back, reverted to human form, then gripped the bars and shouted, "If you don't let us out, you'll *all* end up hurt!"

The burned troll named Zoth roared with anger, apparently understanding just fine. He stomped closer and pounded his fist on the door, and the whole thing rattled on its hinges. Travis couldn't help leaping back in alarm. Luckily for him, Zoth stomped away again, taking his interpreter with him. He slammed the main door so hard that dust shook loose from the vaulted ceiling.

"Rez?" Travis called. "You okay?"

His friend moaned and coughed. "Yeah, I guess." After a pause, he appeared at the barred window in his cell door. "I thought they were going to string me up or skewer me or something. That big one, Zoth—he's pretty mad. Kept pointing at his burnt chest and barking at me. But he was mad about something else, too. He dragged me to see the cocoon, which was lying right where they cut it open."

"Ooh," Travis said.

"Yeah. He went on and on about it, and that funny little troll tried to keep up with the translation. Zoth was saying something about giant bugs squirming all over him. He looked pretty disgusted."

"Can't blame him for that."

"No, we can't."

They fell silent.

Outside, voices rose as if an argument had started up. Travis tuned them out. "Rez, I'm gonna get us out of here."

"Yeah? How?"

"Not sure yet. But I'll think of something."

"I'm waiting, Trav."

If only I were a faerie, Travis thought, reluctantly agreeing that being like his mom would actually be useful in a situation like this. To be able to shrink to six inches in height and fly through the bars . . .

He scowled. Better still if he were an ogre so he could simply bash the door down!

"How's your head?" Rez asked from his cell.

"Fine. I transformed a few times, and now I'm as good as new."

Rez nodded. "That's one thing about shapeshifting I envy."

"So you wouldn't want to be an ogre right now? Or a snake so you can slip through the bars?"

The idea hit him like a thunderbolt—but before he could open his mouth to tell his friend about it, the commotion outside grew louder, more urgent.

He frowned. "Do you hear that?"

"I hear something, yeah."

"I'm gonna take a look," Travis said, heading over to the window in the curved external wall.

He gripped the bars, again wishing they were spaced a little wider. The opening was bigger, and there was no glass, but none of that helped him when the bars were so stubbornly secure.

Outside, trolls were darting here and there, looking over their shoulders as they ran, leaving clouds of dust in their wake. And in the dust, a few of those tentacled scorpions scuttled about. Travis gasped at the grisly sight. The bugs were huge like the ones he'd seen in the forest, the size of the one that had wrapped itself around Rez's feet. And it looked like they were trying to capture a few trolls.

Travis shuddered, suddenly glad to be locked safely inside. He counted six or seven of the bugs, and they zipped around at frightening speed. One leapt onto a troll's back, and the tentacles lengthened rapidly, slipping easily around his neck. The troll let out a roar and stumbled sideways before dropping to his knees.

Two female trolls rushed to help, stamping at the scuttling bugs but missing every time. As one wrenched at the tentacles around the male's neck, the other let out a screech as two more bugs leapt at her.

"They're attacking!" Travis yelled over his shoulder to Rez. "The bugs from the forest—they found their way here and are jumping on the trolls!"

"I can see that," Rez shouted back, his voice distant. "I'm looking out toward the river, and there's a few squirming all over a troll who fell a minute ago. They're wrapping their tentacles around his neck and legs!"

"How did they get across the river?" Travis wondered aloud. "I doubt they swam. They must have come across the bridges. I'm surprised the sentries let them, though . . ." A horrible thought occurred to him. "Unless . . ."

"Speak up!" Rez yelled. "Unless what?"

"Unless they were already here."

"Huh?"

Travis gripped the bars and squinted into the thickening dust clouds as trolls sprinted about the place. And then he saw it—an army of ugly tentacled critters emerging from the ground, from cave openings, from under rocks, even from the long grass. They swarmed into the settlement, spreading wide and overrunning the trolls in a matter of seconds.

"Travis!" Rez demanded. "What's going on? What are you seeing?"

"Uh . . . well, you remember those hundreds of harmless, teeny-tiny baby bugs that came out of the cocoon earlier today?"

"What about them?"

Travis swallowed. "They grew up. Really, *really* fast."

Chapter 20
Overrun

Travis couldn't tear his gaze from the horror unfolding outside his window. Whether trolls were standing, stumbling around, or writhing on the ground, the scorpions swarmed over them in groups of five or six at a time, scuttling this way and that, their tentacles slithering around limbs and necks and drawing tight.

When the dust cloud cleared, an ominous calm descended on the settlement. The shaggy trolls seemed to have given up the fight already, and they held still in whatever position they'd ended up in, in the grip of numerous slippery appendages. The rest of the bugs spread farther out, exploring, hunting for more prey.

As Travis peered out, one of the scorpions leapt up out of nowhere and slammed against the bars inches from his face, gripping them with its eight powerful legs and pressing the underside of its shiny body against the frame. The tentacles slid out from the end of its abdomen and through the glassless window, reaching for Travis.

He threw himself backward in disgust and eyed the nasty critter from a safe distance. The wriggling tentacles stretched about three feet. He imagined they would be six feet long in no time, probably growing at a much faster rate than the bug itself.

Another scorpion slammed against the bars, its underside just as shiny. The arachnids were almost identical to each other.

"What's going on back there?" Rez called. "I see the giant bugs now. They've . . . they've got some trolls pinned down."

"Same here," Travis said loudly. "They're all over the place. We're lucky we're locked up."

"We'd be luckier if we were never captured in the first place."

"True."

Rez's voice was closer now, and Travis turned to see him pressed to the small window of his cell door. "Hey, Trav—I don't really want to go outside right now, but I don't want to be trapped forever, either. What if the trolls never let us out? Or what if these bugs get in?"

Travis nodded. "I have an idea. Hold on."

He grasped the heavy wooden bench seat and dragged it nearer to the door. Then he transformed. As expected, he found himself in the mind of the snake at the rear end.

As if anticipating his plan, the lion jumped up onto the bench seat with his butt against the door. Travis grinned to himself and rose higher. *Now* he could escape the bars.

It felt like that, at least. He turned his head to one side and eased through, his snake body following. Unlike a real snake, his tail end was tethered to the chimera's body . . . but, standing on the bench, he had plenty of length to slither down to the bolt on the other side.

He gripped it in his jaws and struggled with it. It took some effort, but he managed to ease it upward and then across.

"Holy cow," Rez said from a few feet away, staring out of his cell. "That's not something you see every day."

With the bolt slid open, Travis retreated back into his cell. The lion jumped down. At this point, Travis knew he needed opposable thumbs again, so he reverted to human form and dragged the bench aside.

"Done," he said triumphantly as he threw open the door.

He released Rez from his cell, and the two of them stood together to plan their next move. None of the bugs had made it inside yet, and maybe they never would . . . but if they did, it all might be over very quickly. Travis had seen how the trolls had failed to stamp on the things, and he didn't expect to do any better himself.

Would fireballing them help? It would if his aim was true, but one fireball every half-minute wouldn't help much against a swarm of the things.

"Plan?" Rez whispered.

Now that they were together, maybe keeping a low profile would be best. Travis closed the cell doors and headed into the main part of the building, which spanned twenty-five feet at its widest. It had a table and some chairs, perhaps for jail guards.

"There's nowhere to hide," Travis muttered. "All we have are the cells. We could stay inside one and keep the door shut if the bugs get into the building—and if they break in through a cell window, we can get out fast and lock them in."

They stood there, uncertain. The bars in the windows were too close together for the scorpions to breach, and certainly strong enough. The gap under the main door had to be a couple of inches but nowhere near big enough to squeeze through. The jailhouse seemed impenetrable. The bugs would surely give up on them soon.

"Let's just hunker down here and wait it out," Travis suggested. "Maybe they'll move on or something. I think we're safe for now."

He spoke too soon. From high above came a scrabbling sound, and both boys glanced up to see dust trickling down where the tightly woven roof jiggled. Two stubby pincers penetrated the thatch, and one of the scorpions forced its head through.

"No!" Rez gasped. "Travis, do something. Burn it!"

Travis transformed, and to his surprise ended up inside the lion's head even though shooting fireballs had been on his mind. To be fair, he'd also been thinking about where to run if they had to escape the building.

He turned in a tight circle, studying the roof. Another slit appeared, and a bug squeezed through with wriggling legs. The first was already halfway through by now, the widest part of its carapace having cleared the hole. Its legs flailed in mid-air, and then it turned upside down to get a grip on the underside of the thatch. As its backend made it through, the tentacles emerged and seemed to sniff the air . . .

And then it fell. The bug landed on its back with a terrible *crack* and lay still for a moment, apparently stunned. Then its legs started moving, and its tentacles flopped about, pushing at the ground in an effort to turn over. The whole thing began to tilt to one side, and Travis saw a split in its carapace, thick yellowish blood oozing out.

"Travis!" Rez yelled.

He broke from his trance and looked up. The second bug was squeezing through, and more were following. With two holes opened up in the ceiling, the place would be overrun by the things in less than a minute.

His goat's head had been busy forming a fireball. The ball of flames blasted upward and smacked into the thatch next to the second bug, punching a hole right through. Bugs went flying amid a shower of twigs and straw. Liquid fire splashed all over, and this quickly set the roof alight.

Travis had a moment of glee that the fire had dispersed the invaders. But now the roof was on fire, a problem in itself.

Also, the injured bug on the ground had turned itself over and was scurrying toward them.

"Watch out!" Travis shouted, pushing Rez to one side.

He pounced on the bug, throwing his entire weight onto its back and lying on it the best he could. His snake-head tail snapped at the creature with its fangs while Travis dug in with his lion claws. The thing's hard shell broke apart, and he viciously dug deeper, using his teeth to tear into the softer body within. It tasted horrible, and he grimaced as he ripped it asunder.

Clumps of burning thatch began to drop from the ceiling. Flames spread fast. Smoke rolled across the underside, and an acrid haze descended on Travis and Rez as they stood there watching in horror. The giant bugs had scurried away, but the fire was a far worse danger.

"We have to go," Rez said, pointing toward the door. Without waiting for a response, he rushed over and yanked on the handle. The door opened easily despite its impressive size.

Travis steeled himself, aware that his goat-head companion was working on another fireball.

Outside, at least a dozen bugs lurked at a safe distance. More dropped down from the roof, landing nimbly on eight legs with their tentacles fully retracted.

"They haven't seen us yet," Rez whispered, motioning for Travis to move to one side of the door. "The smoke is helping."

He lowered himself to the dirt floor where the haze was a little thinner. He was grimacing and squinting, and Travis felt the same stinging in his own eyes, and the urge to cough. They couldn't remain inside the burning building for long. But they couldn't leave, either.

Some of the bugs had turned to face them. They *knew*.

"Uh-oh," Rez muttered. "Man, they're smart. They won't come in because they don't need to. All they have to do is wait."

Travis nodded his agreement. Meanwhile, it seemed a fireball was ready to launch. But where to aim it? The bugs were spread wide, forming a semicircle twenty feet out from the door.

We have one chance at this, Travis thought. *We gotta run together, and fast! I'll fire ahead and clear a path.* He nudged his friend and tried to convey his meaning with a series of nods.

Rez simply stared blankly at him.

Travis tensed and crouched, hoping his friend would get the message that he was about to sprint out the door. Rez paled, but he nodded and readied himself.

With a snarl, Travis bolted forward. The bugs came to life, rising up on their legs and making an awful chittering noise. They advanced, closing the circle a little tighter.

The goat's head shot a fireball directly ahead. It exploded on the ground right in front of the arachnid wall, and several of the critters flew in all directions, legs and bits of shell blasted loose. As the debris showered down, Travis hurdled the crater and sprinted to safety, glancing back to make sure Rez was behind him.

He was, but only just. Bugs recovered their composure and leapt at him, missing by inches as he ducked past. They scuttled after him at a terrifying speed, but Rez, now stiff and upright with his back arched, ran faster than he'd ever run in his life, his eyes wide with fear.

Travis, a little way ahead, had time to think about where he was headed. Open ground wasn't safe. But nor were the trees. He made a wide circle and headed for the river instead.

He would have leapt into the water without hesitation except that one of the bridges was nearby, so he made a beeline for it. He kept glancing back to check on Rez. His friend had pulled ahead, his wide-eyed fear replaced with a grimace bordering on a beam of triumph.

Keep that fireball stewing, Travis told the goat's head. *We'll need it in any second now . . .*

He pounded across the narrow footbridge to the other side and spun around just in time to see Rez trip on the first plank. He sprawled flat on his stomach, gasped, and stumbled to his feet to carry on, limping now, his face screwed up in pain. The bugs closed the gap a little, but Rez was still way ahead of them. He barreled on, thudding on the planks, his breath ragged.

As Rez left the end of the bridge and tore past, Travis leapt into position and faced the army of bugs as they streamed on at the far end. "Now!" he snarled. Whether it needed to be told or not, the goat launched its fireball.

The fiery orb smacked into the bridge dead center, and its low angle meant the damage was long and shallow. Plank after plank ripped apart, ropes tore and burned, and the whole structure of the bridge weakened. The hole in the decking had to be eight feet long, and there was barely an inch left to stand on at the sides. The scorpions halted, quickly filling one half of the bridge like some kind of traffic jam at the scene of an accident.

But the bridge wasn't completely impassable. Its main supports remained intact, as did the fences along the sides. The bugs began clambering, and Travis felt his stomach flip-flop.

"Oh no," Rez groaned.

They both fled, heading west along the riverbank toward the next bridge.

Chapter 21
Escape

"What do they *want* with us?" Rez gasped as they ran side by side along the riverbank.

Travis grunted, unable to answer in his current chimera form. His goat head bleated and began working on another fireball. On his backend, the snake hissed and reared up in anger as if wishing it could tear itself loose and attack the mob of scorpions that pursued them.

The lake lay just ahead, stretching wide. The Parched Plains were visible beyond, an expanse of land that started a few hours to the south and stretched far to the north. Before the lake, another bridge spanned the river, even skinnier than the last. It was their only hope.

They turned sharply and pounded across the bridge. This one was barely two feet wide, and the whole thing wobbled badly, held together more by rope than anything else. As soon as they reached the other side, Rez collapsed on the ground while Travis turned and shot a fireball.

As before, the superheated ball hit the planks at a shallow angle. The explosion proved too much for the flimsy structure, blowing the decking apart and severing most of the support ropes. The bridge split in two with a series of snaps and bangs. For a few precious seconds, a single frayed rope held the two swaying halves together with a curious creaking sound—and then it snapped, and everything plunged into the river with a tremendous splash.

Thwarted, the army of giant bugs amassed on the grassy bank on the far side. Travis sensed the goat preparing another fireball, and he waited, intending to lob it across the river.

"Travis," Rez said, climbing to his feet. He pointed.

Some of the bugs had already returned to the other bridge and were making their way across the damaged platform. But more of the ugly critters were approaching from the troll settlement, apparently answering some kind of summons.

They're telepathic, Travis reminded himself. *They're the Seer, a single consciousness. And they're coming to get us.*

He was tired of running. He knew Rez had to be, too, especially nursing a knee injury or twisted ankle or whatever he'd done to himself earlier. But what choice did they have? Stand still and be taken over by these persistent creepy-crawlies? He shuddered and nodded toward the hills a little way north of them. A steep path led to the top where trees stood. He doubted a simple slope would stop the bugs, but it seemed the only option except into the water.

They ran. Travis gave some thought to the river, wondering if the rushing water would be their best hope after all. Obviously the bugs were afraid of it. They'd probably get washed downstream to the lake. But so would two twelve-year-old boys, even one in the form of a chimera. And if they stood their ground right there in the fast-flowing current, what then? The bugs would wait on the riverbanks on both sides.

He surged onward, aware that scorpions were streaming across the loose gravel toward them, already anticipating the boys' next move and beginning their ascent up the hill to cut them off.

Travis shot another fireball just ahead of them, and the explosion of dirt and rock was spectacular. By the time the dust cleared and the bugs reorganized themselves, he and Rez had reached the top of the narrow path. Travis paused for a second, shocked at the sight of several trolls heading their way. The nearest was a female, and she had a single bug clamped to the back of her head, tentacles wrapped tight around her throat. She made no attempt to claw it off. Clearly she was in its throes, acting as part of the Seer. And the other trolls seemed to be in the grip of its influence too, each with a giant bug clinging on.

Thankful for the level ground after such a steep incline, Travis and Rez stumbled onward into the trees.

"Where are we going?" Rez gasped. "They'll follow us!"

For once, Travis was grateful to be in chimera form just so he wouldn't have to admit he was out of ideas. What to do? Those bugs seemed tireless, and they were agile. Climbing trees wouldn't help. It seemed only water would cut them off.

They darted between trees, on the lookout for reddish-brown Gnarlers. It wouldn't surprise Travis in the least to find the Seer had already infiltrated this patch of woods. But Gnarlers and Shufflers were ponderous, easy to avoid.

Exhausted, they slowed to a walk after a while. The woods were quiet, and Travis heard nothing behind him—no telltale pitter-patter of arachnid feet, no rustling of bushes, no creaking and groaning of moving trees. He dared to hoped they'd escaped the threat for now.

Rez looked relieved too. "Think we lost 'em?" he whispered.

Travis felt it was a good time to become human again. He transformed and took a moment to check himself over. Smart clothes intact, two legs, two arms, one head . . . *All good*, he thought.

"I don't know," he answered at last. "But this is getting on my nerves. How are we supposed to get home? All three bridges will be guarded now—well, the remaining two bridges, anyway—and I don't think it'll help if we swim across because they'll still come after us. And we can't leave anyway. Not until we've fixed this."

Rez narrowed his eyes. "*Fixed* this? What do you mean?"

"Well, I mean we need to find a way to stop these bugs, the Seer, from spreading. They tricked us into bringing a load of baby bugs across the river and into the troll settlement, took 'em over, and now they're probably planning on spreading even more."

"How do you know that?"

Travis shrugged. "Seems logical, right? They won't stop at taking over the trolls. I think the trolls are just carriers." The more he spoke, the more sense it made to him. "Seems like the Seer aren't satisfied with being plants anymore. They've had a taste of trolls. And humans," he added, raising an eyebrow at his friend. "Can you imagine these things taking over every troll, human, goblin, even the plants for miles around? A single consciousness controlling everyone and everything?"

He and Rez stared at each other for a long while as the ramifications of such an invasion hit home. Whether they were responsible or not didn't matter. The Seer would have found a way to spread no matter what.

A distant rustling drew their attention, and they both looked that way.

"Should we run for it?" Rez whispered, looking like he wanted to do no such thing.

"Let's walk," Travis said. "Quietly. We'll go *this* way."

He wished he had his compass. It had been in his pocket for much of the journey, but now everything was in his or Rez's knapsack—which were lost somewhere. He headed in what he guessed was a northwesterly direction. If he was right, this should take them back out to where they'd been clobbered by trolls just north of the main bridge. What he planned to do once he got there wasn't clear in his mind yet. He just wanted to be away from the bugs.

They crept through the undergrowth, wincing at every snap of a twig. *If only I had wings*, Travis thought longingly. *I could just fly away and be done with this. If I were a dragon, I could blast the whole area with fire and burn everything.*

The town council's decision to forbid would-be dragon shapeshifters annoyed him now more than ever. He understood it made sense to stop irresponsible students from becoming such fearsome beasts . . . but he was *different*. He was the son of Hal and Abigail Franklin! And anyway, he could only be a dragon once, for a very short time, so if anyone was a safe bet, it was him. Right now would have been the perfect time.

With a jolt of fear, he realized he was already into his second day of being a chimera. Two days was his limit, or thereabouts. After that he would become *normal* again. He resolved not to sleep that night. That would be a colossal waste of shapeshifting power. He had to take care of this problem while he could still shoot fireballs.

The woods had gotten gloomy except in front of them to the west, where orange sunshine filtered through the trees. He pressed on, hoping to emerge into open land soon.

Figures materialized ahead. Travis and Rez froze. At least a dozen tall, man-shaped silhouettes stood waiting. "Trolls," Travis hissed. "They're onto us."

"More over there," Rez said, pointing to the left.

Glancing behind, they saw yet more of them lurking in the gloom. "It's like they were *waiting* for us," Travis moaned.

They both looked to their right, to the north. They saw nobody. Rez frowned. "Okay, that's suspicious. Are they herding us?"

"Looks like it."

As one, the trolls began to close in all around from the east, south, and west.

"Stay here and be captured, or walk into a trap?" Travis muttered. "What do you prefer?"

Rez scowled. "Is there any chance a chimera can fly and you just don't know about it yet?"

"No. I don't have wings."

"Can you breathe fire in one long stream like a dragon? Or does it have to be one fireball every few minutes?"

Travis sighed. "I don't make the rules. If I could be fire-breathing chimera with wings, trust me, I would be."

The trolls were close enough to see clearly now. Each had a scorpion clamped to the back of its head, tentacles around the throat. And the varying shades of brown and grey hair that had distinguished the trolls had been replaced by a weird reddish hue. Now they looked much the same. Only one stood out— Zoth, with his burnt chest.

"We have to run," Rez said, shaking his head. "It has to be better than just standing here."

Travis wasn't sure he agreed. However, he'd made enough decisions for the two of them already, and they hadn't gotten very far. It was Rez's turn to call the shots. "Okay, let's go."

They hurried north, somehow knowing they'd be given all the time they needed. The trees thinned a little, but more bushes and thickets appeared, and Travis eyed them warily, guessing they were part of the Seer. *Now they're funneling us*, he thought with dismay, seeing how they formed lines to the left and right. *We're already trapped.*

It was pointless trying to escape now. Travis considered transforming into a chimera and working up a fireball or two, but what would that achieve? He'd punch a hole through the line of bushes, and maybe they'd slip through . . . but for how long? Trolls were everywhere, and they were much faster.

Tired and subdued, the boys walked at a moderate pace, still seeing nothing of interest ahead. The walls of bushes continued to close in, now just thirty or forty feet apart. Behind them, trolls crowded the makeshift corridor of vegetation, some spilling outside. There was no going back.

"The trees," Rez said flatly.

Travis blinked, suddenly realizing that all the trunks they walked past now had the same reddish quality, and the ones just ahead had a much more gnarly look about them. In fact, one was twisting around very slowly, its branches brushing against the neighboring trees. Now that he looked closer at the leafy boughs, Travis could see four or five scorpions the size of dogs, with legs spanning six feet or more. They clung to the trunk, legs akimbo, their thick tentacles threaded into knotty holes. Those appendages stuck out from the bottom of the uprooted tree, splayed wide and incredibly strong.

The boys stopped. It seemed like it was over for them. Beyond this Gnarler stood others. Their branches hung low. And all around, prickly bushes and brambles shuffled closer, while trolls formed a fearsome wall behind.

"It was nice knowing you," Rez said, sounding defeated.

Travis didn't know what to say.

Chapter 22
Assimilation

The Gnarler formed a human face halfway up its trunk. The bark moved aside as a hole opened wide and became a mouth. Eyes appeared, and a nose, and deep creases furrowed its forehead. The features of an old man.

"Thank . . . you," the tree rumbled in a voice that seemed to erupt from the earth underfoot.

Travis frowned. "For what?"

"For . . . helping us."

Anger welled deep inside. "I wasn't *helping* you deliver a bunch of baby Seers to the trolls! You tricked us!"

"You misunderstand," the tree interrupted, its mouth moving in a disconnected, out-of-sync fashion with its ponderous, drawn-out words. "Thank you . . . for what you are *about* to do."

Travis shivered. Beside him, Rez let out a low moan.

Shufflers pressed in tight all around, their tentacles sliding around in the dirt. Trolls advanced, their faces impassive, eyes staring. Adult scorpions scuttled closer.

"You . . . will stand still," the tree said, softly now.

The urge to run was strong. Travis glanced at Rez, who raised his eyebrows and lowered his stance just a little bit, getting ready to sprint.

I'm not gonna stand here and let them do whatever the heck they want to me, Travis thought.

He transformed without warning and just had time to see Rez's face light up before several bugs leapt on them both. Travis stumbled as one gripped the side of his lion neck. Another landed on his back in front of the goat's head, and two more simply clung to his front legs and prevented him from running.

Tentacles wrapped around his neck and squeezed. He choked and staggered, and to his surprise, three of the four bugs fell off. The fourth remained attached. Apparently, when a bug claimed the prize, the others simply lost interest. He felt a strange sensation on the back of his neck as though something was leaking on him. The liquid, whatever it was, sank deep into his skin and flesh, then spread up into his head and down into his shoulders and chest.

He swung around to help Rez, who had fallen to the ground with a bug of his own clamped to his back. *Come on*, Travis urged the goat's head. *Gimme a fireball!*

He could sense one being formed, and he turned toward the Gnarler. He roared and hunkered down, giving the goat a clear target. But trolls came shuffling forward, and they blocked the way just as the fireball hurtled over his head.

The flaming projectile glanced off a troll's shoulder, sending the shaggy beast flying, then arced past the Gnarler and landed somewhere beyond. Fire broke out among the bushes, and the Shufflers quickly retreated.

Another! Travis demanded. *Let 'em have it!*

While he waited on the goat, he spun around and around, expecting to be jumped by a gang of trolls. But they did nothing except stare at him. The one in front held its smoldering shoulder.

Trying to ignore the horrible feeling seeping into his body, and the alarming weight of the giant scorpion on his back, Travis sprang into the air with his claws out, aiming for a female troll that stood there with her head cocked to one side. She was the same reddish-brown as the rest, her gaze lifeless.

Before he could knock her down and spring to safety, the troll swiped at him, catching him around the face with one large-fisted punch. He sprawled on the ground and shook his head, struggling to his feet.

But now he felt dazed and lethargic. The urge to run away abandoned him, and he stood there confused, wondering why he was being so hostile. The trolls were no more than puppets, part of a single consciousness. The trees and bushes, too. If it wasn't clear before, it certainly was now. The enemy wasn't *here*; it was somewhere else. He shouldn't be clawing at trolls or shooting fireballs at trees. It was no use being angry toward the tentacled bugs, either. All were pawns—just like him.

With this simple but powerful epiphany came a sense of hopelessness. This unseen enemy, this collective mind, couldn't be fought. An array of images flitted through his mind, like memories escaping from a part of his brain he never had access to before. He felt these images were important but couldn't quite latch on and study them.

He shook his head. The trolls stared at him. Bushes waited patiently.

Turning, Travis spotted Rez climbing to his feet. His brown skin had taken on a familiar reddish hue, and he looked dismayed. "Oh," he muttered.

Vague though his single-word exclamation was, Travis knew exactly what he meant by it. "Oh" indeed! It was like they'd both been handed the answer to one of life's great mysteries, and the answer was surprisingly obvious and logical.

"And now," a loud voice suddenly echoed in his head, "you are one of us."

Travis winced. A giant might as well have yelled directly into his ear. But he felt oddly comforted by the voice despite its volume. *I'm one of you*, he marveled.

"Walk with us."

As one, all the trolls in the vicinity turned and began marching. Shufflers quivered but remained where they were. Instead, tentacles writhed and retracted, and moments later, giant bugs crawled out from the foliage. As they left the bushes behind, the leaves turned brown and withered, the thick stems twisted, and most of the shrubs simply toppled over.

The giant Gnarlers, however, moved with ponderous determination, tilting from side to side as they went, branches swaying up and down. Travis counted eight in all, spread out among the ordinary, untouched trees of the forest.

Who are you? he asked in his head, knowing the consciousness could hear him perfectly well. He frowned and adjusted his question. *Who are we?*

"We are the Seer."

I know, but . . . who are the Seer?

After a pause, the booming voice said, "We have been in hibernation for some time. Now we have woken, and we require sustenance. We must spread quickly."

What? Why?

"A speedy propagation is essential for a successful takeover. If we move too slowly, they will try to stop us."

Who?

"Everyone."

Travis twisted around to see if Rez was following. He was, and he seemed to be muttering to himself, perhaps asking similar questions to the same booming voice.

But what's our purpose?

"To assimilate. We require multicultural, multispecies ethnography of animals, plants, and fungi to understand the interconnectedness and inseparability of all living things. It is what sustains us. We have no purpose otherwise."

Travis almost faltered in his steady marching through the forest. *What?*

When the consciousness next spoke, it was as though it recognized Travis was not able to grasp a scientific explanation. Its voice softened. "We have always been here. We were here long before you. We have what you might call *feelers* projecting from the earth. These give us a taste of life on the surface and keep us alive, but it's barely enough to whet our appetite when we are awake. Once in a while, we must spawn and assimilate on a widespread scale for a short time. Then we may descend into hibernation and digest a wealth of new information."

Feelers? I don't understand. What are we doing? Where are we going?

Ahead, the forest opened up—but the sun was already setting, and the hilly landscape looked dismal in the fading light. Travis spotted a bridge ahead, the very first one he and Rez had come across. Despite everything, the Seer was leading him in exactly the direction he wanted to go.

Only now he didn't care which way he went. He cared only that he was part of the collective. It could lead him and the trolls wherever it wanted.

The Seer fell silent for a while. Instead of the booming voice, images sharpened in Travis's mind, those fleeting memories he'd been able to latch onto earlier. He watched and began to understand.

The hideous scorpions were merely drones hatched from the ground. From the *feelers*. Travis saw one of his dad's infamous Treentacles sticking up out of the ground, white and smooth, its thick arms spreading in all directions. The scope of reach was impressive but nowhere near enough. Very few living creatures wandered near. If they did, they sank into a stupor that they imagined lasted several weeks or even months.

Like Rez, who had grown despondent at wasting so much time when in fact he'd only been affected by the plant's power for a matter of minutes. The eerie white plant had poked around in his brain and absorbed a lot of information. Travis's dad called it *feeding the brain*. He swore up and down that the Treentacles were connected to a massive organism under the ground.

The Seer, he thought.

Watching the images flash by, he saw the first scorpions spreading outward, taking over small weeds, assimilating them, and growing rapidly so they could move on to bigger plants. Bushes and shrubs, then saplings and entire thickets, and finally stout trees—not too tall and ungainly, only the thick and short ones, which would be easier to mobilize.

And at that point, the Seer had established itself aboveground and was preparing for the next wave of their takeover—animals.

A human stumbled into the vicinity of the feeler. Rez! In those moments, the Seer saw his friends and family, a whole town of intelligent humans. He ran away, but another animal was left behind, this time an unconscious troll. The Seer wrapped it in a cocoon with an army of young drones.

Travis didn't need to be told the rest. He saw it all, and he found himself nodding with satisfaction at such a simple and efficient takeover. Trees and bushes were readily available but horribly slow. Trolls were faster, and a whole settlement of them lay outside the forest to the north, across the river. Better still, a town full of humans lay to the south . . . and from there, both Old Earth and New Earth beckoned. Assimilation would be rapid once the new scorplings were safely delivered.

Scorplings, he thought wryly. Like spiderlings, born rather than hatched. Except these weren't scorpions at all. They had tentacles instead of stingers!

He frowned, realizing that the procession had halted by the bridge on the north side of the river. "This is where you continue alone," the Seer boomed in his head. "Do not pause on your journey."

Travis stood quite still, four legs planted wide, as trolls surrounded him. One approached with something held high. His missing knapsack! Its flap was open, and just before the troll closed it, Travis glimpsed a writhing mass of tiny, baby scorpions just like the ones that had emerged from the cocoon.

He guessed the plan immediately. *Walk home, deliver the package to the town of Carter, and let the Seer take over.*

As trolls hung the knapsack on his back, a feeling of panic rose in his chest. *Don't send me away!*

"We will be with you all the way. Distance will not separate us."

Relief flooded through him. For a brief moment, he saw himself through the eyes of the trolls—a chimera standing there with a knapsack slung over its shoulders. It covered most of the giant eight-legged drone that clung there. Even its tentacles were obscured thanks to his thick mane. The ruse wouldn't stand up to close inspection, but very few would suspect anything was wrong until too late.

It was a decent plan. Not as good as walking into town voluntarily, but better than nothing. Trees and bushes would take forever traveling across the Parched Plains, and they certainly wouldn't be able to shuffle into the town of Carter without causing an uproar! Trolls with scorpions on their backs wouldn't make it past the perimeter fences without being searched. A troll could dump a package just outside and hope the scorplings made their own way in, but a truly successful delivery was to the heart of the town itself, and that had to be carried out by Travis, whom nobody would suspect.

Trolls returned Rez's knapsack to him as well. It, too, was full of scorplings. The relatively small drone on his back maneuvered itself head first into the open top of the bag so that only its rear end stuck out, with the tentacles wrapped around his neck. A female troll finished off the disguise by draping Rez's spare shirt over his shoulders. It concealed the tentacles quite well and hung over the top of the knapsack.

Travis felt a sense of excitement, though he struggled to make his joy known. His body felt oddly drained of emotion, and all he could do was walk stiffly across the bridge and hurdle the broken section on the far side. Rez followed him. After that, they headed south without a single word to each other.

But no words were necessary. They had a mission, and they intended to walk all the way home without stopping. They'd arrive well before dawn before most people were up. They'd walk right past the goblin sentries and brush shoulders with early-rising marketers. Nobody would stop them.

And when they reached the center of town, they'd put down their knapsacks and release the Seer's drones. An army of tiny creatures spilling forth and scurrying to hide.

Shortly after, they'd attack.

Chapter 23
A New Mission

Travis felt at ease, calm and confident that his new mission would go well. He and Rez marched through the forest, following the narrow path back to the main road. They came to the makeshift blockade the dryads had built. It was dry and withered now, still and lifeless, and it took only a moment to clamber under the stretched vines and through the tangle of dead weeds. This time, nothing tried to stop them. Travis glimpsed movement in the trees, though. Probably dryads.

A little farther along, several gnarly trees twisted around to watch him pass. Prickly bushes and tangled brambles quivered. Travis wanted to wave cheerily at them all, but he lacked the energy for such pleasantries, and anyway was still in chimera form.

Rez walked alongside, looking like a programmed automaton though he most likely felt the same way as Travis, full of awe for the Seer and excitement for the mission ahead.

On Rez's back, beneath the shirt that draped around his shoulders, the visible part of his knapsack bulged and squirmed with movement. The scorplings would need to settle down when Carter came into view or else they'd give the game away. But the town was a long way off yet. It would take many hours to get there. By the time they arrived, the darkness of the night and the emptiness of the streets would be a blessing. Travis doubted he'd bump into a single person.

Just drop the knapsacks and release the scorplings. They'll scuttle away to hide and suckle on delicate roots. They'll grow in no time, then find hosts. Human hosts.

The only flaw in the plan was that Travis knew he'd need help to remove his knapsack. It seemed a silly problem to be faced with. The trolls had somehow yanked the straps down around his lion body and tied them off underneath. The knapsack was on tight. He'd never struggle free without Rez's help.

Unless I switch to human form. Then it'll be easy.

For some reason, he'd forgotten all about being a shapeshifter. He tried switching to human form and found he could do so without effort despite being one of the Seer now. The scorpion drone shifted its grip, its tentacles tightening around his neck. The knapsack now hung really low on his back, the straps long and loose, so he paused to adjust them . . . then decided he should leave them alone and return to his far more formidable chimera form. If anyone tried to thwart their mission, be it humans or goblins or centaurs, he could easily lob a fireball in their direction.

With that in mind, he transformed again.

To his surprise, he found himself inside the goat's head.

He resumed walking, though his legs moved of their own volition, still controlled by the lion. Travis stared at the back of the lion's head and the giant bug that hunkered low on its shoulders. The shaggy mane partially obscured the tentacles.

Travis peered down at the knapsack. It was tight again. But it didn't matter so much anymore. For some reason, the mission now seemed a little less . . . important? He frowned, wondering what had brought on this change of heart. He kept pace with Rez, who marched with purpose alongside, but now Travis felt his enthusiasm ebbing. Why, exactly, did he want to dump two bags full of tiny bugs in the middle of the town? Why would he want to help the Seer spread their consciousness throughout human settlements and across into Old Earth?

He and Rez emerged from the narrow lane and turned right onto the main forest road. This would lead them back out to the Parched Plains, and it was a straight shot south from there to Carter.

But so what?

Puzzled, Travis watched as the scorpion creature squirmed before him, its four tentacles disengaging from the lion's neck and twisting toward him. He recoiled as far as he could, but the slippery appendages snaked around his goat neck and tightened.

Moments later, the purpose of the Seer's mission came into sharp focus again, and he understood and appreciated its importance.

Only . . .

On impulse, he reverted to human form again and stopped dead in his tracks. The scorpion still clung to his back, but now he felt its tentacles flailing in mid-air. *Because the goat head's gone*, he thought, trying to clear his mind. The knapsack again hung low and heavy, and he slipped out of it. Something was wrong. He felt confused.

Rez, who had marched on another few paces, now paused and turned back. He looked awful, his eyes glazed, mouth hanging open with spittle running down his chin. He had an unnatural reddish-brown skin color.

Tentacles again tightened around Travis's throat. He reached up to grab them and flinched as his fingers touched the nasty cold flesh. Panicked, he beat at them and jerked this way and that, hoping to throw the creature off.

His panic quickly subsided, and a reassuring calm settled over him. *It's okay*, he told himself. *I'm on a mission for the Seer. These tentacles are good, even if they do feel like snakes around my neck. Everything is all right. Just relax and be a chimera again. Continue the journey, deliver the Seer to the humans.*

He picked up his knapsack and slung it loosely over one shoulder, careful not to disturb the scorpion on his shoulders. He transformed once more, then blinked in surprise when he saw the backs of both the lion's and goat's heads before him. *Too busy thinking about snakes. Now I'm one myself!*

Not properly fastened, his knapsack fell to the ground again, its precious cargo wriggling within. The scorpion was clearly confused at all the shapeshifting. Standing on the chimera's back, it studied the lion's head, then the goat's head, its feelers twitching frantically and pincers snapping as it turned this way and that.

It's looking for me. Hey, doofus, I'm back here!

Apparently sensing his whereabouts at last, the bug spun around and scrambled toward him. Suddenly wary, Travis backed up—which in snake form meant arcing high over the rear end of the chimera. His mind whirled. Just a second ago, he'd embraced the Seer's plan to deliver a knapsack full of scorplings to the town of Carter. Now he was appalled by the idea.

The scorpion lunged, snapping with its pincers and reaching high with its front legs in an effort to cling to him. Its tentacles writhed frantically. But Travis was merely a snake in the guise of a tail, and there was very little of him to grab hold of. He jerked from side to side like an angry cobra, daring the drone to leap at him again.

Travis felt his mind clearing. As the hazy fog of confusion dissipated, he was left with the sickening realization that he'd been violated, his mind and body hijacked. And Rez, too! His friend was still walking, unaware of what was going on behind him, intent on the Seer's mission to deliver—

With a jolt of horror, Travis—or rather the lion aspect of the chimera—bucked and lurched, almost dislodging the scorpion on its back as it kicked at the knapsack. The flap at the top fell open, and a dozen or so miniature bugs spilled out. The drone chittered with anger and leapt at him, but Travis easily ducked aside, then lunged. His fangs sank into one of the flailing tentacles.

Instinctively, he injected every available ounce of venom before the weight and momentum of the creature yanked him off. The scorpion spun loose and landed heavily, and Travis—or again the chimera—danced around in a moment of exuberance. The hunt was on!

But the hunt, if it could be called that, ended quickly. The scorpion twitched and shuddered, and the tentacles thrashed wildly as the legs lost coordination and buckled.

It stopped moving a few seconds later.

Travis noticed more of the ugly scorplings spilling from the knapsack on the ground. They were everywhere now, scuttling about, diving into every nook and cranny on the road, burrowing into the dirt, dashing for tufts of grass and clumps of weeds. More and more emerged, a whole stream of them.

He stood perfectly still and watched them scatter.

After an army of the things had disappeared from sight, Travis let out a sigh. Or rather, his lion head did. The distinction seemed to be blurring. As a mere serpentine tail, he could hardly claim to take off running after Rez, yet that was what it felt like. The three minds of the chimera worked so closely together now, and were so finely synced, that Travis began to understand how a three-headed monster existed without going crazy.

"Rez!" he called, and this time his voice emerged from all three heads—a hiss from his own, plus a bleat and a roar from the others.

Rez continued marching. Maybe his mind-controlling bug had ordered him to ignore the commotion.

Travis trotted up alongside and studied the nasty creature clinging to his friend's back from within the knapsack. The shirt draped over his shoulders had slipped a little, and Travis reached out and yanked it away with his fangs. The tentacles tightened around Rez's neck, and this caused Rez to falter.

I have no more venom, Travis thought with dismay. *I used it all up on the other bug. I should have saved some.*

He could still bite, though.

He lunged and dug his fangs into the soft tentacles as close as he could to the hard carapace where the creature protruded from the knapsack. It was a dry bite, so he bit again and again as the scorpion jerked and thrashed in its confined space. Two of the four tentacles flailed wildly. The other two maintained their grip around Rez's throat.

Rez stumbled and glanced over his shoulder with a look of consternation. Fearing his friend might act on behalf of the

Seer, Travis attacked even more viciously than before, bite after bite until his jaw ached.

Suddenly, the scorpion released its grip and leapt to safety. It scuttled about on the ground as blood oozed from multiple wounds. Rez blinked in confusion.

Travis reverted to human form. "Wake up!" he urged. Without waiting for his friend to respond, he ran at the scorpion and kicked it—then hopped in pain with a throbbing toe. Smart shoes and tough exoskeletons didn't mix.

Still, the scorpion darted about in obvious panic, finally dashing off the road and into the nearest bushes.

Travis ripped the knapsack from Rez's back and threw it aside. Then, as it writhed and bulged, he fell on it and closed the flap with shaky fingers, zipping it tight. Some of the tiny scorplings had already escaped, but most were trapped inside. He leapt up and stomped on as many as he could, grimacing at the sticky mess he left on the bottom of his shoes.

He barely had time to catch his breath before a soft moan filled the air, accompanied by a frenzied rustling of bushes and trees. The Seer was coming. He rushed over to Rez and pushed him. "Move! We have to go."

They ran, Rez still frowning with confusion. But his puzzled expression quickly turned to one of anger. "They messed with my head!" he growled.

"They messed with both our heads," Travis agreed, glancing over his shoulder. Giant scorpions were bursting from the undergrowth on both sides of the road. "And I had *three* heads at the time! Let's not get caught again."

Running without the weight of knapsacks felt good, though it was a shame to leave them behind. He shuddered at the thought of all those tiny scorpion creatures squirming about inside one of them, and he wondered if some of the larger creatures would be dexterous enough to undo the flap and let them out. If so, the woods would be filled with the things.

They hurdled a fallen tree. Travis remembered the obstruction well. It was close to here that the trolls had attacked them the first time, which meant the Treentacle couldn't be too far away. They picked up speed and ran on.

Gradually, they left the scorpions behind. When Travis spotted a low-hanging branch overhead, he knew the way out to the Parched Plains was just ahead, around the next few bends. They walked the rest of the way, panting and sweating, until a dazzling arch of bright daylight came into view. They were safe.

"They'll never catch up now," Rez said, emerging into the warm sunshine. The hard-packed flatland stretched before them. "I'm done with this. Let's get home as fast as possible and tell your dad. Maybe he can come out here and burn down the forest or something."

"Burn down the—?" Travis repeated. He paused in the daylight and looked back at the forest entrance. "There's no way he'd burn down the forest. All those dryads, the wildlife, even the trees! No, there has to be a better way."

"Well, poison, then. Or smoke them out. Miss Simone needs to call an exterminator."

Travis frowned. Even then, numerous other species would be caught up in the attack. He had no love for giant ants and millipedes and wasps and spiders, but what if much of the bug life was killed off and yet the massive scorpions survived? And if the Seer parasites died, what would happen to the trolls? He hoped they'd shake off the effects and get back to their lives without any trouble. But trees and bushes everywhere would keel over and die, a shameful but unavoidable tragedy.

"What are you thinking?" Rez said, his eyes narrowed.

Travis felt a chill, and he swallowed. "I, uh . . . I just remembered something. Yesterday, when the bushes herded us toward the Treentacle, and we had to turn back? I punched one of those white tendrils. Then I tried to strangle it. Did you see how the bushes reacted?"

Rez nodded slowly, looking suspicious. "They cringed."

"Yeah, exactly!" Travis edged closer to his friend, lowering his voice. "They reacted like I was hitting and strangling *them*. The Seer is all one consciousness, right? What if the Treentacle is its brain? I mean, it kind of *is*, right? They called it a feeler. It's connected directly to a giant brain underground. The brain is the consciousness, and the feeler is like . . . like an antenna sticking up out of the dirt, broadcasting a signal and receiving information. Without it, the scorpions might not be able to connect to the brain, and if they can't connect, maybe they'll die. So all we have to do is—"

Rez closed his eyes and shook his head. "Whoa. Stop. Just . . . just stop right there. I know where you're going with this, and you can forget it. We're going home, and we're going to tell your dad and Miss Simone, and they can come and bomb the entire forest for all I care. It's not our problem."

Travis stared at him. The idea of heading back into the forest to destroy the Treentacle terrified him. But somehow he knew it had to be done. One decisive attack would bring about an end to the Seer before they spread too far. And he had to move quickly, because there were two bagfuls of scorplings on the road. One, actually—the other was already empty. The tiny bugs would be fully grown within hours, and then the entire forest would be a death trap.

"We have to deal with this," he said softly.

Chapter 24
Plan of Attack

Rez pointed south. "Look, Travis—you see that? Do you know what that is?"

Travis sighed. "The Parched Plains?"

"It's *safety*, man! We walk that way, and we're back home before bedtime, and then your dad can take over and sort things out here."

"Okay, first, it might be too late by the time my dad gets here. Those baby scorpions will have grown up by then and spread everywhere, taking over trees and bushes and the whole forest. Or it could be worse. Now that we've escaped, the Seer might send trolls in our place. They'll pick up those knapsacks and march off to the nearest towns—humans, naga, elves, whatever—and dump the bags nearby. If those baby scorpions make it into the settlements and villages, then this thing will *really* be out of control."

"Yeah, but—"

"And anyway," Travis went on, "I don't want to go home and say, 'Hey, Dad, we're safe, but there's a huge problem you have to deal with, because we were too chicken to fix it ourselves.'"

Rez shook his head and looked away. "That's not fair. Don't play the chicken card. I'm not eight."

The sun was descending. "Time's running out," Travis said. "If we're going back into the forest, then we're doing it now, today while I can still transform, in daylight. Or would you rather wait until the middle of the night?"

"No, I'd rather do it now," Rez said quickly. He scowled. "Hey, quit that. Don't make me choose between two options I never agreed to in the first place."

"Should we go in fast and furious, or slow and silent?"

"Shut up."

"Would you rather stab the Treentacle with a long spear, set it alight, or let me take care of it while you watch my back?"

Rez clapped his hands over his ears and stepped back. He stood that way for a long moment, then dropped his hands. "This is madness, Trav."

"Why? Think about it. They're just *bushes*. They move slowly. The trees are just as slow. Even if there are trolls . . . well, I can blast 'em with my fireballs."

"And the giant scorpions running a million miles an hour?"

"All right, so we'll go in quietly. We'll tiptoe, and—"

"It's a single consciousness, Travis. If one single scorpion sees you, or even a Shuffler, they'll *all* see you. You don't have a hope of getting close without them knowing about it."

Travis clenched his fists with exasperation. He knew his friend was right, but every minute they stood around discussing it was yet more time for the Seer to muster their forces and protect their feeler. "Maybe they won't be looking for us. They can't hear us talking right now, so they have no idea we're planning to head back. They have no reason to gather an army and guard the Treentacle because we never gave them a clue we were coming after it."

"I'm pretty sure they know," Rez said sullenly.

"I doubt it." Travis spun around and faced the forest. All looked quiet. "I'm going in. I'll be quick. You wait here."

"Travis—"

But he took off running, leaving the warm sunshine and plunging into the curiously arch-shaped corridor of dense vegetation. It felt cool immediately, but the air was still and a little clammy, and sweat dribbled down his face as he jogged. He glanced back once and was both pleased and disappointed that Rez stood still in the sunlight, watching him—pleased because it meant he would be safe, and disappointed because friends were supposed to stick together no matter what.

Then again, Travis wasn't exactly sticking with Rez, either. Returning to the forest was probably a foolish idea . . . but necessary, too. His logic was sound. Going home and reporting the problem to his parents would take way too long. He had a chance to deal with it *now*, to nip it in the bud before it got out of hand. Apparently, Rez didn't understand that.

Or he's chicken, he thought grumpily.

He tried to control his breathing as he ran, though his chest burned. He vowed to run more often in his spare time. He needed to stay fit if he was to go on missions for Miss Simone. There would likely be lots of running throughout his career. Running and fighting.

Then again, the beauty of shapeshifting was being able to cruise along on four legs at a much faster pace than mere humans.

He slowed and shifted to chimera form. Finding himself inside the head of the lion, he growled with satisfaction and picked up his pace again, this time padding along with ease. And while he ran, the goat worked up a fireball just in case.

The wide road, with its densely formed walls and curiously arched canopy of branches above, curved first to the left then the right. He passed by the low-hanging branch and focused on the bushes at either side of the road, looking for danger. He started to get the sense that this was, as Rez had suggested, a foolish plan. Even if the scorpions had given up the chase and retreated, they would still be there in the undergrowth, most likely surrounding the Treentacle. They probably considered the creepy monster their *master* and would defend it at all costs.

They don't know I'm planning to kill it, he told himself. *They're probably still trying to figure out a Plan B—someone to carry their knapsacks full of scorplings into a populated area. Maybe they'll try and nab a few dryads to do their dirty work. Makes perfect sense. Dryads can sneak into a town undetected. Yeah, that's gotta be what they're doing.*

He picked up his pace a little, looking for the fallen tree somewhere ahead. Just before that tree, the Treentacle would be deep in the woods on his left. He shifted his focus to the task ahead. How would he kill it? Blasting it with a fireball seemed the obvious choice, but he worried it wouldn't be enough—and coughing up another would take time. How many scorpions would be dashing toward him at that point? How many prickly bushes shuffling forward? Gnarlers lurching closer?

He paused and listened. For a moment there was silence as if whatever he'd heard had paused at the exact same moment. Then it came again, a clear rustle just off to the side of the road. He tensed and waited. Maybe an innocent groundhog?

A scorpion launched itself from the undergrowth, scuttling across the road and scattering pine needles in its haste to reach him. Travis jerked backward, and the goat let loose with a fireball. The flaming projectile slammed into the ground inches ahead of the scorpion, and the creature flew apart in a shower of legs and tentacles mixed with dirt and pine cones. When the dust settled, only a crater remained.

But now he'd expended his ammunition, and a dozen or more new scorpions burst forth and came at him. He turned and fled, leaping over those that blocked his way. Glancing back, he let out a shudder at the sight of a dozen more joining the ranks from both sides of the road. A stream of the ghastly creatures tore after him, and he sprinted away. He knew he'd make it safely back to the Parched Plains, but he also knew his mission to destroy the Treentacle was doomed to fail.

He didn't stop running until he saw daylight ahead. He half expected to find Rez silhouetted there, standing with feet apart and hands on hips . . . but there was no sign of him. Travis left the forest behind and emerged into sunlight, and only then did he stop and look around, blinking in the glare.

Rez waited some fifty yards out, sitting cross-legged on the hard ground, his back stiff, looking like a meditating hermit. He raised a hand in greeting. "Over here," he called.

Travis trotted over, glancing back to make sure no scorpions followed. There seemed no reason why they couldn't pursue the boys onto the plains, but they stuck to the forest. If an army of them spilled out into the open, Travis felt certain he and Rez could outrun them. And maybe the Seer knew that.

Travis reverted to human form. "What are you doing?"

Rez shrugged. "Waiting. I knew you'd be back. I guess you ran into a bunch of scorpions?"

"Yeah."

"Figured you would."

Travis kept his eye on the forest entrance. "So I guess you were right," he said with a sigh. "We have to head home and bring some reinforcements. My fireballs aren't cutting it."

"Well . . ." Rez pursed his lips. "I had a crazy idea. Probably won't work, but maybe something worth mentioning."

"Spit it out," Travis urged.

But Rez took his time. "I waited on the road for you until I heard a shuffling in the trees. I assumed it was a giant bug or a walking tree, so I bolted. But when I looked back, I saw a blurry movement. A dryad."

The mention of dryads caused Travis to recoil. "Oh no! The Seer captured one!"

"Huh?" Rez frowned. "No, I don't think so. It was just standing there watching. Then it took off. I saw the bushes moving where it squeezed past."

Now Travis frowned. "So what are you saying?"

"I'm saying that maybe the dryads are on our side here. Remember that fence they put up? They tried to stop us taking that cocoon to the troll village. They know what's going on, and I'm sure they'd help if we asked."

With a surge of excitement, Travis spun around and scanned the fringes of the forest. He saw no sign of dryads, but that meant nothing; there could be twenty of them standing there right now, staring out from the trees. "Yes! If they could help us, maybe we can sneak up on the Seer somehow."

"They could make us invisible," Rez said. "I mean, that's how they work, right? They touch you, and you turn invisible?"

Travis arched an eyebrow at his friend. "Uh, no, not exactly. They have the power to blend in with the background, but they can't cause other people to be invisible as well. Now, if they hid something under their clothing, I suppose it would become invisible . . . but that's not much help."

"They wear clothing?"

"Uh, sure. I guess. Why not?"

Rez looked puzzled. "Are you saying their clothing is magical like yours? I mean, a chameleon can change its color to blend in with the surroundings, but if it wore a cute little jacket and a pair of pants, they'd stand out a mile. Unless the clothes are magical like yours."

"Well . . ." Travis said, faltering. He realized he had no clue whether dryads wore clothes or not. "Look, does it matter? The point is, dryads can't make *us* invisible."

Rez climbed to his feet. "Listen. You're wearing a magical shirt. I remember the story about Darcy O'Tanner, the dryad shapeshifter. She wore the same magical clothes. And they turned invisible along with her skin. So these smart clothes, as you call them, somehow mimic whatever power the wearer has. Right? Otherwise they wouldn't be much good."

Travis stared at his friend. Apparently, Rez knew more about shapeshifting than he'd let on.

"So," Rez went on, "if you gave your shirt to a dryad, that shirt would turn invisible, right?"

"I . . . I guess so. But how does that help us?"

"It doesn't." Rez grinned and held up his hands in a placating gesture. "But maybe I still have a crazy idea. First, we have to make friends with some dryads."

Looking toward the forest, Travis saw no sign of anybody. And even if dryads were watching, they were notoriously reticent. Very few people had ever met one. Even Darcy, the dryad shapeshifter, had struggled for years to integrate herself into their community.

And now Travis and Rez needed their help.

Chapter 25
Dryads

They stood on the fringes of the forest just west of the commonly used entrance. Thick vegetation spewed out between the close-set trees. Travis saw no easy way in. He suspected the dryads had deliberately made it this way, forcing travelers to stick to the main road and abandon attempts to wander into the woods.

"I'm pretty sure it was here," Rez said. "I saw movement, and whatever it was—something invisible—squeezed past some of these bushes here."

Travis saw nothing but dense undergrowth. "Hello?" he whispered as loud as he could. His voice came out as a weird rasp.

Rez raised an eyebrow at him. "Something in your throat?"

"I don't want the Seer to hear me."

"So keep your voice down."

"But I want the dryads to hear me."

"So what was that? A half-whisper? Something halfway between a full whisper and a shout? I'm pretty sure that makes it normal talking volume. So why not just talk normally?"

"Shut up," Travis said. He tried again, this time speaking normally, perhaps raising his voice a notch or two. "Any dryads out there? We need your help. Can you come talk to us?"

Yeah, right, he thought. *Just like that.*

Rez took over, talking to the forest. "We're pretty sure you want to stop the Seer from spreading. So show yourselves and help us. We have a plan."

Well, not exactly a plan as such, more like a vague notion . . .

"They're doing some pretty bad damage to the forest," Travis offered. "Taking over trees and bushes, eating them from the inside out, using them . . . and dumping them when they're finished. Nothing survives once the Seer moves on. The forest just withers and dies."

Go ahead, lay it on thick.

It was Rez's turn. "There are a load of new baby scorpion things. In a few hours from now, they'll be fully grown and looking for something to latch onto. Maybe they'll use trolls to spread to the nearest human town—"

"Or maybe they'll find some dryads," Travis broke in. "You guys can hide, but can you hide forever? With millions of those scorpions swarming about the forest?"

They paused and waited, listening hard, searching the gloom beyond the wall of brambles.

Nothing.

After a half-minute of silence, Travis sighed. "I don't know, Rez. I feel like we're wasting time."

"What choice do we have?" Rez grumbled. "You said yourself there are too many giant scorpions lurking about. We can't get close to the Treentacle without help. If you had wings, maybe you could drop down on it from above—but you don't have wings."

"If I were a dragon like my dad," Travis said, "then I could blast a path through the woods with my fire, and nothing would stop me. Or if I were a faerie, I could just buzz along out of reach. Instead, I'm a chimera. Seemed a good idea back at the lab, but now . . ."

He shrugged and fell silent.

Rez gave him a light punch. "Hey, your fireballs have come in handy plenty of times, and so has your snake-tail. It's not your fault you're utterly useless right now."

"Thanks."

They fell silent again, staring into the darkness of the forest. The wall of brambles before them seemed to be just that—a wall. Everything was a little clearer about ten feet in.

"Well," Travis said with a sigh, "I guess we'll just have to go home. We can't do this without help. Come on, Rez, let's go.

We'll be back in the morning with my dad, and he can burn the forest. I guess he'll have to burn pretty much the whole place, otherwise he might let some of those scorpions escape."

Rez nodded. "Yeah, we can't take the risk. This entire place will be black and dead by the time he's done." He raised his voice slightly. "Sorry, dryads—you'd better move out while you can. Don't be here when Hal the Enormous Dragon arrives."

They both backed away, listening for the slightest noise, hoping for the crack of a twig or a slight rustle in the bushes, just something to indicate a dryad was nearby.

Nothing.

Travis felt crushing disappointment inside. Enlisting dryads had been a long shot, but it clearly wasn't happening. He turned to leave.

Then Rez sucked in a breath and grabbed his arm.

Travis paused and turned back. "What?" he whispered.

Rez simply gave a vague nod.

Looking again, Travis scanned the gloom. "I don't see anything," he muttered.

And then he jerked backward in surprise as a figure slowly materialized just in front of him. A dryad stood there, leaning back against the wall of brambles, close enough to reach out and touch.

Though still translucent, its features were clear to see. This one was female, with a curious headpiece of twisted wood. She wore the ring of bark like a crown, but it seemed permanently fixed to her head, blending seamlessly with her rough, earthy skin.

She was the size of an ordinary human woman, very slender, a mottled dirt color wrapped in spiraling swaths of bark as though it had grown around her. Currently, her lower legs were invisible, but she'd allowed herself to solidify from the knees up, a very curious effect. Travis had to blink several times, certain he was imagining her. How could she have been there the whole time?

"Uh," he said in a strangled voice. "Hello. I'm, uh . . . I'm Travis, and this is Rez."

The dryad simply stared at him. Then she moved, and suddenly it seemed impossible she'd stood there for so long without being spotted. Movement gave away her camouflage, though her body somehow continued to blend perfectly with the background no matter where she positioned herself.

The dryad edged closer, mere inches away, and Travis caught a sweet scent on her breath. He racked his brains, trying to place the aroma. Eucalyptus? Meanwhile, she moved closer until her cheek brushed against his—a strange sensation, because part of it was smooth and warm, the rest rough and cold.

"Nepta."

She eased away, and he swallowed and forced a smile. "N-Nepta? What does that mean?"

"That's her name, doofus," Rez murmured. He raised his voice. "You're Nepta? That's your name?"

She tilted her head, then pointed at his chest. "Ress."

"Rez, yeah."

Nepta looked at Travis. She squinted, then tentatively said, "Tre-vas."

"Travis. Are you able to help us?"

She didn't seem to understand, not fully anyway. Perhaps she'd gotten the gist of what he and Rez had tried to convey earlier. Maybe she had a rudimentary grasp of English. Chatting to humans wasn't something they were famous for.

He opened his mouth to say something else, then almost let out a strangled cry as he realized dryads had materialized all along the bramble wall. Some were more visible than others, but they were definitely *there*. And had been all along, silent and watchful. All of them, both male and female, had the same earthy skin tones and sweeping, swirling bark coverings. Travis couldn't decide if the bark was a form of clothing or actually part of them, but it had a supple quality about it, indicating it wasn't real wood. He guessed dryads could blend into the woods quite successfully even if they remained opaque.

Rez had taken a step back, looking flustered. "Wow," he muttered. "Dryads everywhere." He raised his voice and said, "Uh, so, can you help us? We need to get to the Treentacle. To the, uh . . ." Here, he glanced at Travis for help.

Travis took over. "The white-tentacled plant thing. Do you know it? It sticks up out of the ground and has white tentacles, and if you stand too close, time slows down."

Nepta's eyes grew round with fright, but she didn't flee. Instead, she ducked low and peered over her shoulder, fading a little more so she was harder to see. Then she frowned and nodded, and suddenly Travis felt a hand grasping his.

Surprised, he allowed himself to be tugged into the woods. It shocked him to see Nepta march easily through the brambles without breaking a step—because the thick bushes parted and allowed her through. Travis stumbled after her, astonished at the turn of events. Wait until his parents heard about *this*!

Behind him, other dryads had taken hold of Rez and were urging him through the wall of brambles. Travis shrugged at him and offered a smile, and his friend put on an expression that clearly said *Whatever*.

Dryads knew how to move quietly. In single file—with Nepta leading and Travis right behind, then two male dryads, followed by Rez, and then probably another half-dozen bringing up the rear—the procession crept between trees with hardly any noise at all. Travis realized he and Rez were the only two spoiling the peace with their clumsy footwork. The dryads moved smoothly, not once pausing, their transparent feet somehow avoiding every brittle twig and dry leaf. Maybe their chameleon magic affected sound, too. Maybe they *were* making noise, but their strange power dulled it.

Travis still couldn't help wondering how the dryads were planning to get him and Rez close to the Seer without being spotted. Maybe they had a distraction in mind. He wanted to ask about it, but he dared not utter a word while they stole through the forest.

They walked for a long time, weaving quietly in and out of trees. A darkness descended, but there was still plenty of light to see by at the moment. It would be another hour or more before they'd have to worry about being lost in the woods at night.

Nepta stopped suddenly. Travis almost crashed into her. He halted and waited.

Just ahead, bushes moved as though teased by a gust of wind. But there *was* no wind, and only certain bushes quivered. The Seer! And as Travis stood holding his breath, a giant scorpion appeared, its tentacles held high, tasting the air.

Dryads eased past Travis on both sides. He couldn't believe they made no noise. Their invisibility spell had to be dulling their sounds. Every one of them had turned transparent by now, though their individual movements could be tracked by the bizarre blurring effect that played tricks on his eyes.

Rez sidled up and stood by his side. The blurring increased all around as the dryads formed a tight circle around them. It was hard to see which way they were facing, but it made no sense to be looking inward. When the circle was complete, Travis felt an invisible hand on his back, and he tiptoed forward with Rez matching his pace.

The circle of dryads moved with them, their formation unbroken. They pressed in tighter, and Travis became aware of hands touching the top of his head, causing him and Rez to stoop a little. Surprised, he squinted and came to the conclusion they were attempting to shield him and Rez, hiding them in case anyone looked down from above, like the Seer-controlled trees. But the dryads were *invisible*. What good would—

Travis had a moment of realization then, and he mentally kicked himself. If Darcy O'Tanner could hide an object under her smart shirt and cause it to turn invisible, then perhaps the dryads could do the same for two human boys.

Walking together in such a tight cluster was difficult. Travis constantly tripped on invisible toes and stubbed his own at the same time. He felt breath on his neck, felt hands gripping his arms and pressing down on his head. And all the while he bumped shoulders with Rez.

The blurry view all around made him blink and squint as though he had sleep-gunk in his eyes. The dryads were utterly invisible, and Travis felt exposed—but rather than dwell on his fears, he marveled at the impressive magic that hid him from sight. He spotted three scorpions scuttling about, and not one of them spun around to face the dryads. A reddish-brown Gnarler turned, its branches swinging around . . . but then it lurched away, massive tentacles slithering about at its base. Several Shufflers lifted and moved, and one even brushed past a dryad without its Seer scorpions realizing it.

No way, Travis thought in astonishment. *Being invisible is one thing, but making us invisible just by shielding us . . . ?*

He couldn't fathom how that worked. Someone looking into the circle from the outside must somehow see *all the way through* to the other side. Which meant the dryads on the far side had to be projecting their background onto the ones in the front. Or something like that.

He shook his head, perplexed by the whole thing. But excited, too. He saw the Treentacle up ahead. He saw scorpions scurrying here and there, and several Seer trees looming over what they must perceive as their master—the creepy white plantlike trunk, with its massive limbs spreading out in all directions, and thinner tendrils reaching through overhead low-hanging branches.

Nothing glanced his way. He and Rez had successfully crept up on the Treentacle without a single sign of alarm.

Now they just had to pull off their mission and destroy it.

Chapter 26
The Treentacle

Travis realized, belatedly, that they had no real plan of attack despite Rez's promise.

As the dryads eased closer to the giant Treentacle sticking out of the ground, he sensed time slowing and tried to shake off the effect. His brain went into overdrive picking out tiny details—the grass and weeds growing up around the white trunk, a patch of moss clinging to one side, a generous pile of acorns stacked in a shaded area among some tangleweed. The canopy of branches overhead appeared to support the weight of the Treentacle's heavy limbs, though that might be an illusion. Everything was intertwined, branches and tentacles and vines and tendrils, all woven together and spreading wide.

The dryads inched forward, maintaining their tight circle and grasping each other's hands over the center. Travis and Rez kept their heads down, peering through the transparent bodies at their target, now less than ten feet away.

Travis felt something crunch underfoot and heard a dull, drawn-out *snap*.

Though the dryads kept moving, forcing Travis and Rez along, the noise did not go unnoticed. A scorpion—a huge one, with four tentacles raised high above its head—turned to face their way. Off to the right, a reddish-brown tree slowly stood up straight. If it had ears, they would be pricked by now.

"Tra-vis," Rez whispered, his words emerging lazily, each syllable spaced apart.

Travis raised a finger to his lips, wishing he could do so faster. He felt like he was underwater.

He glanced back toward the giant scorpion. It was staring right at him, or so it seemed. Maybe staring *through* him. In any case, it hadn't reacted yet.

The dryads arrived at the trunk of the white Treentacle. It looked as thick and solid as a two-hundred-year-old tree, easily four feet across, its surface white and smooth. Travis counted nine separate limbs arching up and out, threading through and over the boughs of neighboring trees.

How are we supposed to destroy this thing? Travis thought, his heart thumping hard. *My dad already tried burning a tendril. It turned black, but then the charred bit crumbled away, leaving clean white skin underneath. It's indestructible.*

The one good thing about time dragging was that he had a moment to gather his thoughts and make a plan. How to destroy something that could not be destroyed?

The dryads stopped. The woods all around fell silent. More scorpions appeared, all of them giants, with splayed tentacles standing higher than six feet. These monsters were big enough to take over trees, yet they hung around to protect their master. They faced Travis and Rez, clearly alert even though the dryads' magic continued to confuse them.

Nearby, the reddish-brown Gnarler continued twisting around with a groaning, creaking noise.

"They're onto us," Travis whispered.

Rez didn't react. Or if he did, he took his time about it.

So I'll transform, Travis thought, trying to calm his nerves and clear his head. *The dryads will move out of my way, and I'll—No, wait, I need them to hang around for a minute after I've transformed, because it'll take the goat that long to make a fireball. Dang it! I wish I could form a fireball now while I'm still human . . .*

To his surprise, a warm feeling immediately flared in his throat. Something burned there, and excitement chased away his terror. Was he actually creating a fireball while still in human form? Well, why not? His dad could do it.

He frowned in concentration, only vaguely aware that Rez was tugging on his arm. "Tra . . . vis," his friend intoned.

Then he noticed what his friend was trying to tell him. The dryads were breaking the circle and sidling away, still invisible, blurs in his periphery as the massive white trunk in front of him came into sharp focus.

Scorpions jerked into action and scuttled toward him. Luckily, they traveled at a snail's pace. But Travis's fireball was equally slow in the making. How long had he been at it now? Five minutes? He knew it couldn't possibly be that long, but it sure felt like it.

You're too close!

This realization hit him like a ton of bricks. He had a clear shot of the Treentacle, but his fireball would simply spatter in liquid form against its solid trunk. Yes, it might sizzle and smolder, but there'd be no destructive force.

It took all his strength to lift a foot in an effort to back up, but several scorpions had already closed the gap by now. Three of them leapt.

In panic, Travis spat his fireball at them, catching the first full on and knocking it out of the air. It fell to the ground screeching and thrashing, a molten mess, sizzling noisily. But the other two scorpions slammed into him and Rez a split-second later, sending them both reeling.

The weight of one creature pinned Travis to the ground. With his head turned sideways and one cheek pressed into the dirt, he squirmed and yelled as their tentacles flopped about and sought out his throat. Meanwhile, he heard Rez shouting something, but his words seemed slurred. The whole moment had a surreal, dreamlike quality about it.

The scorpion on his head finally climbed off, and Travis blinked and moaned. Tentacles tightened around his neck as the scorpion settled heavily on his chest. Rez lay to his side, equally incapacitated. Both of them had ended up back in the Seer's control, this time by much bigger creatures.

And mere inches from their silent, motionless master.

"Great," Travis muttered. He should have thought it through better. The dryads had successfully delivered him to the target, and he'd royally screwed up.

"Not . . . again," Rez complained several minutes later. Or it *seemed* like several minutes later. Maybe it was just a few seconds.

Travis lay there panting, slowly recovering his composure. A sense of calm settled over him. This wasn't so bad. The Seer had no intention of harming him.

They simply wanted his help.

* * *

Travis guessed several hours had passed since being recaptured by the Seer, though it still looked like dusk as he peered upward through the branches to the reddening sky. It didn't matter either way. He was happy to lie there and wait for instructions.

He turned his head, possibly his first movement since the scorpion had tightened its tentacles around his neck. Rez lay nearby, perfectly still, staring sightlessly upward, blinking occasionally. Drool ran from the corner of his mouth down his cheek. He, too, had a giant scorpion on his chest, its tentacles looped easily around his throat, cradling his head.

Turning to face the other way, Travis's gaze fell on the monstrous Treentacle, which towered over him, so close he could reach out and touch it. It looked so much like a bizarre plant that it was no wonder scientists had pooh-poohed the idea of it being a living, sentient creature. They had admitted it was more animal than vegetable, but since it grew like a weed and never moved, further studies hadn't been a high priority.

The slender tendrils moved, though. They were moving right now, writhing like snakes among the trees. Travis thought he saw the massive trunk shift as well, a barely perceptible pulsing across its surface, almost like the twitching of great muscles or the rise and fall of a chest. Maybe it always moved this way and nobody stood around long enough to notice.

Or maybe something unique was happening.

Trolls loomed in the fading light. At least a dozen of them slipped out of the trees and into the clearing holding baskets. One by one, they stepped closer and placed their baskets on the ground. One troll—the one name Zoth, with his burnt chest—brought his basket all the way up to the pulsing trunk of the Treentacle and placed it at its base. Travis tried to shuffle sideways to allow the troll more room, but the scorpion on his chest was heavy, and he couldn't muster the energy.

Zoth waited by his basket. The scorpion that clung to his back, with its tentacles around his neck, hadn't gotten any bigger lately despite a speedy infancy. As Travis wondered about this, the answer leaked into his brain courtesy of the Seer. Quite simply, drones grew only as big as they needed to be. Those attached to the backs of the trolls were plenty big enough to get the job done, while those destined to take over the trees ate ravenously, their rapid growth essential for the mammoth task of burrowing through the trunk and uprooting it from the ground. It took six or more.

But they no longer needed the trees. A greater plan was afoot. Travis had a vision of more scorplings, a vast army of them, carried by trolls and delivered to multiple towns and settlements in the region—human, naga, centaur, elven, and the rest. The miniature scorpions would spill from the baskets and hide, feed for several hours until they were bigger, then re-emerge and attack. It would be a spectacular moment when they all leapt out of hiding and took over entire populations.

Then the Seer would get its multicultural, multispecies ethnography of animals, plants, and fungi. It would study the interconnectedness and inseparability of all living things for the next few months, absorbing information until they were sated.

Just for a moment, Travis felt a jolt of fear. The Seer would control everyone and everything for a *few months*? He imagined his friends and family stalking about the countryside like zombies with scorpions attached to their backs. How could they survive that way? Would they be allowed to feed? They had to eat and drink, or they'd drop dead.

He caught a fleeting glimpse of the Seer's drones finally departing from the region, leaving behind gaunt and wasted figures. Many would die, just as bushes withered and trees toppled over.

Travis had been staring absently at the Treentacle's trunk the whole time, but now he blinked and refocused. Something was indeed happening. The slow pulsing on its side had become more pronounced. Just above the basket, the surface of one massive jutting tentacle bulged outward like a blister. The dull-white skin thinned to a delicate transparency, revealing dark movement within.

Abruptly, it split open. A stream of tiny scorplings poured out, pure white and fragile, their trailing tentacles like squirming maggots. The basket below filled quickly. Travis watched, amazed, as the newborns flowed like foamy ale from a punctured barrel.

Zoth calmly switched out the full basket with an empty one and handed it off to another troll, then prepared to switch out again as the scorplings kept on coming. Those that had missed the basket squirmed on the ground at Travis's feet, and a feeling of revulsion swept over him.

How many more? he moaned to himself.

On closer inspection he noticed that a couple of other tentacles at the base of the Treentacle's trunk had similar blisters that had already burst and closed up again. This was perhaps the third outpouring of scorplings, with potentially more to come.

Basket after basket filled up with the things, and the massive trunk quivered and pulsed the whole time.

Where are they all coming from?

He felt them clambering over his legs, a teeming mass of blind, helpless bugs. Half a dozen baskets were already filled by now, with Zoth handing the most recent to a colleague and quickly inserting another under the gushing flow. Looking around, Travis counted at least another ten baskets waiting to be filled.

Not hundreds of babies. More like thousands. And this is just one tentacle, one spawn.

Whether the horror of the situation had gotten to him or the Seer was simply distracted, Travis found himself thinking freely again. Fighting the weight of the giant scorpion straddling his chest, he struggled up onto his elbows, sweating profusely and panting hard. He'd been released, at least temporarily. Yet Rez remained calm and quiet, a faint smile on his face.

Travis fell flat again as the scorpion shifted. The tentacles tightened around his throat. The Seer's booming voice drifted back into his head . . .

"No!" he yelled.

He transformed and thrashed wildly, taking the scorpion by surprise and throwing it off. He slashed at it with his powerful lion claws, then roared and snapped, gripping the creature at the soft base of its rear end where the tentacles sprouted. He had a sizeable spongy mass to get hold of, and the long limbs writhed as he bit down hard and drew blood.

During the frenzied struggle, he knocked against the latest nearly full basket and send it toppling, spilling its entire contents. The squirming scorplings spread out across the ground and sank into whatever holes they could find. The stream of newborns continued unabated while Zoth hurried forward to right the basket, accidentally squashing a dozen bugs underfoot.

Trolls jerked into action as though woken from a daydream. They stumbled forward, obviously intent on subduing Travis.

He pounced on the rapidly filling basket and sent it flying again, then stood directly in front of the torn blister where the scorplings gushed out. *So not just a thick tentacle, then*, he thought in amazement. It was some kind of delivery tube, the babies being sent up from far below. Fighting his intense disgust, he dug his claw into the aperture and ripped it open, widening the hole as the wriggling creatures continued spewing out.

Now! he ordered the goat, leaning forward.

With a flash of heat, a giant fireball erupted from the goat's mouth behind him. It shot over his head and straight into the aperture, a ball of molten lava rammed down the throat of the delivery tube. Some of it blackened the edges and caused a lot of sizzling and popping, and some of it was blocked by the onslaught of scorplings . . . but most of it tumbled down inside.

The stream of newborns ceased immediately. Amid the squirming, sizzling mass at his feet and the horrified gasps of several trolls as they stumbled to a halt, Travis felt a sudden lurch under his feet as the monstrous Treentacle reacted to a sharp stab of pain.

It's not enough, Travis thought as a silence descended. *Goat, we need another—*

But then the ground gave way.

Chapter 27
Into the Depths

Crying out, Travis scrambled for a grip as dirt poured into a widening abyss surrounding the Treentacle—which was rapidly sinking into the ground.

Travis briefly arrested his fall with four paws spread wide, but the earth continued to crumble and sink beneath him. Just for a second, though, he gaped in amazement at the sight of the monstrous Treentacle descending into the abyss—first the thick mass of its trunk, then the individual tentacles, which thudded down amid a shower of branches and leaves. The white limbs thrashed and strained at dozens of delicate tendrils still wound through the surrounding brush. Rather than unravel neatly, they were wrenched away, vines and small bushes and all.

Stunned, Travis watched over his shoulder as the whole thing disappeared, all the while losing his grip as the earth slid out from under him. When the last tendrils vanished down the hole in the center of the funnel-shaped depression, he realized with horror that he was going down with it, along with several uprooted bushes and numerous baskets of scorplings.

Most of the trolls had stumbled away from the danger, but the one named Zoth lay flat on his belly on the slippery slope, looking like he was swimming in crumbling dirt. His scorpion came loose at that moment, apparently lifeless, its legs curling up and tentacles going limp. The troll's eyes widened as if finally waking from a dream state . . . but it was too late. They slid together into the abyss and were gone.

"Travis!" Rez shouted.

His friend clung to the rim of the funnel-shaped crater, one hand outstretched. Travis reached for him with a clawed paw and knew an instant later he needed to revert to his human form. He did so just as he grasped his friend's hand. Suddenly feeling lighter, he tried to dig his feet into the dirt to climb up, but the slope was steepening by the second, the black hole at its center growing wider.

"Pull me up," Travis urged.

"I'm trying!"

But now the rim of the crater was giving way, and Rez found himself leaning a little too precariously over the edge. Realizing this, his eyes widened in terror.

In that moment, Travis felt his world slow down. A sense of calm came over him. He knew he had to let go, otherwise they'd both die. And when he looked up at Rez and met his gaze, he knew his friend had come to the same conclusion.

Travis relaxed his grip.

Rez tightened his.

The look on his face had turned from terror to anger. "Don't you dare let go!" Rez yelled, sweat pouring from his forehead.

Travis didn't need to look over his shoulder to know this couldn't end well. The hole at the center of the crater had widened so much that his legs now dangled in midair from the thighs down, and the crumbling, slippery, ever-steepening slope was unforgiving. He was going in no matter what. And Rez was too, if he didn't let go.

Travis swallowed. Pouring an entire childhood's worth of friendship and gratitude and regret into one word, he said, "Thanks."

Then he yanked his hand away and hurtled into the abyss.

* * *

Falling into the blackness, Travis gasped with terror. He waited for the impact, hoping it would be quick. The longer and farther he fell, the harder he would smack down on a slab of rock, which would be a merciful end. Or maybe he'd glance off the side of a wall and crack his head wide open, knocking him senseless so he wouldn't feel anything else.

What if I break every bone in my body but don't die right away? What if I lie in agony for hours in some snake-infested pit?

He fell with air rushing noisily past his ears, making his clothes flap. Panting, he glanced up. Far above, the pinprick of daylight quickly faded. The blackness below was terrifying. Expecting to hit rock at any moment, he closed his eyes and gritted his teeth.

And waited.

In the darkness, he brushed against something and jerked in fear, lashing out with his hands. It felt like something was falling with him. Wait—*was* he falling still? Yes, he was . . . but the noise of the wind had eased a little, his clothes not flapping quite as much.

Startled, he reached out, groping blindly. He touched something long and stringy. A rope? A vine? No, something else—probably one of those eerie white tendrils. He recoiled, his heart hammering in his chest.

But the implications of this hit him hard. Could he actually be falling alongside the Treentacle? He reached out again, this time finding a limb as thick as his wrist. He couldn't hold onto it, though, because it slid upward out of his grasp; he was falling much faster, passing it by. He was in freefall, whereas the giant tentacled creature was not. At this rate, he'd reach bottom before it did.

Yet his descent slowed further. "What *is* this?" he muttered.

His fear drained away. He still expected to die, but there was only so much terror a person could feel. He'd reach his peak earlier. Now he was past it, and fascination was kicking in. Shouldn't he have smacked down onto rock by now? How could he be slowing? Gravity didn't work this way. If anything, gravity should be stronger this deep below the surface.

Unless there's some kind of magic down here.

So much of New Earth was shrouded in mystery. Scientists from Old Earth had been exploring and forming opinions about magic for decades, trying to explain it in ways that conformed to their established laws of physics. But even Miss Simone, who had spent much of her earlier scientific life dismissing magic, had given up and accepted the inevitable: that some things just could not be explained by mere humans. She often quoted a great author, Arthur C. Clarke, who'd said, "Any sufficiently advanced technology is indistinguishable from magic." While that might be true to some extent, she also argued that a powerful, unfathomable force was probably just magic.

Travis wondered if there was a scientific explanation for his slowing descent. More likely it was something more sinister, something unearthly. After all, he was falling alongside a weird time-skewing, knowledge-absorbing, white-tentacled monster that had until recently projected from the ground like an antenna for a colossal underground brain! It had spewed thousands of tiny scorpion bugs into the world, which had animated bushes and trees, then attacked an entire village of trolls and altered their way of thinking. It had planned to spread its consciousness across the region, tap into a vast pool of information, and feed until sated.

If there was a scientific explanation for all this, then it was so far outside the norm, so alien to New Earth, that it might as well be called magic.

Travis continued falling. His clothes flapped quietly now, more like he was floating on a gentle breeze than plummeting into an abyss. He reached out again, finding thick tentacles within easy grasp. He matched the speed of their descent now.

With hope flaring in his chest, he pulled himself toward the appendage and wrapped himself around it. The cool tentacle was so thick he could only just cling on. *I feel like Jack climbing a beanstalk*, he thought in amazement.

All kinds of parallels with the fabled beanstalk sprang to mind. But instead of sprouting from the grass and stretching up through the clouds to a kingdom of giants, the monstrous Treentacle grew out of a massive subterranean brain and poked up above ground.

A massive subterranean brain.

He still found it hard to believe, even now. Nevertheless, the Treentacle had certainly risen from the depths. But was it really long enough to stretch to such heights?

He squinted, seeing a faint glow in the darkness below. It gradually brightened until he could make out the shapes of tentacles all around him. They undulated like sea serpents in deep water, and he realized with astonishment that the abyss he'd fallen into was not just a narrow shaft but a vast cavern. He could see white, snakelike appendages looping in all directions. The Treentacle really was fantastically tall, and now it had collapsed on itself, spreading in all directions.

It fell slowly, though, almost lazily. Travis clung tight, starting to believe that he might in fact survive this fall.

His limbs quickly grew tired of holding on. Gripping the tentacle would be much easier if only it were a little slimmer. As it leaned to one side, he moaned and gritted his teeth, knowing he was about to slide off. And when he did, he let out a gasp and tumbled away into the gloom.

Yet he didn't plummet quite the way he'd expected. He simply floated alongside, sinking rather than falling, drawing ever closer to the brightening haze below. He focused on it, trying to make out some details. The glow spread over a large area, too massive and far-reaching to take in. A bioluminescent floor of some kind? Or . . .

A giant brain, he admitted. *It has to be.*

He could now see where the single, massive trunk of the Treentacle sprouted from the luminescent floor. It really had stretched all the way to the surface and poked out of the dirt, then split into various limbs like that of a tree. But down here at its base, it had to be fifteen feet thick, smooth and white, unblemished by moss and mold and whatever else the forest had smeared on it over the decades.

How long has it been here?

His dad had first discovered these things twenty years ago. They might have been there much longer. Did they die of old age? Did new ones take their place? Or did they last as long as trees, perhaps hundreds of years? All he knew was that *this* one, the one he drifted alongside, had pulled itself loose or been yanked down. He'd harmed it with one tiny but superheated ball of liquid fire.

The surface below came into focus at last. The light was almost blinding at close quarters, but as his eyes adjusted, he made out a bumpy terrain. It was too white to be rock but not white enough to be snow and ice. It reminded him of a frozen sea caught in dazzling moonlight.

The tentacles had stopped falling. They hung in space like a colossal wilting weed, spread far and wide in the cavernous subterranean gloom. Travis drifted on down, trying to judge the speed of his descent. *Like being underwater*, he thought. *Sinking to the bottom of a lake.*

He caught his breath as the weird, glowing, rocklike surface came up to meet him. He bent his knees, expecting a sudden jolt. It occurred to him that if this truly was the source of the time-slowing Treentacles, then his perception of speed might be terribly skewed. What if he was falling much faster than he thought? What if he was about to smack into the ground at terminal velocity and spread himself all over the place?

He'd hoped for a quick death earlier. Maybe it would be—but he'd experience it in slow motion.

Chapter 28
The Giant Underground Brain

Travis landed on something a little warmer and softer than rock. His initial fear of smacking down hard while his overactive mind soaked in every tiny detail proved unwarranted. Instead of watching his legs crumple in slow motion and turning into a red mess of broken bone and torn flesh, he simply touched down like a spaceman on the moon.

He stood there with his knees bent and arms outstretched for balance as the sloping rock under his smart shoes yielded like putty. He sank into it a few inches, and light flared under him, rippling outward as though he'd triggered a few synapses.

"No way," he whispered.

He spotted an upturned basket along with a widespread scattering of scorplings, all twitching on their backs or scuttling in random directions. He made out a fine sprinkling of soil and small rocks, too. A few small branches and leaves lay here and there.

His heart thudded, and his breath came in ragged gasps. There was no way he could ever get back to the surface now. What scared him most was the uncertainty of what, eventually, would kill him off. How long might he spend shuffling around in this bleak, underground horror show before collapsing from thirst, hunger, despair, or much worse? Maybe Zoth the troll would come after him. He had to be down here somewhere, probably full of hatred.

Travis tried to put aside the overwhelming feeling of despair and concentrate on the sheer spectacle of the place. "My dad would love this," he mumbled to himself. "Twenty years he's been going on about a giant brain under the ground, and he was right all along. And if he were here, he could fly out. But me? Nah, I'm a wingless wonder. Never again. Next time I choose what kind of shapeshifter I want to be, it'll be something with wings."

If there's a next time, he finished silently.

He turned in a circle, taking in the vast expanse of the frozen ocean glowing in a nonexistent moonlight. Darkness pervaded the horizon in all directions, so it was impossible to see how far the brain actually spread. Or how deep. Was it one gigantic blob filling the planet's core? Travis shook his head. That was impossible. Still, theories abounded that those white-tentacled monsters, those Treentacles or *feelers*, could be found all over the world. So either this brain filled the core like a stone inside a peach . . . or there was more than one brain.

He slowed his breathing and listened carefully. Not a single, solitary sound.

"Yeah, lots of brains," he whispered, eager for the sound of conversation. "That has to be it. Maybe this one has a bunch of feelers sticking up all around where I live, the ones my dad has seen. And maybe the next brain is thousands of miles away, across the sea."

He looked again at the oceanlike surface. It was as though time had paused. Maybe it had. Maybe this really was an ocean, and when time started ticking again, he would plunge below the surface and sink to the bottom. He gasped at the nightmarish idea. What horrors might lurk below? He bent his knees again, trying in vain to be lighter than air.

"It's rock, it's just rock," he told himself.

Gradually, he controlled his trembling nerves and steadied his knocking knees. He took a few tentative steps, and each caused a faint flicker of light underfoot.

Okay, so now what?

He looked around again. He had no plan whatsoever. Walking into the darkness in any direction seemed like a bad idea, though he knew he would never actually reach the darkness; it was like fog, always thicker in the distance no matter where he was. But even if he walked in light the whole time, what could he possibly find that would help him? A ladder? A convenient rope dangling somewhere? A bored pegasus looking for a rider to take on a flight?

"I'm so screwed."

With his fears giving way to frustration, the glimmer of an idea came to him. If this was indeed a brain, it wouldn't want to be injured.

"Let me go!" he yelled as loudly as he could. His voice echoed a little in the darkness overhead. "Send me back up or I'll . . . I'll *hurt* you!"

To punctuate his point, he stamped on a tiny white scorpion that happened to scuttle past. It squished underfoot.

Absolutely no reaction.

"Okay then," he muttered, and abruptly transformed into his chimera form.

He padded about for a minute while his goat head worked on a fireball. He felt a little cheated; he'd wanted to be the goat this time, but he found himself inside the lion's head yet again. He growled and raked his claws across the weird, slightly spongy surface, then hopped up and down as though pouncing on a rodent.

When the goat was ready, a silent understanding passed between the three heads. Travis stopped jumping around and stood still. Moments later, the fireball shot over his head and arced through the air. It punched into the brain twenty feet away.

The thud of the explosion was surprisingly loud. The force tore a bathtub-sized crater in the spongy surface, and heavy chunks of *something* flew everywhere. There was no dust, but a fine grey mist drifted on a barely perceptible breeze.

Light flared under the crater, pulsing outward. The oceanlike surface swelled upward several feet while the lightshow continued. Inside the crater, something churned and bubbled.

Fascinated and terrified at the same time, Travis stood perfectly still until the swell of the ground eased and settled. The pulsing flashes slowed, and the crater seemed to collapse in on itself until, gradually, the surface completely repaired itself. At that point, everything dimmed again, returning to its former subdued glow.

Travis let out a soft growl and padded over to where the crater had been. He saw nothing out of the ordinary. The giant brain had certainly felt the force of the fireball and reacted swiftly, but its healing powers were second to none. Yet a similar fireball had caused a kneejerk reaction in the Treentacle while spewing forth its scorplings, and now it hung limp and lifeless, thick tentacles floating aimlessly high above.

Making sure he could be understood, Travis reverted to his human form so he could challenge the brain again. "How about another?" he demanded loudly. "I can keep shooting fireballs all day, you know. So if you know what's good for you, you'll find a way to send me back to—"

He broke off and listened hard. He heard a thundering sound in the distance, a strangely familiar noise that he couldn't place. Not *actual* thunder but something else . . .

"What *is* that?" he whispered.

Whatever it was, it grew louder, echoing out of the blackness in one direction or another. Travis swallowed, suddenly fearful. Maybe challenging the brain had been a bad idea. What if it had giant antibodies or something grotesque stampeding around on the surface? Maybe more of those scorpion things, extra massive ones with legs as thick as his waist.

An icy chill swept over him, and he jerked and stumbled sideways, swinging around. "Whoa!"

The thunderous noise continued in the background, but right now he was distracted. A hooded figure swept toward him, seeming to glide over the uneven surface, the blade of a scythe glinting in the glow from beneath.

"Death," he moaned, backing away.

The Grim Reaper's pale, ghostlike skull grinned maniacally. A skeletal hand rose and stretched toward him. "You must come with me," Death hissed.

"No way!" Travis exclaimed, almost falling over himself as he backpedaled. "Stay away from me! I won't shoot any more fireballs, I promise!"

"It is too late," the Reaper whispered, his voice rising above the approaching thunder. "Come with me now. Before it arrives."

Travis faltered, confused. "Huh? Before *what* arrives?"

"The dullahan."

The nature of the rising thunder suddenly clarified in Travis's mind. He swung around in horror as a horse and rider emerged from the distant gloom, silhouetted against the underglow, a cloak billowing. It seemed impossible for one horse to make so much noise. Amplified in a supernatural, nightmarish way, it was probably meant to instill terror. Which it did.

"Come with me," the Reaper insisted, his skeletal hand still reaching for him.

Though Travis instinctively knew his best bet was to trust the Grim Reaper, he couldn't help pausing to see what kind of monster the dullahan was. He didn't need more than a couple of seconds to make out that the colossal black horse wore an iron facemask and heavy, dull-metal barding around its neck and shoulders. The armor clanked noisily, though this sound was almost drowned out by the creaking and clattering of a four-wheeled wagon trailing behind. It seemed to be made of bones and rotten wood, covered with a pale, tan-colored leathery material that looked suspiciously like skin.

As the cloaked rider drew near, Travis saw that he wore armor smeared with oily-black grime. In one hand, he swung a long ivory whip, the spine of some large creature or other. It made a sharp cracking sound every time he flicked it, though it didn't ever touch the surface of the brain underfoot. Nor did the horse's hooves, for that matter.

The dullahan had been decapitated at some point in his ghastly life. He carried his own laughing, wide-eyed head under his other arm.

"We go now," the Reaper whispered.

The headless horseman brought his steed to a halt twenty feet away. The chilling laughter ceased, and the dullahan's face turned into a grimace. "It is your time, Tra—"

At that moment, the Reaper gripped Travis's shoulder, and he felt a wrenching in his gut. When he staggered and blinked, the dullahan was gone.

"Wh-what happened?" he stammered, glancing all around. He shuddered and brushed at his shoulder, which felt unusually cold now. "How did you do that? You made him disappear!"

The Reaper gave a single shake of his skull. "I made *us* disappear. We have relocated. But the dullahan will find you again." He leaned closer. "Never hear him say your name."

Looking around, Travis saw much of the same—an oddly bumpy and softly lit ground stretching into darkness all around. He had to concede it looked a *little* different, though. Cleaner, for one thing. No dirt and rocks and feeble scorpion scorplings.

"How far did we come?" he asked shakily.

The Reaper said nothing, and he didn't need to; in the distance, Travis heard the thunder of hooves again.

"Not far, then," he muttered.

The skeletal, hooded figure leaned close, and a blast of icy air chilled Travis to the bone. "The Seer has become aware of you," he hissed. "He has sent the dullahan to dispatch you."

Travis nodded, scouring the blackness and trying to pinpoint the direction of the approaching horseman. "Why are *you* helping me?"

"Because you helped me. And because it pleases me to defy the dullahan." With the scythe held high in one bony hand, the Reaper held out his other. "We will keep moving. The dullahan will grow bored eventually."

Travis looked into the lifeless face of the Grim Reaper, trying to find a spark within the empty eye sockets, something to confirm this wasn't just a pile of bones in a robe. The Reaper stared back impassively.

"Okay," Travis said, grasping the long, ivory hand. "Thank you."

As the thunderous noise of hooves and the creaking rattle of a wagon rose in volume, a deathly cold feeling swept up Travis's arm. Suddenly, the scene shifted.

As if being reset, the dullahan was once more far away, a distant echo.

Travis and the Reaper stood at the foot of a gigantic Treentacle, a pure white trunk some thirty feet across and stretching directly up into darkness.

"Whoa," Travis said. "This is a different one, right? How many are there?"

Annoyingly, the Reaper chose not to answer directly. "The Seer has shifted its focus to this one. It will spawn in a few days from now."

Travis gaped. "It's gonna have babies?"

The Reaper tilted his head. "This new brood is preparing to rise and will emerge above ground in the vicinity of your town."

"What? Carter?" Travis felt sick. He looked up at the towering trunk. "Are you saying this is the one that sticks up next to the Prison of Despair?"

He jumped back in alarm as a sudden pulse of light illuminated the inside of the trunk around its base, proving that its thick walls were not as opaque as they were in broad daylight. He guessed that, above ground, the trunk and tentacles were sheathed in a hardy skin to guard against the elements. There was no need for such protection down here.

In those few seconds when the light pulsed and flickered, Travis saw something that confirmed the Grim Reaper's announcement of a new brood: a vast mass of tiny, wriggling, squirming scorpions just inside the translucent walls of the massive stalk.

Chapter 29
The Passage of Time

Travis backed away from the faintly illuminated trunk, his lips curling at the sight of the wriggling creatures within. "I'm going to blast a hole in the side," he said with steely determination. "I don't care if the brain throws a hissy fit. Those things are *not* making it to the surface."

The Reaper reached out and gripped his arm. "It will do no good—"

"We'll see about that. I killed one of these tentacle monsters with a single fireball. I can do it again."

"Your attempts will be futile," the Reaper whispered.

But Travis shook him off and transformed, this time willing himself into the head of the goat. Triumphantly, he began working on a fireball as his lion counterpart circled the massive trunk, padding lightly across the spongy ground.

He became aware of the rising thunder of hooves in the distance. Clicking his tongue with annoyance, he guessed he would only have time to cook up one fireball, two at the most. He'd better make it count.

While the heat built in his throat, he studied the giant trunk. The flickering illumination spread from the base up to about six feet in height, bathing the mass of baby scorpions in light. The trunk walls were thick, but Travis was confident his fireball could punch a hole through. If he hit it at the base, then the scorplings would spill out.

"We need to move on," the Reaper warned as maniacal laughter echoed around the endless cavern.

The lion's head growled at the hooded figure, and the snake-tail hissed. Travis warmed to his unseen traveling companions. They were a team, a united front.

When he felt the fireball was as ready as it could ever be, he waited until the lion had backed up to a safe distance then coughed it up with all the force he could muster. The flaming ball smacked into the trunk about a foot from the bottom. The boom was deafening, and the surface of the brain reacted with a violent jolt that sent Travis tumbling. He rolled and scrambled for a grip as bright flashes strobed wildly beneath him.

When the noise died down, he picked himself up and firmly planted all four feet. The Reaper stood there apparently unperturbed by the earthquake. Though his robe draped on the ground, Travis remained convinced he floated a few inches in the air.

He surveyed the damage to the trunk. Or rather the lack of it.

Dismayed, he gaped at the pitiful smudge of soot across the translucent wall. Apart from that, nothing had changed except that the chamber of scorplings seemed brighter now, a bioluminescence that flitted around inside the thick walls. Within, the critters writhed as before, agitated by the disturbance.

As Travis watched, the whole mass rose a few inches up the delivery tube.

"We must go," the Reaper said.

Without a word, Travis reverted to human form and reached for the Grim Reaper's bony hand. The thunder of hooves had once again reached a crescendo, and just for a moment, the horseman appeared out of the shadows, underlit by a ghostly glow . . .

The scene shifted, and the noise cut off.

This time, Travis and the Reaper stood on the edge of a giant crater, so big that the other side had to be half a mile away. Unlike most craters, though, the walls fell away gradually and grew steeper toward the center, more like a funnel. The surface underfoot was smooth and bright, rising and falling, trembling and shuddering, *alive*.

"What's this?" Travis whispered.

"I want to show you something," the Reaper said icily.

Travis couldn't work out if his guide was irked, scornful, or something else. He followed the hooded figure anyway, treading carefully, not liking how the ground sloped away. If they went much farther, they'd surely fall in.

The Reaper held a hand out to his side, palm up. Feeling rather like a dance partner, Travis sighed and suffered the indignity, noticing that the Reaper really was floating now—carrying on out across the abyss while the ground fell away.

"Whoa," Travis muttered as the familiar deathly chill swept throughout his body. When he looked down again, he realized he'd left the ground behind. Startled, he stopped walking . . . but he continued moving, somehow caught up in the Grim Reaper's levitation magic. The two of them glided toward the center of the giant abyss where, directly below, a rapidly narrowing shaft led to the pits of the Earth. Its walls were illuminated in a glow that darkened to an ominous red deep down. "Seriously, what the heck—?"

Once more, the sound of hooves rose in the distance. Travis huffed and scowled. He should be terrified of the life-snatching demon, but right now he felt only annoyance at the constant interruption.

"The dullahan cannot follow us below," the Reaper said softly. "His role is merely to end lives. He does not collect souls and has no jurisdiction here. You will be safe. In time, I will help you back to the surface."

Without warning, the two of them dropped. Travis couldn't help crying out, and as his clothes flapped around his body in the sudden downrush, a stream of pleas escaped his lips. "No, stop! I don't want to see what's down there! Take me home! If you can help me back to the surface, then help me *now*, not later! I don't want—arrgh!"

The words choked in his throat as they plummeted at a dizzying speed into the ever-narrowing shaft. But just as Travis thought his heart was about to explode in his chest, the shaft ended and let out into a vast cavern of almost complete darkness.

At least he *thought* it was a cavern. It was impossible to tell. All he could see were thick, grey clouds all around. *This is the Underworld*, he thought with horror. *There's an inferno below, with smoke everywhere!*

But smoke would cause his eyes to sting, and he experienced no such discomfort. It didn't even smell like smoke. It was everywhere, dark and rolling, only marginally paler in color than the blackness all around. Yet it seemed harmless.

It took him a while to calm his thudding heart. He floated in silence with the Reaper alongside, still holding hands. He had to admit it was peaceful. Then he spotted orange glows here and there, drifting aimlessly, adding to the serene if bizarre landscape. He watched them with interest as they crisscrossed back and forth. He thought he could see a bright light in the distance, but it only became visible when the rolling, pulsing clouds moved aside.

After a while, he shook his head to clear it. "I feel like I'm falling asleep."

"It is mesmerizing," the Reaper agreed.

Travis sighed. "Okay, so where are we?"

The Grim Reaper gestured vaguely with his scythe. "You might think of this as the place between life and death. It is where I bring souls."

Travis gaped at him, and his heart once again began to thump—this time with excitement rather than abject fear. "This—this is—this is the *World of Darkness*?" He shook his head in astonishment. "This is where my dad came when he was turned to stone by a gorgon. Well, his *mind* came here while his body lay around for two weeks. But . . . but I'm *actually here*? In the flesh?" A horrible thought came to him. "Wait—am I dead? Am I a soul? Is this why you're helping me?"

The Reaper maintained his firm, cold, bony grip. "No, young Travis, you are not dead. I will return you shortly when the dullahan has moved on."

Travis processed this in silence. "Wait," he said after a while. "I think I get it. My dad said time slows down in this place. He was only here an hour or two, but weeks passed by outside. So—"

"If you wait here, the dullahan will forget you. His memory is weak. He will search for two or three days, then forget you exist and move on. We will wait the equivalent of four days, just to be sure. Four days is twenty-four minutes here."

"But—*four days?*" Travis exclaimed. He shook his head vigorously. "No, we can't wait that long. You said the next brood of scorpions will be ready in a few days. That's at the Prison of Despair, right outside Carter. I have to kill them all before they're born!"

"If we leave here too early, the dullahan will come after you."

"Not if I'm back home in Carter."

"It doesn't matter where you are. The dullahan will find you. He travels by horseback, but he is unnaturally fast."

Travis couldn't argue with that. He and the Reaper had hopped from one giant Treentacle to another, and they were a day's walk apart on land—yet the dullahan had covered the distance in a matter of minutes.

"He will sense your whereabouts and track you down," the Reaper went on. "He is relentless. Your only hope is to hide in a place he cannot enter and hold out until you slip from his mind. We must wait four days."

"And then it'll be too late," Travis argued, trembling with anger. "Take me back up. I'd rather be chased everywhere by the dullahan than wait here and let everyone in Carter be taken over by the Seer."

The Reaper fell silent for a moment. "You cannot escape the dullahan if he's bent on taking your life. You've been marked for death, and his job is—"

"My life isn't worth living if I get back home and find everyone walking about like zombies with tentacles wrapped around their necks," Travis said stiffly.

"You can still save the ones you love as you did before, by severing the link between—"

"No!" Travis yelled as a hopeless vision flitted through his mind. He saw himself walking about among zombified people, carefully prying loose a few select scorpions to free his parents and friends, then running like crazy to avoid hundreds of other scorpions. If he destroyed the Treentacle at the Prison of Despair, it would release its hold on everyone . . . but what if he *couldn't* destroy it? What if he was overrun by scorpions before he could get to the prison? "No, I have to stop the babies being born. Take me back now before it's too late!"

After a moment, the Grim Reaper gave a nod and gently dragged Travis up through the thick, dark, rolling clouds, somehow able to propel them both without a single movement of his skeletal body. They headed toward the reddish glow overhead that marked the opening at the bottom of the shaft.

"I should imagine two days have already passed by now," the Reaper said. "You will have time to carry out your mission—but the dullahan will not have forgotten you yet. Your re-emergence into the world will not go unnoticed."

"Okay," Travis muttered. "Just hurry up."

They drifted up into the shaft, which suddenly looked far more inviting than it had before. It was narrow, just ten feet across, its walls throbbing with deep-red energy, but as they rose at a steady pace, the light slowly turned white and became more sporadic and fleeting.

"Those floating balls of light," Travis said, remembering what he'd seen among the ominous clouds below. "That was pure magic, right?"

"Processed souls," the Reaper said. "The cycle of life."

"Yeah. People die, you take their souls, bring them to the World of Darkness, and the souls are turned into balls of magic by . . . by the Gatekeeper."

The Grim Reaper said nothing.

Travis pressed on as they continued rising up the shaft. "I wish I could have seen her. If we'd had time, I mean. My dad said she's really tall, a lady full of blinding light, and she leads all the souls into a pit, where they're turned into magic. And those balls of magic leak back into New Earth."

Again, the robed figure said nothing. He didn't need to. Travis believed he had it all figured out, though his mind reeled at the enormity of it all. *Wait until my dad hears about this!*

"Hey, will I remember anything from below?" he asked suddenly. "My dad said that people who visit the World of Darkness—mostly dead people, and people in deep comas or just going through a near-death experience—he said they forgot everything they saw once they returned to life. He said people might have vague memories like dreams of a white light, but mostly they just forgot."

"You're a special case," the Reaper said with what sounded like a hint of amusement.

Travis nodded. "I guess so. I'm actually here in the flesh."

They ascended out of the widening shaft and drifted across to the rim of the massive funnel. Thankfully, there was no sign of the dullahan. It felt good to touch down on solid ground again, even if that ground was essentially brain matter. Travis looked into the distant darkness, listening hard.

"I don't hear him," he whispered.

The Grim Reaper reached for his shoulder again. "Only the passage of time sours his lust for death, and very few have ever outlasted his patience. I fear we have returned too early."

But all Travis could think about was the prospect of returning home roughly two days after he'd left Rez behind. It was hard to believe. It felt like he'd only been in this underground cavern for an hour at the most, and just ten minutes or so in the World of Darkness. Two days outside! Rez probably would have waited in the woods for hours, perhaps overnight, then eventually returned home to break the news of what had happened. . .

Travis swallowed. By now, his parents already thought he was dead. The whole town assumed he was gone forever. What else had been happening? Had Rez brought townsfolk out to the forest to investigate the dead scorpions and confused trolls? Had he thought to destroy the Treentacle at the Prison of Despair?

"Take me up," he said to the Reaper.

Chapter 30
Homeward Bound

Instead of relocating directly to the surface, the Reaper delivered Travis to the foot of the towering trunk where listless tentacles swayed in the darkness above. Dirt, rocks, and dead branches littered the glowing surface of the brain, along with dead scorpions.

"We're back where we started," Travis said, stepping away from the Reaper's ice-cold touch, which chilled him to the bone. "I thought you were taking me up to the forest?"

"I have a client."

Puzzled, Travis watched as the Grim Reaper glided across the peaks and dips of the terrain. He headed toward an unidentifiable heap on the fringes of the darkness. The hooded Reaper held his scythe stiff and upright, his black robes flowing behind.

Travis hurried after him. What kind of *client* could the Reaper possibly have down here in this empty, subterranean landscape? But then, as he drew closer, he identified the strange heap and sucked in a sharp breath. It was a shaggy-haired troll lying on his side with his legs drawn up. Motionless, he was either asleep or—

"Wait!" Travis whispered sharply. "You can't take his—I mean, he's not dead, is he?"

"He will be shortly."

The Reaper stood over the troll, waiting. Travis knelt and peered closely at the shaggy face. This was Zoth, who'd fallen with him into the abyss. His eyes were closed, his breathing shallow.

"What's wrong with him?" Travis asked softly. "It's only been two days, right? He can't be *that* bad already."

"He did not descend as gracefully as you," the Reaper said in a quiet, respectful voice. "He bumped against the shaft wall three times on the way down and broke several bones. He also hit his head on the tentacles as he tried to arrest his fall, after which he clung on for several hours before a brain bleed caused him to lose consciousness. He fell the rest of the way and landed softly, woke for a while, crawled, and then suffered a hemorrhage. He has lain here, unmoving, for the past thirty-three hours and is due to die several minutes from now, at which point I will take his soul and—"

"Stop!" Travis hissed. He glared sideways at the Reaper's hood. "Why didn't you say something? If you knew he was here the whole time, we could have helped!"

The skull turned to face him. "We were otherwise engaged."

"Yes, but—"

"It is not my place to save lives. This troll is fated to die. His plight came to my attention a short time ago, and now I must wait. It is my duty to safely deliver his soul."

Travis balled his fists and chewed his lip, feeling utterly helpless. "But . . . he's not dead yet. We can do something, right? Let's get him to the surface. Maybe the other trolls can help? We should let them try. And if he dies, at least he'll be in the right place."

The Reaper said nothing.

"Please!" Travis begged. "Just—just do *something*. You stopped the dullahan from killing me, so I know you can bend the rules a bit. Let's save this troll."

"Fate has already determined—"

"I don't care about fate! He's not dead yet! *Help* him!"

The Reaper tilted his skull and stared at Travis with black, eyeless sockets. "He means that much to you?"

Travis nodded vigorously. "Of course he does. Why shouldn't he?" He frowned and shrugged. "Okay, I know he attacked me and everything, but . . . well, he's a troll. It's what they do. It's just not right to leave him here to die when you have the power to do something for him."

"I have no such power. My duties are clear: collect the souls of those who die."

"He's not going to die," Travis said firmly. "Do trolls even *have* souls? And why do you—? Never mind. Please, Mr. Reaper. Help him!"

In the back of his mind, he marveled at the craziness of the situation. Here he was, a mere twelve-year-old boy, arguing with the Grim Reaper while standing on top of a giant brain deep underground. Arguing for the life of a troll who'd ambushed him in the forest.

The Reaper lowered his scythe a few inches. "This . . . is most irregular."

The moment he said that, three figures materialized one by one out of nowhere less than twenty feet away. The first two were human, the third a massive hound. The human figures were nothing but bones. One was wrapped in shabby grey rags that hung off his skeleton. It looked like he'd just crawled out of a grave. The other wore a wide-brimmed hat and a long coat. Despite his skull, he had wispy grey hair hanging past his shoulders. Both carried scythes.

The hound was absolutely black, with paws as big as a bear's. Its eyes glowed bright white.

Travis shuddered and sidled closer to the Reaper. "Who are they?" he whispered.

"Other Reapers."

"*Other* Reapers?"

"There are many of us. You caused me to falter in my task, and that moment of doubt summoned others." He raised a hand and pointed to the shabby, grey-robed figure. "The Meager Hein, sometimes called the Bone-Man. The one with the hat is Ankou. And the hound is a Gabble Ratchet."

"Gabble Ratchet," Travis repeated. He swallowed. "Are they, uh . . . are they friendly?"

All three inched forward, their eyes on the troll.

Still holding his scythe upright, the Reaper knelt beside the troll, peered at him for a moment, then looked up at the newcomers. He raised his voice above the usual harsh whisper. "I believe I will relocate this one to the surface. He will die as fated, and then I will reap his soul myself."

The Gabble Ratchet let out a soft growl. The other two merely glanced at one another. Travis swore he could feel a blast of cold air rolling off them, and a smell of death lingering in the air.

The Reaper laid his scythe across the troll and planted his bony hand on the upturned hairy shoulder. He held out his free hand to Travis. "We will go now."

Travis shot his hand out. Right before he made contact, the hound let out a howl.

* * *

Travis blinked in dazzling daylight and shielded his face. It took a while for his eyes to adjust, and he stood there studying the palms of his dirty hands for a good thirty seconds.

"Thank you, Mr. Reaper, you saved me. And you saved Zoth, too. I'll do my best to get help for him, and then I'm heading home to see if . . . if . . ."

He trailed off as his eyes finally adjusted to the bright light. He stood in the middle of a clearing in the forest, near the large crater where he'd fallen into the abyss—literally back where he'd started. Only the hole was no more. It had closed up. A few empty baskets lay here and there, and thousands of tiny, dried-up scorpion carcasses littered the place as well as some much bigger specimens with flies buzzing around them. Travis wrinkled his nose in disgust as their rotting smell filled his nostrils.

The eight-foot troll named Zoth lay stretched out on his back, still unconscious.

The Reaper was gone.

"Well," Travis muttered, "I guess I'm on my own again."

Except he wasn't. He jumped when, over his shoulder, he spotted two stout goblins staring at him. Both wore rough leather clothing and had deep frowns on their piglike faces.

"You're dead," one said.

Travis opened and shut his mouth a few times, then managed to get a few words out. "Obviously not. What are you—?" Then he remembered two days had passed. Of course goblins were here. Miss Simone had probably ordered them to come out and investigate.

"Who were you talking to?" the other goblin demanded.

Travis looked around again. "Uh, nobody. Look, this troll needs help. He's hurt pretty bad. Broken bones and a brain bleed. He's dying."

The goblins remained where they were, motionless, looks of deep suspicion and bewilderment on their faces. One pointed at him. "Where'd you come from? How'd you get here?"

"I'll explain later. Please help this troll before he dies, okay?"

He watched anxiously as they huffed and grumbled then stamped over to kneel by the troll. Goblins often traveled with at least one field medic in their group, and these two were likely the tail end of a rescue crew or perhaps an investigation team. Travis expected there were more around somewhere.

"He doesn't have long," one of the goblins muttered at last. "In a bad way. Can't do nothin' for him here. He'd probably die even if he was in the 'ospital. Best let the trolls take him home."

Without a word of argument, the other goblin stood up and shuffled off through the bushes. Travis noticed then that many bushes in the vicinity stood at weird angles, dark and withered. At least half a dozen trees had toppled over as well, their trunks completely hollowed out and rotting tentacles splayed out from the bottom end.

"Where's he going?" Travis asked, tearing his gaze from the carnage.

The goblin scowled at him. "To fetch the trolls." He said it as though it were obvious, and Travis suddenly felt stupid. "There's a bunch of 'em nearby." He stood up. "You got some explainin' to do. Come with me."

"I'll explain on the way home," Travis said firmly. "We don't have much time."

"That's why I said come with me."

The goblin stomped past and pushed a withered bush aside. Travis wrung his hands, looking down again at the poor troll. Even if nothing could be done for him, he couldn't stand the idea of leaving him alone to die. Zoth had been a mean one, demanding payment and then attacking ... but Travis had burned his chest in return, and they were square. Everything else was the Seer's fault, a common enemy to both humans and trolls. Zoth seemed more like a fallen comrade now.

"Zoth—" he said, awkwardly, moving closer.

"COME ON!" the goblin roared from behind him.

Travis jumped and swung around. The goblin gestured fiercely, his scowl deeper than ever. They were *always* bad-tempered, though. It was perfectly normal. This one just seemed a little more peeved than usual.

Travis sighed and followed the goblin through the trees. But as he glanced back again, he spotted movement in the trees and paused again. A group of very tall, shaggy trolls towered over a stout goblin as they pushed through the undergrowth toward the clearing. Maybe Zoth would get to die in the company of his own kind after all. Better than alone, deep underground.

The Grim Reaper appeared out of nowhere. The mysterious robed figure stood in the way of the approaching group, but they walked right through him without pause and knelt around the dying troll. A minute passed while the four trolls and short goblin inspected Zoth closely, and as one, by some unspoken agreement, they straightened up.

Travis knew Zoth was dead.

So did the Reaper, who passed through the crowd and bent to reach into the troll's chest. When he straightened, he pulled out a wispy dark-grey cloud . . . and then vanished with it.

"You done gawking?" his goblin guide snapped from behind him.

Travis nodded and followed after him, filled with sadness. Then his sadness gave way to anger. The Seer had to be stopped. He had to get back to Carter and destroy the Treentacle at the Prison of Despair before it gave birth to thousands more scorpions.

He stared at the ground the whole time as the goblin led the way through the trees to the main road. Only then did he look up to find an entire campsite pitched there, blocking the way. Three tents, a couple of wagons, four horses grazing by the roadside, at least ten goblins, and—

Travis stared in surprise. Rez stood there, his mouth hanging open and his eyes wide.

"Hey," Travis said, offering a wave.

Rez's mouth worked up and down, but it was still a few more seconds before he was able to get a word out. "TRAVIS!" he yelled, and came running over.

As Travis was nearly bowled over by his jubilant friend, two more figures appeared from behind one of the tents—his mom and dad, both looking weary and pale.

Ignoring Rez's barrage of questions, Travis looked past him to his stricken parents. His dad stood absolutely still as if a gorgon had turned him to stone again, while his mom sank to her knees, her hands flying to her face and tears flowing down her cheeks.

Oh boy, Travis thought. *This is gonna be rough.*

Chapter 31
The Prison of Despair

Travis clung to the knobby ridges on his dad's broad reptilian shoulders, his legs straddling the rock-hard armor plating. His mom hugged him from behind, using the excuse that it was *very* important to hold tight while soaring through the sky on the back of a dragon. It was, but she didn't need to hold *that* tight.

Rez clung on, too. He was farther back, moaning with terror. This was actually his second time in the air. Travis had tried to persuade his friend many times in the past, saying "Honest, my dad won't mind, come for a ride with us!" but always receiving a polite and somewhat appalled refusal. All that changed after Travis's fall into a bottomless pit. Rez had stayed the night in the woods staring mournfully into the darkness, surrounded by dead bugs. He'd ignored the disgruntled trolls, and they'd left him alone. He'd headed home the next morning and tearfully told his story, and then a ride on the back of a dragon had been mandatory; he and Travis's parents had returned to the scene of the incident with a team of goblins following on the ground.

That was yesterday, and it had been grim. Now they were all riding home together.

Travis nearly jumped out his skin when his mom yelled in his ear over the wind. "Tell us again! Say it louder so your dad can hear."

So Travis retold his story, starting with how he fell into the abyss and followed the white-tentacled monster down. He skipped some of the details simply because it was hard work shouting over the wind, but he included all the important bits—the massive underground brain, the Treentacles sticking up in certain locations, the weird shaft leading down into the

World of Darkness where time crawled—all of it. He made sure to include the Grim Reaper and the other three weirdos that had popped up toward the end, but he glossed over the dullahan part, suggesting the headless horseman had lost interest in him.

He hoped that was true. It just had to be! And if so, there was no point worrying anybody about it now. They had enough to think about.

"So do you think Miss Simone cut the tentacle monster down yet?" he called over his shoulder.

"We'll see," his mom said. "That was her intention after Rez told his version of events, but we left in a hurry, and she's been *very* busy lately. I'm sure she got her best team of goblins on it. They probably relished the challenge of cutting down an indestructible plant."

"It's not a plant."

"I know, I know. It's just . . . Even now, it's so hard to believe. I never doubted your dad all these years, but still, it's one thing being told there's a giant brain under the ground, but quite another to . . . to . . ."

Travis laughed. "To be told by someone else as well? You should *see* it, Mom. It's gigantic. It goes on and on for miles. It's under us right now, stretching from the Treentacle in the woods all the way to Carter—and even bigger than that."

His mom said nothing. Travis suspected she still had trouble swallowing the idea.

His dad, however, did not. He let out a grunt, which Travis knew meant, "Yup."

They thumped down in Carter at last. Rez walked about stretching his legs while the immense dragon reverted to human form.

Travis's stomach growled. "Is it dinnertime?"

"Oh, you must be starving!" his mom exclaimed. "It's probably after six by now."

Travis had already noticed how low the sun was. It had also been low before he'd fallen down the shaft. The Reaper had

propelled him forward almost exactly forty-eight hours. "Yeah, I'm hungry. But I want to go to the prison first. That monster's due to open up."

As it happened, his dad wanted to go there straight away, too. He'd landed on the outskirts of the town, and from here it was a winding walk through dense woods. The prison had never been easy to get to from the sky; landing through the trees was dangerous.

"Let's go," his dad said, leading the way. "We can eat later. Or we'll ask a goblin to grab us something."

The four of them walked together, and Travis felt a moment of happiness. Together with his parents and best friend again, taking a stroll in the evening, nothing in the woods about to jump out at them. It felt good. For now, anyway.

Rez kept giving him sideways looks. "Thought you were dead, man," he grumbled at last.

"Me too," Travis replied. "I would have been if gravity had worked properly down there."

His dad clamped a hand on his shoulder. "I reckon there's a reason for that. A brain that size, all that weight? Maybe it wouldn't survive if normal gravity applied. So it generates a kind of magical field and just floats down there."

Travis couldn't argue with that. His descent had definitely slowed, and he'd touched down lightly, like a man on the moon or a diver on the seabed. Either comparison worked. After that he'd walked normally across the surface of the brain, yet it seemed all the Reapers managed to float about the place. Of course, they were supernatural beings, so . . .

"But where did it come from?" he wondered aloud.

His mom nudged him. "Why didn't you ask the Grim Reaper?"

"Oh man, I never thought to!"

"You were busy."

"Yeah," he agreed. *Busy being chased by the dullahan.*

As they neared the prison, his dad said, "I want you to know, buddy, that I was prepared to come down after you.

When Rez told us his story, we flew straight out, and I planned to throw myself down into the abyss after you."

Travis slowed. "That would have been nuts!"

"That's what I told him," his mom said. "But there *was* no hole. The shaft had closed up, collapsed in on itself or something. It was gone, no way down."

"So we've been here ever since, trying to figure out what to do," Travis's dad said shortly. "We considered grabbing some heavy equipment from Carter, or better still Old Earth—something big and mechanical to dig with. I'd still like to go down there sometime." He looked at Travis. "Just how deep *is* that pit?"

Travis had no idea. "Deep," he offered. "I fell for ages."

His dad clicked his tongue and shook his head. "I can't help thinking that destroying these things—these Treentacles—is nothing but a nuisance to whatever's down there." He looked sideways at Travis and lowered his voice. "I don't talk about this much, but from what the Gatekeeper told me, that giant brain down there created New Earth as a social experiment. It was meant as an alternative version of Earth with a mixture of other intelligent species to rival humans. It worked, too. People behave themselves better in this world. They respect the planet more. The existence of centaurs and elves and the naga is a positive influence on the human race. New Earth is better than Old. The tradeoff is that the brain needs to study us, so it wakes every few hundred years and craves information, like a briefing, and it does that by plugging into us for a few months."

Travis listened intently. Never again would he doubt his dad's wild ideas. "But . . . plugging into us? *Using* us and taking over our minds?"

"Oh, don't get me wrong. We can't allow that. We need to destroy these Treentacles. I just wonder what it will do next . . ."

They rounded a corner and came across the infamous Prison of Despair. Nestled in the woods, the trees hung over the top and crammed up all around. The stone steps were wide, the large double doors solid oak. Two goblin sentries stood outside, but the real muscle was the enormous three-headed cerberus that stood up and growled.

"Down," one of the sentries muttered, and the grey-furred hound lay back down, still baring its teeth.

The goblins asked no questions. If the famous shapeshifters Hal and Abigail Franklin wanted access to the prison, then so be it. One of them opened a door and gave a dutiful nod as he stepped aside.

Travis's parents entered first. His mom turned and winked. "Don't linger."

He and Rez followed them in. There were no guards inside, and for good reason—white tendrils snaked about the ceiling, wrapped around the ivy and vines that had long ago crept into the building. The whole place looked like it was losing a battle with the encroaching woods, and even the thick glass in the barred windows had cracked open to allow more vegetation in.

The main trunk of the Treentacle was out back, but still the delicate milky-white tendrils on the ceiling caused time to skew for those foolish enough to end up a prisoner here.

"Two inmates this week," his dad whispered as they crowded into the wide lobby. An old office stood to the left, generally used for storage. Ahead, around a corner to the right, lay a corridor with cells on both sides. "One savagely beat up his brother over a girl. The other is in for robbery. Both are spending time contemplating their errors. A few days here will feel like weeks, and a week or two will feel like months."

Only the cell fronts were barred. Thick walls separated them. The group walked single file down the corridor to avoid groping arms, but neither prisoner seemed interested. They sat in neighboring cells, each perched on a bunk, staring into space. One blinked and frowned as if noticing in his periphery that people had arrived, but if he glanced over at all, Travis and the rest had already passed by.

The ceiling was so thick with vegetation that it reduced the headspace a foot or two and hung down the walls. Travis peered up at it as he walked, repulsed by the number of thin white tendrils. So innocuous . . . yet part of something so dangerous.

They all turned left at the end of the corridor into a darker passage leading to the back of the prison. This place had been like a jungle at one time, but most of the vines and ivy had been cut away, leaving only the white appendages—and they were thicker here, actual tentacles, because this end of the prison was much closer to the source.

Solitary confinement on the right had not been used in a very long time. In fact, Emily Stanton, the naga shapeshifter, had been the last to spend time in that awful room back in the days when Queen Bee had locked up all the shapeshifters while she took control of Carter.

Travis's dad marched straight to the end of the corridor and threw open the external door. Outside, a twenty-foot portion of the woods had been chopped away to clear some space around the trunk of the Treentacle. It stood there against the back wall of the prison, its limbs splitting off in all directions overhead. Half of them had threaded their way into the prison through cracks and openings a long, long time ago, along with the ivy and vines.

Travis had been here before, but normally the enclosed clearing out back was empty and silent. On occasion, his dad sat with his back against the white trunk. Travis's job was to wake him after fifteen minutes or so, which felt much longer to his dad. *Sharing information*, his dad had always said with a grin. *Doing my bit to feed the brain.*

How sinister all that seemed now.

Today, the clearing wasn't empty at all. Three goblins sat cross-legged on the dirt, staring into space. They had a collection of tools scattered around them—several hammers, shovels, picks, a heavy ax, a long two-handled saw, a large hand-drill, even a motorized chainsaw from Old Earth.

"Aw, come on," Travis's dad muttered. He kicked one of the goblins' boots. "Wake up!"

The goblin jerked and blinked. "Wassat . . ."

After the other goblins had been roused from their slumber, Travis's dad stood with his hands on his hips and a frown on his face. "How long have you been sitting here? Wait, don't answer that. It probably felt like a week to you. One of you was supposed to stand outside the prison and check on the others every ten minutes. Did you forget?" He shook his head. "Have you done anything at all?"

The three goblins were standing now, looking grumpier than usual. One snarled and pointed at the chainsaw. "Try and see, Mr. Franklin."

"How about you show me?"

So the goblin got to work, yanking the cord and firing up the chainsaw. Travis stepped back in alarm as the machine roared and belched a plume of smoke. The goblin stepped toward the thick white trunk and pulled the trigger, and the saw roared even louder as it cut into the surface.

Or rather, *didn't* cut into it.

The chain skipped and bounced, leaving a series of scuffs and a couple of gouges. But the gouges quickly filled in, and the trunk smoothed out again. Even the scuffs faded.

The goblin gave up, disgusted. He tossed the chainsaw down and threw up his hands. "See, it ain't doin' nothing."

"And you've tried burning it?" Travis put in.

The goblin pointed to a can of gasoline that he'd presumably brought along for the chainsaw. "Poured it around the base of the trunk and set it alight. Burned good and hot for a while, but—"

He gestured to a faint coating of soot on the smooth, white surface on the backside of the trunk. It looked like the goblin had succeeded in burning up any dead leaves and twigs on the ground, and had left a black smudge on the prison wall, but the trunk itself stood unharmed.

"We tried digging around it," another goblin said, his words a little slurred. He looked like he might be sliding back into a dream state again. "Spent days doing that."

"Minutes, more like," Travis's mom muttered. "Shame we can't get a crane out here. One of those big things from Old Earth might work. We could just lift this plant right out of the ground."

"Uh, no," Travis said. "There's no way you'd pull *that* thing out of the ground. It's massive, Mom. It stretches all the way down to the brain. It's like a beanstalk."

As everyone turned to stare at him, he felt his face heat up and looked away. *Really? Like a beanstalk?*

"So we can't cut into it," his dad said, "and we can't dig it up, and we can't burn it. What's left? Any ideas?"

Travis turned to find Rez standing there with a droopy look to his eyelids, his mouth open slightly. "Hey, wake up!" he said, clicking his fingers in front of his friend's face.

Rez jerked. "What? What do you mean? I wasn't asleep. I'm just bored. Seems like you've been talking about this thing for hours now."

Travis had to admit it felt that way, though he knew it couldn't be so. He looked at his dad. "If we could just poke a hole in it and force something hot down inside . . . That's pretty much what I did, except it opened itself up when the baby scorpions poured out."

His dad turned to the goblins. "You tried drilling, right?"

"Barely made a mark. Anyway, as soon as we pulled it loose, the dent filled in."

His dad sighed and nodded. "Well, we may just have to wait for the newborns, then. Let's get away from here. We'll come back every hour to check on it. Heck, every half-hour if we need to. You said it forms a blister when it's about to happen, right?"

And then splits open and spills thousands of miniature scorpion-bugs everywhere, Travis thought with a shudder.

He resigned himself to a long night.

Chapter 32
Night Watch

"See, this is what's wrong with being a shapeshifter and having big adventures," Rez complained, batting at a mosquito. "You have to stay out all night in case some monster-plant opens up and sprays deadly brain-eating scorpions everywhere."

Travis sighed. "Go home, then."

They huddled over the fire. Several goblins snored nearby. Two more sat on a log having a muted conversation while chewing on roasted chestnuts. Travis's parents had stretched out on a rug to study the stars, though it looked more like his dad had fallen asleep.

Camping on the narrow lane outside the Prison of Despair wasn't unheard of. That was what the convenient logs and ready-made rock-walled campfire pits were for. Goblins had been roasting chestnuts here for decades.

"How long's this going to take?" Rez asked. "I mean, you said those bugs were ripe, so they should be spilling out soon, right? It's gotta be past midnight by now."

"Ripe," Travis repeated with a laugh. "Yeah, well, the Grim Reaper said it would be a few days, and it's been slightly more than two days already, so it should be tonight or tomorrow."

"Great."

"Look, I said you could go home. Seriously, you don't have to be here. There's nothing you can do anyway. You don't have fire breath. You have *bad* breath, but not fire breath."

Rez ignored the slur. "Nor do you, actually. Your chimera power has worn off."

This gave Travis pause. "Actually," he muttered . . .

And he transformed, making Rez yell out and stumble backward. Travis couldn't help chuckling to himself as he padded around in a circle. He felt a little warmer now thanks to the thick mane around his throat.

"Interesting," his mom said, sitting up. "Rez is right, your power should have worn off by now."

Travis reverted back so he could speak. "It's been four days for you, but only two for me. It should be wearing off soon, though."

One of the goblins got up and shuffled away. They'd been taking it in turns about every thirty minutes to check the status of the monster behind the prison. This time, though, he returned in a hurry. "There's somethin' new," he barked. "A bulge."

Everyone immediately jumped up—Travis, his parents, Rez, the two chestnut-chewing goblins, and another couple who had been sound asleep.

They hurried along to the prison. The cerberus immediately stood up and growled, and a goblin told him to shut up and lie down. Seeing the approaching group, the sentries came down off the steps, obviously eager to help with whatever was going on.

"Go ahead and get those prisoners out of here," Travis's dad ordered. "Move them to the jail in the middle of town. And take the hound with you."

The sentries grunted and hurried inside.

Without another word, Travis's dad led the way around the side of the prison. Long ago, he'd created a very narrow passage between the wall and the dense vegetation, but it was hard to maintain. Since they'd had nothing else to do while waiting this evening, he'd spent a bit of time in dragon form yanking and pushing at the brambles, burning bits of it, trying to clear it back a little. The passage was awkward, but it beat traipsing in and out of the prison and down the corridor every time.

The indestructible trunk stood just around the back corner. The group marched into the clearing and peered suspiciously at the monstrosity, which seemed to glow in the light of several lamps hanging from branches.

Travis moved closer, already feeling that they'd been standing there too long. He was surprised the thing hadn't split open already. He studied the smooth surface of each thick tentacle. Where they stuck out of the ground so tightly clustered together, they'd long ago formed a skin over the surface that made them seem like one large trunk. Still, Travis knew each tentacle was a potential delivery system, each one capable of splitting open and releasing the Seer's new brood.

He gasped when he saw a bulbous mound. It pulsed gently, breathing in and out.

"It's about ready," he whispered.

Two of the goblins, each wearing heavy leather gloves, brought forward a short section of a black-painted iron drainpipe they'd pulled off the side of the prison. It was useless anyway; the gutters had hung loose for a long time, and even the drainpipe had broken apart at the joints. Tonight, that four-foot pipe would have another use.

They readied themselves, holding the drainpipe horizontally like they were about to pole-vault over the bushes. They pointed one end toward the white trunk and waited.

And waited.

Time passed, and Travis's dad had to keep barking at them all to wake up. He seemed less affected than everyone else, perhaps because he'd spent so much time feeding the brain. Meanwhile, Travis's mom took off into the air with her faerie wings buzzing, so she could watch from above and not get sucked into the time-skewing magic.

Still, Travis couldn't believe how long they waited. Despite the constant wake-up calls from his parents, time dragged horribly. Rez kept saying he was bored.

"How long's it been now?" he groaned.

"About ten minutes," Travis's mom called from above.

The trunk pulsed more now, and it illuminated in a ghostly light. Everyone let out a murmur of awe. It was really happening. A flicker of movement inside the trunk—inside one particular tentacle—suggested the scorpions were on their way.

A distant cackle of laughter sounded. Travis pricked up his ears, distracted. Then, as he stood there with bated breath, he thought he heard a low thundering sound carrying across the night sky. His mouth fell open. *No way*, he thought with mounting horror.

He glanced around. Nobody else seemed to have noticed. And maybe it really was just thunder. But if it *wasn't* . . .

"Travis," his dad whispered.

Refocusing on the trunk, Travis gasped when he saw that the blister had started to split. It was a ten-inch horizontal opening, and as it widened, clear liquid oozed out and dribbled down the side.

Then, abruptly, tiny white scorpions spewed forth.

"Now!" Travis shouted.

The goblins didn't need telling. They rammed the pipe into the split and lifted their end as high as their short arms allowed. Scorpions continued streaming around the blockage and falling to the ground, but they also began scuttling up the pipe and out the end.

Travis transformed, thinking of the goat. He immediately started working on a fireball.

Meanwhile, his dad ran to the end of the pipe and gripped it, trying to ignore the miniature creatures that toppled out onto his shoulders. The group had talked about this plan earlier. His dad had suggested breathing fire down into the split, but getting the angle just right would be difficult, and fire had a tendency to spread out, so he'd have to be uncomfortably close to the blister. Hence the pipe, to avoid both issues.

It helped that he could breathe fire while in human form . . . except that the scorplings continued streaming out. With a grimace, he pressed his face to the end of the pipe and let loose with a blast of fire. The roar was surprisingly loud, and the goblins immediately reared back as the iron heated up. They kept hold of it, though, their gloves smoldering a little.

Fire licked out the lower end of the pipe and into the blister. The whole trunk lit up inside, and though scorpions continued streaming, now they came out black and smoking, twitching as they hit the ground. The trunk visibly shuddered, and the ground cracked. The trees rustled above as numerous tentacles jostled against the branches.

"Again!" Rez shouted.

Travis's dad took a deep breath, then pressed his face to the pipe again and let loose with another long blast of fire. But this time the goblins yelled and let go of the steaming pipe, and the whole thing dropped to the ground with flames licking out the end. It squashed some of the scorpions where it landed.

There had been a momentary falter as the trunk jerked in pain. But after a brief sputter, the stream of newborns resumed, almost spraying from the blister now.

"Pick it up!" Travis's dad yelled at the goblins.

"Too hot!" a goblin yelled back.

Without hesitation, he shifted to his dragon form and instantly filled the clearing, pushing everyone aside. He backed up as far as he could and blasted the trunk with fire. The entire thing was engulfed, and the heat was terrible. Hundreds of scorpions instantly turned black and curled up, and those that continued spewing from the split caught fire on their way to the ground.

But the brood kept on coming.

Travis was sure of two things. First, his dad was likely to spray the entire area with fire and burn every last one of the scorpions no matter how many more came out. That was good. Second, the trunk would eventually finish its job and close up, and then it would be indestructible again. That was bad. And more scorpions might be forthcoming. There might another two or three batches in the coming days.

He rushed forward the moment his dad paused to catch his breath. He heard his mom yell at him from above to get back out of the way, but he ignored her and leapt over the pile of smoldering scorpions. They stung his paws—which he felt despite being inside the goat's head—but fresh ones spilled out on top of the rest, and he ended up slipping and sliding on top of those instead.

He closed in on the blister, and his lion head ducked. Travis was ready. His fireball had been brewing the whole time, and now he coughed it up and shot it out. It hammered straight into the open blister and down the tube, a red-hot ball of lava burning everything it touched on the way down.

He leapt backward, aware of what might happen next— what he *hoped* would happen next.

As his dad resumed his fire-breathing and torched the rest of the scorpions, the Treentacle shuddered violently and thrashed about in the trees above. The split closed up, but it was too late. Like a choking giant in quicksand, the monster descended into the ground, slowly at first, then quickening. Cracks opened across the clearing, and everyone darted to safety as dirt tumbled in.

The clearing suddenly didn't seem big enough. "Everyone inside!" Travis's mom shouted from above. "All the way through to the front! Go!"

Rez, nearest to the door, wasted no time leading the way. He dashed inside, followed by a line of goblins, then Travis's dad as soon as he'd reverted to human form. Travis ran with him, still in chimera form.

They were no safer inside, though. It was like an earthquake was ripping the place apart. The thickest tentacles yanked loose, pulling parts of the wall down. The tendrils followed, bringing with them a great deal of the ivy and vines across the ceiling throughout the prison, and everyone had to throw themselves down as the whole lot swept by overhead, snagging and whipping at them. It seemed impossible for the tendrils not to be severed, but they remained intact, bringing down chunks of the ceiling and walls wherever they'd wound through nooks and crannies.

It was a good thing the goblins had relocated the prisoners earlier, because the whole backside of the prison seemed to be collapsing. The group rushed out the front door to a safe distance, then turned to watch as the thunderous noise continued for another few minutes. If the cerberus had still been here, it would have been barking all three heads off at the commotion. There wasn't much to see from the front, but trees swayed in the moonlight, and Travis knew a massive abyss had opened up. It had probably swallowed a section of the prison.

And then maybe closed in on itself afterward, like the last one had.

Travis reverted to human form and stood with his parents, Rez, and a group of goblins. A sense of calm settled over them all, and they grinned at each other. As it had turned out, burning the scorpions might not have been necessary. They'd most likely fallen back underground along with the Treentacle. And anyway, they'd all die or run around aimlessly without the voice of the Seer to guide them.

"The brain's really gonna be upset," he said to his dad.

"Yeah. We'll have to form a plan. There are plenty of other brain beasties to take care of, even if that means rigging up some sort of equipment at each location—I'm thinking metal pipes, a cauldron of boiling liquid or molten metal, that sort of thing." He thought for a moment. "Or I'll enlist the Army from Old Earth. They have grenades. It would be easier to drop a few of those in."

After a pause, Rez said, "Not as much fun, though."

They all laughed.

The thundering continued, now distant but persistent. "Well, let's go take a look," Travis's dad said, heading for the prison.

"Uh, shouldn't we wait?" Travis asked. "Sounds like it's still rumbling back there."

"Nah," Rez said, marching past. "Quiet as a mouse now. It's over, dude. We did it."

As the group headed toward the right-side of the prison and disappeared along the narrow path there, Travis hung back. A chill had crept in, and his heart thumped. "Mom?"

Hovering a few feet off the ground, she turned back. "Honey?"

Travis swallowed. "Don't you *hear* that?"

Buzzing back to him, she looked at him with a frown. "Hear what?"

"That . . . that *rumbling* sound. Sounds like thunder."

She dropped to the ground, retracted her wings, and listened. "I don't hear anything, sweetie. It's completely silent out here tonight. Even the crickets and cicadas have gone quiet."

Travis felt the bottom drop out of his world. The rumbling, thundering noise continued, rising in volume, echoing through the night sky. The thunder of hooves.

Just then, he heard a distant cackle of laughter.

Chapter 33
The Dullahan

"Travis," his mom said with wide eyes. "You look like you've seen a ghost. What's wrong?"

"It's the dullahan," he moaned. "He's coming for me."

She frowned. "But . . . you said he'd forgotten about you—"

"I know what I said, but he's coming for me, Mom! Can't you hear him?"

She shook her head and approached him, reaching for his shoulders. "Honey—"

The thundering of hooves increased suddenly, and Travis swung around, searching the forest all around. There really wasn't room for the dullahan to be galloping about in the trees, especially with a wagon, but nothing was certain when it came to supernatural beings that only he could see. The Grim Reaper had passed right through a group of trolls and goblins like they weren't there. The dullahan might come tearing out of the dense woods at any moment.

"Travis Franklin!" the dullahan roared, still some distance away, his voice floating through the trees.

Travis fell to his knees as a terrible feeling swept over him. It was like being cocooned in ice while squeezed by a giant hand. And he smelled death, as though he'd come upon a pile of rotting corpses. He felt sick and giddy, trembling all over.

"Travis!" his mom cried, bending to hug him. "What's happening? Do you see him?"

He'd never felt so scared in all his life. He wanted to collapse into a ball, but his mom held him upright, so he buried his face in her shoulder, painfully aware that tears streamed down his face. The dullahan had *said his name* . . . but he'd said it from a distance, its effect weakened. Spoken up close, it would certainly kill him. Travis had no doubt about it. His insides would shrivel up and rot in an instant, his heart squeezed in a viselike grip.

Paralyzed with fear, he almost slipped away in a state of shock, preferring to give up on life and block out whatever came next. But his mom shook him roughly, clasped her hands to his face, and spoke fiercely. "Fight him, my darling! Do you hear me? *Fight* him! You can still be a chimera, so be one right now and blast the dullahan with a fireball! Do it!"

He blinked at her.

"*Now*, Travis!"

Branches cracked and splintered, and when Travis looked to his left, he saw movement in the woods—something fast approaching, trampling over bushes without the slightest hesitation. And then it came into view, a headless man on a powerful armored horse, his cloak billowing, a wagon bouncing around behind, all lit up in a hazy glow. Though it couldn't really be crashing through the woods, it sure looked and sounded like it was.

Travis felt a sharp slap across his face.

"So help me—!" his mom growled. "Get your butt off the ground and *fight*."

Feeling the sting on his face, Travis focused—and transformed.

The dullahan exploded from the woods onto the narrow trail, skidding to a halt and swinging around to face them, the rattling wagon tilting to one side and thudding back down. As the horse whinnied and rose up on its hind legs, the headless man cracked his bone-whip. The noise sounded like a gunshot.

Fighting his terror, Travis—now in the head of the goat—worked on a fireball and prayed he could have it ready before the dullahan spoke his name again. But would a fireball even work against such a creature? Not even the Grim Reaper had caused it lasting harm.

"Is it here?" his mom whispered, looking at both the lion's and goat's faces and following their collective gaze.

It seemed impossible that she couldn't see nor hear this towering monster just twenty feet behind her in front of the prison entrance. But Travis could. He worked hard on his fireball. Maybe he could fire it off early, half-formed. It might be enough.

The dullahan's face—which was tucked under his arm—had lost all traces of mirth. Now he frowned and looked about, confused. He looked directly at Travis, at his mom, then beyond them and all around. He sniffed the air. He listened.

Travis froze, a glimmer of hope seeping in. He raised a paw to his mom's mouth, placing it carefully on her lips, his meaning clear: "Shh!"

She stared at him in silence while he stared over her shoulder at the dullahan.

The horseman yanked on his reins, and the horse galloped around in a tight circle, dragging the wagon with it. Its wheels looked ready to collapse and spring off the axles, but Travis guessed supernatural wagons like this could take all kinds of rough treatment and stay in one peace. The skin-colored tarpaulin, tied securely all around, was stretched taut over a load of something lumpy and unidentifiable—and then a skeletal arm flopped out from under the sheet, hanging down the side of the wagon, and Travis knew there had to be a dozen bodies under there. He shuddered.

The dullahan faced the other way now, the horse's tail swishing at a cloud of flies. The ghostly glow had a green tint to it, but as bright as it was, it didn't linger on any of the surrounding bushes, nor the front wall of the prison, nor even its steps.

Travis held absolutely still. The dullahan had seen him and his mom crouching there but didn't care. He was looking for one person only, a boy named Travis Franklin, who had apparently disappeared.

Emboldened, Travis nudged his mom, turned, and trotted off along the trail toward the town. He checked to see if she was following, and she was, hurrying along almost on tiptoes, glancing back every now and then. Behind her, the dullahan continued turning his horse this way and that, dragging the wagon sideways at times.

Don't say my name, Travis thought over and over. *Don't say my name.*

He picked up speed as they passed the goblin campfires, trotting faster than his mom could walk. Instead of breaking into a jog, she sprouted her faerie wings and lifted off the ground. Then she was able to keep up easily.

They left the dullahan behind. Travis began to feel he might make it out alive after all. But just then, a distant but booming voice shouted, "Travis Franklin!"

Again, he was gripped in a fist of ice. The sense of horror that descended on him coupled with the stench of death almost forced him to his knees, but being in chimera form helped, and he stumbled onward. The fireball he'd been storing in his throat belched up of its own accord, and he flung it ahead of him. It didn't go far. Flames roared for a few seconds as he tore past the small crater, but by the time he looked back at it, the ball had dimmed to a red-hot ember.

Finally, as he sprinted to a safe distance, he began to grin to himself. He'd beaten the dullahan, and all because he was a shapeshifter. He literally wasn't himself when in chimera form. But the horseman's booming voice would still have killed him if he'd been close enough.

So stay away, he thought grimly. *He can't find me if I stay in chimera form. I'll stay like this for days if I have to—*

A new jolt of fear made him grimace. He couldn't stay in this form. In fact, by his reckoning, he really only had until late morning at best. That wasn't enough time. The dullahan had been close. He would keep looking, and he would come for Travis the moment his shapeshifter power ran dry.

His mom still followed behind, buzzing with ease and shooting glances over her shoulder every so often. Travis wished he could talk to her, but she would never understand his endless bleats. He would have to find a patch of dirt or something and paw a message into the ground. He dared not revert to human form now.

He had a plan, though, and it involved Miss Simone.

* * *

Travis waited until he and his mom had found Miss Simone before trying to get his message across. She was at home, and she answered the door in a nightgown, looking haggard. She perked up at the sight of him, though.

"I was *so* pleased to hear the news of your return this evening," she said. "It's been a busy two days since Rezner told us the awful story. Among other things, I've been prepping new shapeshifters to explore underground and track you down. Robbie and Lauren's daughter Melinda is one of them. She's a year early, but . . ."

Travis bleated and dragged her outside by her sleeve. He wrote "Need to be new shapeshifter NOW" in a dry patch of dirt to the side of the cottage. Miss Simone stared at the words, then asked his mom to explain what was going on.

She tried her best, and to her credit guessed most of it correctly. "He's being pursued by a *dullahan*? Do you know what that is? Anyway, I think this *dullahan* lost the scent when Travis transformed, which is why he's still a chimera right now. But that power is wearing off soon."

Miss Simone stared at him and pushed her tousled hair away from her face. "Travis, I must say your power's lasted longer than I thought it would—wait, no, I forgot, you lost time in the World of Darkness. Sorry, I've had a busy day." She squinted. "You're two days behind, correct? So I suppose your power will be wearing off in the morning . . ."

"And then the dullahan will find him."

"But Abigail, he can't stay in another form forever," Miss Simone said with a frown. "I mean, he could if his immune system would allow it, but it won't. He'll only have two days. And then what? We perform another procedure? And then another, and another? Is he planning to avoid being human for the rest of his life?"

Travis's mom spread her hands. "I'm not sure. I just know he needs a procedure very soon, before he ends up back in human form and pursued by the dullahan."

They talked about it while Travis waited anxiously. It was well past midnight, and he hoped he would have another five to ten hours as a chimera. That should be enough time for a new procedure as long as Miss Simone didn't wait until morning.

"I'll get dressed," she said, sounding weary. "We'll do this now, tonight."

Yes! Travis thought.

And so the three of them headed to the laboratory. Travis desperately wished he could join in with their discussion, especially when they started throwing in ideas for what he should become next.

"How about a faerie?" his mom suggested.

Travis bleated rudely.

Luckily, Miss Simone shook her head. She seemed to be getting a handle on the predicament. "I fear that may be too close to human. The dullahan may see through the disguise. I think something utterly inhuman would be better."

Something with wings, Travis thought, wondering if he could possibly escape the dullahan by soaring into the sky. Or could the headless horseman fly, too? It wouldn't surprise him. And the wagon probably wouldn't be much of a hindrance to such a supernatural being.

The women discussed the possibility of a unicorn, something much faster than an average horse. But there was nothing average about the dullahan. Then Nitwit came up in conversation. The petite imp had a knack of vanishing very quickly, and it seemed she could instantly transport to another location. An imp would be perfect!

Yet Miss Simone still feared Travis would be too humanlike, so the idea was abandoned. They threw in other suggestions including a few water dwellers—the hippocampus being a favorite—but that meant Travis would be unable to communicate *and* be nowhere near Carter.

"To keep him from being recognized," Miss Simone said, "I think he'll to have go incognito for a while. No speaking, nothing recognizable at all."

Travis's mom sighed. "I suppose so. Do you have something in mind?"

Miss Simone smiled. "You'll see."

Travis bleated noisily. *What is it? Tell me! What is it?*

* * *

Miss Simone performed the procedure herself.

It was strange being in the laboratory this late at night. Hardly anybody wandered the corridors, and most of the lights were dim. A couple of goblin guards looked astonished at the sight of a chimera stalking about, but they eyed Miss Simone and said nothing.

Remaining in his three-headed chimera form, Travis drank the special 'sleep tea' from a saucer and began to feel drowsy. He leapt up onto the table and lay down with his paws dangling over one side and his long snake-tail over the other. He allowed his goat's head to lay against the table's edge, noting that the lion did the same.

Miss Simone peered down at him, looking bemused. "This is highly irregular. It's one thing having such a wonderful beast on my table, but . . . doing a shapeshifter procedure on one?"

"He has to stay hidden," Travis's mom warned.

"I know, I know. But this is uncharted territory. His chimera shapeshifter blood still fills his veins, and now I'm about to give him *different* shapeshifter blood. I suppose it'll be fine, though." She patted Travis on one furry shoulder. "I've had such a busy day that I never thanked you personally."

He grunted weakly.

She leaned closer. "You and Rezner saved us all. You prevented an invasion of something nobody's even heard of before, something that's unknown in recorded history. From what I understand, the Seer would have released their hold eventually, but at what cost? How life-threatening such an invasion would have been in the end is a mystery, but nobody wants to be used as puppets even for a minute. You and your friend were in the right place at the right time."

His vision began to swim. Miss Simone leaned over him, her mouth moving and an endless stream of words echoing softly through his head. He caught some of them, but most blended together.

". . . ordered the destruction of every one of those awful tentacle plants. That's your dad's job, Travis. He can take care of it. He knows where they are. And we need to get the word out to other parts of the world . . ."

What kind of shapeshifter am I going to be next? he wondered. *Not that I care. I'll settle for a squonk as long as the dullahan doesn't find me.*

". . . time for Robbie and Lauren's daughter to become a shapeshifter. She's only eleven, but I'd already starting prepping her, so . . ."

Melinda? he thought sleepily. *A shapeshifter?*

And then everything went black.

Epilogue

He woke.

Instead of opening his eyes to the glare of a ceiling-mounted light fixture as he usually did after a procedure, instead he seemed to be lying on his belly staring along the ground at a patch of grass to one side of a path. He recognized the place immediately. This was the approach to the laboratory. For some reason, Miss Simone had taken him outside while he slept.

He realized with a jolt that it was morning already. He'd been asleep at least six or seven hours judging by the brightening sky.

Blinking, he tried to move his limbs and found them heavy and dull. He let out a groan and frowned. Even his voice sounded strange, not at all like the chimera he'd gotten used to.

He jerked in surprise. He'd been inside the goat's head when he'd fallen asleep, and now—well, clearly that was no longer the case, because the lion's head no longer jutted up in front of him. He must have switched places at some point.

"Good morning, Travis," a familiar voice said. His mom stepped into view, smiling at him. "Just relax. Simone gave you a sedative earlier, because you started thrashing about on the table. We brought you outside just in time."

"Just in time?" he mumbled, but his words came out *really* strange, deep and rumbling, not at all human.

His dad appeared then, and so did Rez and Miss Simone. All seemed happy enough, which reassured him nothing was wrong. So why did he feel so weird?

"The procedure worked fine, son," his dad said. "A few hours afterward, you woke mumbling and fidgeting, and your chimera fur started changing into scales. We all panicked, thinking you were about to transform into your new shape right there in the lab, so we drugged you again and carried you outside. And just in time, because you changed anyway, while you were sound asleep."

Scales? Travis thought.

With a monumental effort, he lifted his head and tried to twist around. He couldn't see much of anything, though—just a large clawed foot sticking out in front where he lay, and a great leathery wing that creaked when he opened it and made a fluttering sound when the wind caught the fine webbing.

Clawed foot, he thought dully. *Wing. Dark-green scales.*

"We felt you'd earned the right," his mom said, reaching forward to stroke his snout.

Snout!

"And it made perfect sense," his dad went on. "This way, you're completely inhuman so can stay hidden from the dullahan—but I can talk to you in my own tongue."

Travis stared at him, excitement mounting. Could it be . . . was he . . . ?

Miss Simone spoke then. "Melinda will be here this morning for her first procedure. We've already decided what kind of shapeshifter she should be. I'd like you both to stick together. I have a task for her, and I want you to be her protector. I know communication between you will be a challenge, but you'll figure it out."

Travis felt like he was in a dream. He heard every word she said, yet she sounded distant. He lifted his head a little more and pulled his front paws together, then pushed himself up. Looking down, he saw two reptilian paws exactly like his dad's. His wings, which he could easily spread out to the sides or lift high in the air, were also exactly like his dad's. And when he swung his long, club-ended tail around, he knew without a doubt that he was indeed a replica of his dad—a younger version, perhaps, but a full-fledged dragon all the same.

"Two days," Rez piped up, grinning broadly. "That's how long you have in this form. Then you're done forever. So make it last. And don't forget you can't be human, otherwise the dullahan will sniff you out again. You have to stay a dragon the whole time."

"And then be back here for another procedure before your power expires," Miss Simone added. "I did some research on the dullahan. As I understand it, you need to lie low for three or four days, and then he'll forget about you. So be a dragon, then be something else, and then you should be good."

Travis struggled to his feet, and everyone stepped back.

"Now," his dad warned, "just remember what you are. Mind that tail; it's easy to forget you have one. And don't go breathing random blasts of—"

Just as he said that, Travis belched up something hot that had been burning in his throat. A flash of fire shot out, and everyone leapt aside. Rez collapsed into laughter, and Travis's dad smiled, but the two women exclaimed and broke into lectures about dangerous beasts and how important it was to be a responsible shapeshifter.

Travis tuned them all out. The excitement he felt was almost overwhelming. A dragon at last! But only for two days. How fitting, then, that he absolutely had to remain in dragon form throughout. Two full days of flying around and breathing fire—oh, and protecting Melinda as she went on her first shapeshifter mission.

The memory of the dullahan still terrified him. He wasn't safe from that awful specter yet.

But he'd have fun hiding.

A SNEAK PEEK AT THE NEXT BOOK IN
THE ISLAND OF FOG LEGACIES . . .

Melinda still felt woozy from the sleep tea and laboratory procedure, but she tried not to let it show. She was a shapeshifter now, her first time ever! Her parents had actually gotten quite weepy when she'd transformed earlier.

But now it was down to business. She had a mission.

She glanced sideways at Travis. He'd spread his leathery wings out wide, providing much-appreciated shade from the hot sun, and his thick tail gently thumped on the grass as he looked off into the distance. Was that a smug grin on his scaly face? Did he really think *he* was going to be in charge?

She stepped out from under his wing. "Just so you understand," she said firmly, "this is *my* mission." As Travis swung his huge head to face her, she folded her arms and lifted her chin high. "Yeah, yeah, I get it. You're the son of Hal Franklin, the famous dragon shapeshifter, and now *you're* a dragon as well. But guess what? That doesn't make you the boss of me. Miss Simone is sending *me* on this mission, and you're just coming along to—"

She paused to choose her next word wisely. Not *protect*, nor even *help*. She didn't need either.

"To *assist* me," she finished. Yes, that was the one.

Travis's yellow eyes widened, his nostrils flaring even more than usual. Muscles bunched up on his shoulders and along his flanks. Fearsome claws dug into the earth. His club-ended tail swung back and forth, then thudded down. A low growl came from deep within his throat.

As impressive as he was, Melinda felt no fear. She had no doubt Travis could kill her any number of ways if he wanted to—burning, chomping, clawing, even squashing underfoot. Of course, there was no way he'd do such a thing. He couldn't and wouldn't, because he wasn't a real dragon, just an ordinary boy a little older than herself, one who happened to be in a spot of trouble and needed to remain in dragon form for the next few days. He could beat his wings and breathe fire all he wanted, but he was no danger to her. *She* was in charge here.

"Just wanted to make sure we're clear," she said. "Or you can stay here if you prefer. It's not like we can talk and catch up while you're stuck in that form." She pursed her lips. "Well, I can talk, but all you can do is listen. Do you think you can listen to me talking for a few days nonstop without being able to say a word back?"

Travis huffed and shook his head, rearing back with what seemed to be a reptilian look of horror.

Melinda laughed. "It's okay, I'll try not to talk too much. If you get bored, just grunt or something." A thought struck her. "Hey, maybe we can figure out some kind of sign language, or you can grunt in different ways to mean different things."

She edged toward him and reached up to pat his snout. He jerked back, and she giggled.

"Sorry," she said. "It's funny, though, isn't it? We grew up together like cousins, and I never would have patted you on the nose while you were human. But now that you're a dragon . . . well, you're like a giant pet."

Travis reversed, stomping hard. He threw back his head and let out a terrible roar, and red-hot flames blasted from his throat. When the fire cut off, a puff of black smoke curled away on a breeze.

Melinda laughed again, but inwardly this time. Having Travis along on her first mission was going to be fun, and she had to admit—secretly—that she'd feel much safer with a dragon by her side. Just as long as he didn't overstep his boundaries and try to take charge.

"Well, I guess we should get started," she said, pretending not to have noticed his outburst. "Before all those gargoyles tear up the town."

Her casual statement had the desired effect. She felt Travis's intense dragon stare on the side of her face as she peered absently into the distance. She waited a moment or two before feigning surprise.

"Oh! I just realized, you don't even know what my mission is yet!"

Travis grunted. It sounded suspiciously like *Duh!*

"Have you heard of a town called Garlen's Well? It's to the west. My mom flew out there last month and mentioned that the place is overrun by gargoyles, which has been perfectly all right for hundreds of years but recently has become a bit of a problem. They're getting mean and destructive, and people are asking for help. They asked for a shapeshifter to come and talk to them. That's where I come in."

The dragon lowered his head, listening intently.

Melinda pointed at her tiny brown suitcase. "I brought some overnight things. It might take a few days, or it might take a week, but you and me are going to find out what's going on and try to fix the problem."

Like our parents used to do when they were our age, she thought with excitement. Except for one tiny issue . . .

"It would have been helpful if I were a gargoyle shapeshifter," she said ruefully. "The easiest way to speak to gargoyles and try to understand their problems is to be one of them. But Miss Simone has never been able to extract DNA from a gargoyle. She made a golem once, which is a person made out of sticks and stones and animated by magic, but for some reason gargoyles are much more difficult, maybe impossible. So I can't be one, which is a nuisance."

She paused, knowing Travis was waiting with bated breath. It would be easy to transform right now and show him what she'd chosen to be for this mission—what Miss Simone had suggested might work—and it would be easier still to simply tell him.

But where was the fun in that?

"Well, let's go," she said, reaching for her small suitcase. "Apparently, you just need to fly west and look for three mountains in a row. Garlen's Well is just to the right of those. It should only take a couple of hours for a strong dragon to fly there."

She looked at Travis's tail, wondering if it were best to walk up its length and onto his back or clamber up over his shoulder. He hunkered there with his head tilted to one side, looking like a dog who'd only been given half of his dinner, still waiting to be told what kind of shapeshifter she was.

This is going to be fun, she thought with glee.

GARGOYLE SCOURGE

ISLAND OF FOG LEGACIES #3

OTHER SCI-FI AND FANTASY NOVELS
BY THE SAME AUTHOR . . .

In *Island of Fog*, a group of twelve-year-old children have never seen the world beyond the fog, never seen a blue sky or felt the warmth of the sun on their skin. And now they're starting to change into monsters!

What is the secret behind the mysterious fog? Who is the stranger that shows up one morning, and where did she come from? Hal Franklin and his friends are determined to uncover the truth about their newfound shapeshifting abilities, and their quest takes them to the forbidden lighthouse . . .

There are nine books in this series, plus a number of short stories available for free at islandoffog.com. It's an expansive saga set in a parallel Earth with plenty of magic and familiar creatures from myth and legend.

In *Sleep Writer*, everything changes for twelve-year-old Liam when a girl moves in next door. Madison is fifteen, pretty, and much weirder than she seems. Sometimes when she's sound asleep, she scrawls a message on a notepad by her pillow. She finds these cryptic words when she wakes the next morning—a time and a place.

But a time and a place for what? Liam and best friend Ant join her when she goes hunting around a cemetery late one night, and life is never the same again.

This fun science fiction series is ongoing, with at least one new novel each year.

In *Fractured*, the world of Apparatum is divided. To the west lies the high-tech city of Apparati, governed by a corrupt mayor and his brutal military general. To the east, spread around the mountains and forests, the seven enclaves of Apparata are ruled by an overbearing sovereign and his evil chancellor. Between them lies the Ruins, or the Broken Lands—all that's left of a sprawling civilization before it fractured. Hundreds of years have passed, and neither world knows the other exists.

Until now.

We follow Kyle and Logan on their journey of discovery. Laws are harsh. In the city, Kyle's tech implant fails to work, rendering him worthless in the eyes of the mayor. In the enclaves, Logan is unable to tether to any of the spirits, and he is deemed an outcast. Facing execution, the two young fugitives escape their homes and set out into the wastelands to forge a new life.

But their destinies are intertwined, for the separate worlds of Apparati and Apparata are two faces of the same coin . . . and it turns out that everyone has a twin.

There are two books in this series, with a possible third (a prequel) planned for the future. This series is co-written with author Brian Clopper.

In *Quincy's Curse*, poor Quincy Flack is cursed with terrible luck. After losing his parents and later his uncle and aunt in a series of freak accidents, Megan Mugwood is a little worried about befriending him when he moves into the village of Ramshackle Bottom. But incredibly good fortune shines on him sometimes, too. Indeed, it turns out that he found a bag of valuable treasure in the woods just a few months ago!

As luck would have it, Megan has chosen the worst possible time to be around him.

This is a fantasy for all ages, a complex and rewarding tale, a little dark in places but also a lot of fun.

Go to **UnearthlyTales.com** for more information.

.

Made in the USA
Coppell, TX
19 March 2020